Catching Red Herring

Judith Sakhri

Querida Juliane,
seu livro é o
primeiro que eu
autografo! :)
Espero que goste
da estória, é simples
mas foi escrita com
carinho.

Judith

DEDICATION

To the ones who made me do it,

To the one who broke my heart,

To the one who gave me shelter and

To the one who held my hand and told me I could fly.

CONTENTS

ACKNOWLEDGMENTS

Also special thanks to my mother, my son and all the friends that supported and encouraged me.

PROLOGUE

Maleventum

She doesn't recognize me. I tap ever so lightly on the foggy window glass, hoping that only she, and no one else, will hear me. But Rori is too drunk with lust to react. Her silky red hair is disheveled, she has bruises all over her so-white arms, and henna tattoos disfigure her hands and feet. Her little bustier, woven from some kind of copper thread and studded with pearls, sparkles in the dim light. Her knees are bent in fetal position, but her spine is twisted as she gazes in the opposite direction. A translucent fabric covers part of her naked bottom, but recent bloody cuts, scars and bruises mar the rest. Grime covers the bedsheets and pillows. Though she is looking in my direction as I stare at her, she doesn't see me.

Standing barefoot in the damp moss that covers the ground, deep in the dense woods, I shiver and hold a sneeze. Tonight is unusually cold. A gust of wind lifts up my hair, striking a sweaty spot on my neck. I hold my breath and rub my arms, afraid that my shivering will attract unwanted attention.

She closes her eyes slowly, opens her mouth, and starts drooling. Afraid of letting her go and still hopeful of some—any—communication, I reluctantly move my eyes away from her face and down to her feet, where I see a hairy, dark masculine arm tickling her legs with a huge peacock feather, slowly and teasingly moving it up and down her legs. After sticking it into her belly button, he slides it down and stops at her navel and strokes lightly around it Ecstatic, she tries to grab the feather with no success. That's when I notice he has handcuffed her wrists to the iron bedposts.

Yet I sense that there is no true will in her body rhythm; like a puppet, she is not in charge here. Just days ago, I watched similar scenes in which she still resisted the strings of the puppeteer. Has she given up? I'm afraid that she's starting to enjoy it.

I feel powerless. My spine tingles with a sense of urgency and failure. I'm running out of time.

3

CHAPTER 1

San Francisco

Two years ago, I started feeling the call of the land. My hands wanted to touch dirt so badly when I was enduring my nine-to-five job at a web technology company that I would spend my breaks sticking my fingers inside the soil of the potted plants around the office. I wonder if that's why my preppie, Ivy-League-educated manager so willingly granted my request for my own cubicle even though our oppressive open-office policy didn't allow any privacy, even to the CEO. When he caught me poking the soil of the plants on the patio where employees usually went to smoke, he was in utter shock.

"Oh, come on," I responded. "It beats cigarettes. And it's free!"

Since he already thought that I was a nut job, anyway, I didn't care. But after that, every time I went over to his desk for meetings and touched his keyboard, he would spray Lysol over it after I left. Now, who's the nut job?

Of course, my coworkers were sure that I was headed for the loony bin when I started saying that I wanted to quit my high-salary dot-com job in San Francisco to apply for a degree in agricultural and environmental sciences at UC Davis and then raise chickens in Petaluma. "Now, you're definitely out of your mind," they would say. But, to me, that plan felt like the only way to stay sane.

I can hear my equally desk-bound friends now.

"But, Cami, farming is the lowest-paying job ever. It's so unprofitable that most farmers have to be subsidized by the government!"

"And, besides, you'll die of boredom. Nothing to do and nowhere to go for miles and miles."

"And aren't you scared? Carmela, you'll be isolated out there. It's a no man's land!"

The more my friends tried to talk me out of it, the more willing I was to make the jump. I even found an old, out-of-print farmer's manual at the used bookstore Green Apple called *Five Acres and Independence*. It made me feel like my hoped-for enterprise was somewhat feasible.

Besides, every morning I would wake up—a burned-out, arthritic twenty-something with a coffee habit—running late and rushing for my double latte. Fridays were triple-shot days. If the lines at the Valencia Café were too long, I would daydream that I was still sleeping as I clutched my buy-ten-get-one-free card and inhaled the smell of freshly ground coffee. The earthy-spicy fragrance would make me sigh and remember one childhood summer spent on a family friend's farm in Hawaii where my cousins and I would climb over mountains of coffee beans drying in the sun. We gathered sticks so that my mom could start the fire in the woodstove, rubbed garlic on our ankles and shins to ward off snakes, and ran downhill to the garden to gather lettuce, fresh caper blossoms, and mustard greens for salad. For us Brooklyn kids, it was like a tropical dream come true.

The farm owner, a native Hawaiian, taught me how to make a cup out of the huge taro leaves that grew like weeds around their tiny, spring-water source, which dripped constantly and made the roots growing around it especially tasty. She would connect the two upper pointy bits of the heart-shaped leaves, making a wide cone that she used to fetch the spring water. Wherever the water touched the velvety surface, the green would turn to shiny silver.

All my ancestors had been farmers until they moved to the Promised Land of the United States and never bothered planting again—apart from some sour grapes that my grandpa grew in his Brooklyn backyard. When I agreed to rent a room at globetrotter-always-travelling-yoga-teacher Aunt Lilly's so I could help her afford to pay her astronomical Bay Area mortgage, I hadn't anticipated not having a backyard, and now I sorely missed Grandpa's little vineyard. From my bedroom window, I could see the neighbor's little plot of land, especially his fig tree heavy with fruit, so close and yet so far away.

Of course, I had another reason for believing in my farming dreams that my friends didn't know about—the egg. One morning, after one too many dreams about chickens, I woke up to find an egg nestled in the empty second pillow of my queen-sized bed. The egg was still warm, just like they are when they've just come out of a chicken. I broke it, and the yolk was blue—as dark blue as the deepest parts of the Pacific Ocean.

But my friends were right about one thing: I couldn't just change careers immediately, so I decided to test the waters. I started volunteering once a week at Hayes Valley Farm, a permaculture-oriented, community-run urban food garden at the site of the old freeway on-ramp that had to be demolished after the 1989 Loma Prieta earthquake. All my nine-to-five days were spent anticipating the weekend and its promise of rakes, shovels, buckets, and mulch, not to mention trimming the tomato plants and catching up with the herbs sprouts' progress in the nursery.

***

On Valentine's Day, an unusually cold day in the low thirties, a bunch of us volunteers were planting fruit trees. Our fingers were so cold that we all had to take breaks and dip our hands in the heat-generating compost. I was up to my elbows in worm-filled dirt when I met Josh, a sun-tanned Australian surfer with bleached hair wearing a flannel shirt missing a button or two. He had just returned from spending the summer in New Zealand.

"Yeah, I just spent the whole summer there for virtually free, working on some organic farms part-time for room and board, and on the weekends I went surfing all over the coast."

"Wow. And what kind of work do you usually do in these places?"

"Anything that's needed at any given time. I've taken care of cows, chickens, geese, plowed fields, harvested cherries. I even built a rock wall once. There is something very liberating about spending a whole day digging holes or chopping wood. Inner peace through hard work. Wiping the sweat from my forehead at the end of the day feeling like I went through a lot and deserved my dinner and full night sleep in a straw mattress."

My eyes twinkled. I guess I even felt a little envious—and the holes and mends in his old shirt suddenly seemed richer than the conflict-free diamond earrings that I'd bought myself with my first big paycheck.

"But my favorite job ever was this last summer: we went on a wild oyster hand gathering effort. We camped overnight, and illegally, at a beach to catch the early morning low tide that let the rocks full of oysters out in the open. I had to use knifes and an ice pick to detach each oyster. And when they were too hard to get, I would slurp them straight out of the rock. Squeeze a little lime right there and fill my belly up!"

I was smiling silly.

"Oh wait, some mud sprinkled in your face." And he rubbed my chin mole trying to clean it away. And I blushed. And he let out a big, hearty, half embarrassed laugh. So open hearted that felt almost like a fart. One of those that you let out in public thinking it will be small and silent and ends up being big and loud. But hopefully odorless. And his breath smelled like the fresh peppermint leaves he had been chewing on.

After washing up, Josh and I went out for coffee. He told me he was a sort of wanderer farmer, a nomad with his feet planted firmly on the ground, if such thing could exist. His plan for the next twelve years was to travel the world to learn the tools of the farming trade and find the perfect spot to buy a bit of land and lay down roots. He had been on farms in Australia, Hawaii, Japan, Brazil, Mexico, France, Spain, the Netherlands, and Italy. That last spot made my heart skip a beat.

"*Il Bel Paese*! I dream of going to Italy. My grandparents were Italian, and I really want to connect with my roots. If I ever manage to spend some time there, I might find the missing piece of my soul puzzle."

"What do you mean by soul puzzle? A puzzle with a picture of The Commodores?" he teased me.

I threw him the last piece of my bacon sprinkled maple donut. "No, I have this yearning for farming, and dirty, and growing food. My grandfather came from Italy, from a family of farmers, so I've always wanted to go."

"You should definitely go. The world is much bigger than your cubicle, you know."

"My mother is against it. I've brought up the idea a couple of times, but she won't budge."

"Well, you're past the age to need your mother's permission to go places, aren't you?"

That was when I realized that I could open up to him more than I could to anyone else. I also noticed the freckles on his nose. I'm a sucker for freckles.

I picked up my iPhone pretending I had just received a text and was checking it, but instead I pointed my camera to him and took a picture. Only I forgot to turn the flash off. So much for acting on the sly. His squinted eyes in the photo are a proof that I should never try to be a spy.

Another big smile from him, but now I was the one embarrassed.

He took out of his pocket a tiny paper sketchbook, sort of a cheaper version of a Moleskine, and a pencil.

"Can I have your number?"

"You don't have a cell phone?"

"I do, but I always forget it at home."

"Wow. Are you from this planet?"

"Maybe I'm more from this planet than Your Highness Queen of Code here." He winked.

"How do you know that I code? I didn't tell you…"

He pointed to my wrist and forearm splint with abducted thumb that I'd just worn after washing my hands.

"Oh, that."

He let out a minuscule, sad smile of compassion lifting up just the left corner of his chapped, sun burnt full lips. He got up from his seat and came behind me, touching the back of my neck and sliding his hands down slowly over my shoulder blades.

"Relax your chest. Take a deep breath."

He rubbed my shoulders. I kept trying to inhale deeply but was a bit surprised by him getting so close so soon.

"Shoulders away from your ears. Close your eyes. Take a long breath all the way down your tummy, and let it out slower than it came in."

I relaxed immediately, like all my troubles went away. A sense of trust filled up my ribcage.

"With this posture, at your age…I can tell you spend a lot of time crunched over a computer."

"Yeah, but who doesn't?"

"I don't."

He was sweet but also blunt, and there was this defiant undertone in his voice that was starting to bother me.

"Unless you are a writer."

"No, I'm not. Unless you count social media updates as writing."

"Oh yeah, I forgot, these days everyone is a writer. And a reader. Sometimes a writer, sometimes a reader."

I turned down my gaze, I don't know why.

He touched my chin. "Look at me in the eyes when I talk to you, will ya?"

I blushed, this time out of annoyance. "Who do you think you are, ordering me around like that?" I looked up almost bursting in anger…and he was smiling.

"Don't you hide these beautiful eyes behind words, ok? That's why I leave my phone at home. I don't want to walk around checking text messages when all I want to see in front of me is the world. I don't have time for this. Life is too short."

Ok then. I didn't even need to open up. I decided that from now on I would just sit back, relax and let him read my mind.

***

One day as we were walking home from Hayes Valley Farm, I decided to tell Josh about the egg that had shown up in my bed one day. I was afraid that he would call me crazy, but I blurted it out, anyway.

He didn't blink. "You know, one summer when I was in Rio, surfing near Ipanema Beach, I saw a penguin swimming right beside me. I couldn't believe my eyes. The poor thing landed in the hot sand, and it was about to faint with the heat. Someone called the zoo, and some guys came to pick it up. Rio's Zoo keeps a lot of penguins that end up there after riding up the cold current from Antarctica."

"Oh, it's just like the tropical fish that come to the East Coast in the summer," I responded. "It's so pretty to see them when they arrive with the warm currents. But then comes winter, and it's sad because they all die since they don't know how to go back."

"Yep. 'The Penguin from Ipanema and the Amazing Angelfish from the Hamptons.' I'm going to write that song."

"But, wait—what does all that have to do with my egg?"

"I just mean that there are more things in heaven and earth, my dear, than are dreamt of in your philosophy."

I stopped walking and took a deep breath before taking the uphill path alongside Dolores Park. He hadn't called me a freak or a weirdo. What a relief.

"Hey, do you have potatoes at home?" he asked. "If you like, I'll cook you rosemary roasted potatoes for your dinner."

"We'll need to buy the rosemary; I don't have any."

"It's right here!" He grabbed a bunch of stems from a big, fragrant rosemary bush that was growing right by the beginning of our path. He picked off the little bluish blossoms, saved the edible leaves in his jeans pocket and filled the many holes in his his thrift store cashmere sweater with the tiny flowers. "Organic embroidery", he winked.

I smiled.

Josh made me smile a lot. For him, life was all so easy, a matter of packing up and leaving, arriving and getting settled. He lived so simply that cooking a meal with fresh local vegetables was his idea of a big night. Whenever he was living in a big city, whether it was Paris, Sidney or Tokio, he worked as kitchen help. Since he was a great cook and always broke, our dates revolved around buying groceries, coming home and whipping up great meals with happy endings.

"Carmela, my caramel, come try the sauce and tell me if this *Calamar en su Tinta* needs more garlic." How would I know? That was the first time ever I was going to eat squid stewed in its own ink, so who was I to judge?

"Gee, I don't know, it's looking kind of black, did you burn it?"

"It's their ink, sweetie. It's supposed to be black."

"Oh, ok. I guess I'll make the salad then." I always made the salad. It was easy and a great escape from whenever he wanted to involve me too much in his concoctions.

"Sure. I'm feeling this needs some Himalayan pink salt. Can you get some for me?"

I looked all over his shelves and all I could find was a box of Kosher salt. I brought it for him.

"No cupcake, it's that over there." He pointed to a pink rock sitting on top of his bedside table. And I've always thought it was decoration. Well, since he lived in a Mission District one-room studio where the stove was just three feet from the bed, it made sense to expand the storage.

"Here, we brake some pieces and sprinkle the crumbles over the stew."

I would just watch mesmerized. And I tried a bit of the delicacy, very intriguing.

"Do you want to do a little salt tasting? Come here."

He opened a drawer and took out some glass containers with different kinds of salt out of it. Poured a bit of each side-by-side on a wooden board.

"This off-white one is my own homemade salt, straight out of the waters from Ocean Beach. Can't get any more local than that!"

I tried a pinch of it. It did taste like the Pacific. Reminded me of my childhood habit of going to the beach, letting salt dry on my arm's hair and then lick it. But then the Atlantic tasted different.

"This one is Maldon smoked sea salt, from England. Check out the chunky crystals."

He sprinkled some of it on a piece of clam for me. It was amazing.

And there was the so white Portuguese Flor de Sal, and the grayish French Fleur de Sel. All of them subtly distinct.

"Boy, look at you going places - you just went around the world with your taste buds!"

He rubbed some salt in my face.

"Now, Miss Carmela, you are my salted caramel!"

And he licked my nose. And picked me up and threw me in bed, and continued licking me like a cat doing his coiffure. Only he was licking me. On his bed. And he bit my ear, kind of too strong for my standards. Or at least what I was used to until that moment.

"You taste so good, I want to cut your ears and eat them with pepper and butter."

I pulled him away, not sure if he was just kidding or serious, and took a good look at him. He had insane eyes, like they were on fire or something. He pushed my arms open apart and squeezed me under him. I was stuck and couldn't move away from his pressure, and he kept kissing me. I resisted—I don't like when I don't have a way out of a situation, no exit or escape. He kept kissing me, his lips so full and soft and hungry. I gave in. I felt a circle of warmth right around my coccyx, like a burning ring, the temperature was rising so much that it started to hurt, physical pain and it was hurting almost to the point I felt I was in danger of injury. Like a branding hot iron making its mark: this cow is mine. I was scared but I didn't want it to stop, until I started to smell actual smoke. And the fire alarm went on. That finally made Josh let me go. He jumped out and turned off the stove. We let the calamari burn!

"Fast, fill up that bowl with cold water!" he shouted, while he got the burning pan out of the burner and reached for a cloth to fan out the smoke smell away from the fire alarm.

"Here, it's ready."

And he immersed the pan into the water, immediately cooling off its bottom and making the water hiss at the contrasting contact. He let it sit in there for a while. The alarm finally stopped.

He smiled at me, scratched his head and combed his fingers through his scalp bringing his shoulder length hair into a ponytail. "Can you get me a spoon?"

I guess ordering people around made him calmer. I almost told him "you get your spoon", but I was too stressed out to create conflict, so I complied.

"Here, we'll scoop out the surface of the stew. Hopefully the cold water did the trick and the burnt taste stayed at the stuck bottom of the pot." and he skimmed the surviving surface saving it on the side in a ceramic bowl.

"Sorry Cami."

"It's ok. Maybe we can order some Ma Po Tofu from Mission Street Chinese?"

He looked at me with a twinkle in his eye. "No, I don't feel like having Chinese." He grabbed me and threw me back in his bed—so conveniently located right by the cooking section of his home—and we ended up having the squid for breakfast. And the cold water did the trick; it didn't taste like burnt at all.

"Buongiorno Carmela!!!" He woke me up holding a plate with a crepe on it and sliced oranges on the side. "The first ever crepe filled with calamari in su tinta. Fit for a queen. My queen Carmela!"

His Australian accent made even my old-school immigrant name sound cool. Because he had learned to cook during his travels, he often didn't know the name of a spice or herb in English. Instead of looking at labels on the bins in the bulk section of Rainbow Grocery, he would smell the powders and dried plants to remember where and how he had used them and come up with ideas for dinner. After smelling and deciding, we would go to the vegetable section where he selected the rest of the menu based on freshness, color, and texture.

I got deep into the I'm-a-foodie-and-the-kitchen-is-my-refuge movement. Me, the geek who once could spend whole weeks gulping burritos in front of my laptop, coding away without even moving my eyes away from the screen to check for bugs in my food. Now I was perusing farmers' markets looking for heirloom tomatoes and edible flowers—and losing weight at the same time, the less the merrier! Hanging out with Josh helped me take the first steps toward exploring a world that until now I had only heard about. Except for that summer spent in Hawaii and moving to San Francisco in my private Internet gold rush, I had never been anywhere except Brooklyn. After joining WWOOF (World Wide Opportunities on Organic Farms), the organic farm volunteer network online, I started looking for places where I could stay once I reached Italy.

My first idea was to visit inland Campania, the region in Southern Italy where my ancestors had once lived, but it was hard to find farms accepting volunteers there. I asked Josh for help.

"But the South, Cami?" he protested. "Why? I think you should try Tuscany or Emilia Romagna. People in the South are big dreamers and can make all these fantastic plans, but when it comes to turning them into reality, they almost never succeed. The South is beautiful, but it's so poor and backward. If I were you, I wouldn't go there. Just my two cents."

"But I want to connect with my roots, and that's where my ancestors came from."

"And they left for a reason, right?"

"Yes, they were poor farmers. With twelve kids, they had a hard time feeding them all. That's why my *nonno* and his brother left all their family behind and moved to Brooklyn."

We were lying down in his bed at his sunny and warm studio I had my head in my favorite spot: the comfort of his strong chest. And I felt his heart beat change pace. He seemed truly upset.

"Yes, that's exactly what I'm trying to tell you. The South of Italy is a place that people run away from, not move to. Apart from the coast, the countryside is dry and inhospitable."

"I think you are mistaken. My *nonno* was rather fond of it. He was always telling stories about his childhood and complaining that the grapes they grew in Brooklyn from the cuttings he brought over in his jacket pocket never tasted the same as the grapes back in his homeland. Sour as hell, but he still insisted on making his own wine in the basement."

"Okay, but he never went back to Campania, did he?"

"No," I admitted reluctantly.

"Childhood memories tend to be happy, baby. Just the simple fact that you were a kid makes it up for you."

After he said that he kept quiet, and sighed a long, sad sigh. Like someone who is giving up on a lost cause. We stayed quiet like that for a while, and I kept my head on his chest even though I felt an energy kicking me out of there, like his heart had little arms and it was trying to push me away, but the rest of his chest didn't mind me staying.

Suddenly, his room became dark like a day of a total eclipse.

"What's that?!" He lifted his head up fast, finally kicking my head out of his chest. There was a black mass of something covering the entirety of his large window, the only source of light to his home. I squinted my eyes.

"Bees!"

"Yes, they are swarming!!"

I ran up and instinctively closed the windows. He joined me and we watched them swarm frantically, an amazing and scary phenomenon. I clutched his hand.

"You don't need to be afraid, sweet bun. They are just taking care of their business, we are safe even if the windows stay open."

Josh's home in Fair Oak Street overlooked his neighbors' rooftop, and the beehives located there. I always saw one or two of the little bees visit Josh's windowsill herb garden; he had a little bunch of White Clover in it just for the bees. But to see them in their totality, moving around in such frenzy, was indeed frightening.

"It's beautiful, isn't it?" Josh smiled, and I secretly thanked the bees for taking him away from his previous dark mood.

"I think it's more scary than beautiful." I replied.

"It's because you don't know what's going on. If you only knew…"

"Well, do you care to share?"

"I wish I knew too. Well, basically, when a hive gets too crowded, they all leave it and have this big conference when they decide who gets to stay in it and who needs to leave and form a new hive. If I only could turn myself into a bee and take part on this congregation. I would love to be talking to them right now." His eyes were bright again, my life loving Josh with his big smile was back.

He took a deep breath, sat down in lotus pose, closed his eyes and called OM. As he progressed through the vibration of the m in the end of the sound, he turned it into a buzzing, and soon enough he was in unison with the bees. He stayed like that for a while, one with the bees.

Later we could see, hanging from the branches of their liquid amber tree, the big mass of bees that needed to start anew. It looked like a big, black, strange fruit, almost like a giant jackfruit if it could hang heavy like that without simply falling to the ground.

The next morning we saw the beekeeper come and remove the swarm from the tree with a catching net in the end of a long stick. He built more hive boxes, and from the three initial hives he went to seven. We kept watching the process from his window for a couple of days; it was one great source of entertainment since my eco boyfriend did not have a television. Josh bought a variety of flowers from the Botanical Gardens sale and planted it in pots hanging from his fire escape even though the landlord had warned him he should leave that space empty. "It's for the bees," he explained to the fireman who came for an inspection once and told him to remove the plants. "C'mon, it's ok to break the rules if it's for the bees…"

His wide smile could melt away even an officer's heart.

***

Since Josh and I couldn't reach an agreement, we stopped talking about Campania for a while. Meanwhile, I had to convince my boss to let me take some time off to travel and I had no idea how to do it. I had been giving him some hints in that direction, suggesting that I was due for some vacation time, but he blatantly ignored me. I guess he thought that I was indispensable.

Besides sticking my fingers into potting soil of the office's plants, I had another dark little secret: I had taken to eating handfuls of dirt. Sometimes I would go to a park or sneak into a neighbor's backyard and fill my mouth with the stuff. Its earthy, mineral-rich flavor tasted good, and eating it somehow relieved my aches and painful yearnings.

"I must be lacking some kind of nutrient," I decided. A checkup revealed the healthiest blood the doctor had ever seen but nothing wrong except tendonitis to explain my ever-diminishing desire to come into the office.

CHAPTER 2

Still San Francisco

One ridiculously sunny spring day, the kind that should have inspired me to call in sick just to enjoy it before the foggy San Francisco summer arrived, I rode my bike to the office, thinking that this was it; I would get permission to leave. I wasn't going to spend the upcoming summer under the fog. I focused on my wish so hard that I kept quietly thinking about it during the entire shift. I hardly talked to anyone, had lunch alone, and didn't take any coffee breaks, causing my coworkers to ask questions and point in my direction.

At 4:17 P.M., I suddenly felt the urge to eat more dirt. Driven by something other than my own will, I got up from my desk, walked toward the huge Mediterranean fan palm that stood in the middle of our office's common area, and stuck my hand deep into the dirt. I noticed the looks aimed in my direction and managed to avoid eating the stuff, but I was possessed. Unsure whether I was commanding my own actions, I climbed into the pot and hugged the thorny palm tree so hard that its thorns started making their way into my flesh. Soon, I was bleeding profusely all over my body, which was rather surprising since the thorns were small. And the cuts didn't hurt, not a bit. It was almost as if the tree had decided to stab me with each one of its little spikes.

Everyone in the office started screaming. Some got up and stood around me, apparently wanting to help me but hesitating because they were scared. A coworker named Joanna found a towel and tried to bring it to me, but some sort of repelling force prevented her. Soon everyone around me stood motionless as if their fear had paralyzed them even though they could still speak. I could hear the humming of the crowd—frantic people telling each other to call 911 or security— but I was locked in a trance and couldn't move or speak.

My boss broke out of the gathering—he was the only one who hadn't fallen into a state of shock—and pierced me with beady black eyes like a hawk's.

"Carmela, what on earth is going on? Should I call an ambulance?" From the look on his face, the ambulance he was planning to call would come equipped with a straitjacket.

"No, Matthew, I need to ask you a favor," I said.

He leaned closer, still avoiding any physical contact as if I were a leper, and whispered in my ear, his voice raspy with anger, "Okay, let's take it somewhere else, shall we? Please leave this tree alone and come see me in the Bora Bora Conference Room, ASAP."

In a snap, I woke up. I looked at my scratched arms, my white top now stained with scarlet; the brightness of my blood always amazes me. I jumped out of the huge pot and made my way through the drop-jawed employees, leaving a crimson trail behind me on the tan carpeting. Why, I wondered, do technology companies always name their meeting rooms after exotic places, planets, or chemical elements?

I opened the door. My manager, Lysol spray in hand, cleaned the bloody doorknob and pointed to a chair covered with a disposable tablecloth. "Please have a seat."

My blood continued to drip, slower now but still enough to form a small puddle on the floor beneath me.

"What's going on? What's happening to you?"

"I need some time off. A personal leave of absence."

"I'm not sure. We need you here now with the expansion of the social media department. . . ."

I sighed, disappointed. My blood started pouring harder, like water from a fountain.

He opened his eyes wide in fear. "Okay, okay. How much time do you need?"

"Six weeks?"

"Deal."

The blood stopped running—immediately. I never felt so light in my life. As I got up to shake his hand and seal the agreement, I noticed that all the blood was gone. The tablecloth covering the chair was just as white as it had been when I'd arrived. The puddle was evaporating quickly. My scratches were healing, too, closing into light scars that slowly faded as if a Photoshop erase brush had gone over my arms, taking away all those wounds.

I left Bora Bora and went to look at the palm tree. No sign of blood on the floor or in the pot. All the employees were back at their respective desks, typing away as if nothing had happened. It was as if a time warp had folded whatever scene they'd just witnessed into oblivion. I went into my cubicle and continued working on the software plug-in I'd started writing earlier that morning. After sipping the coffee I had left behind, now cold, I heard a light knocking on the dry-erase whiteboard wall to my right. My boss peeked over the barrier and looked down at me. "And take the rest of the day off, will you?"

***

Browsing the website of the farming network, I found Rick Zanini, a kid from Brooklyn with an Italian background like mine, who had wwoofed the previous summer at a farm near Benevento, Campania, and was raving about it in a review. That's how farm help volunteers from WWOOF refer to what they do: they are wwoofers and they go around the world wwoofing. I e-mailed him and he wrote me troves of information about his favorite farm holiday (*agriturismo* in Italian) and told me that he was planning to return that summer. Campania happened to be exactly the region where my grandpa was born and raised. How appropriate.

I told Josh that I'd made up my mind and I was going to Campania.

"So you finally found a farm in the South? I remember you telling me there weren't many volunteer opportunities there."

"Yes, but this one showed up, and—"

"Listen, Cami. Don't you think it's strange, this scarcity of farms accepting volunteers around that particular region? I think it's a big red flag."

"Well, maybe the South isn't as open and cosmopolitan as the North, but there are exceptions to every rule."

"Well, why don't you tour the rest of the country before you go to Campania? You would have to fly into Rome, anyway, so you might as well check it out. Then you could go to Tuscany for a couple of weeks before you go down south. Hopefully, you'll give up on this idea."

"Gee, Josh, why such hate? You sound just like my mom, the daughter of a Southern Italian who won't visit or even talk about her own father's land."

"I don't know. I understand your need to go against your mother's recommendations, but I'll have to agree with her on that one. I just have a feeling that it would be better for you not to go. You're not used to the Southern mindset. They're so macho over there, and you'll be a woman traveling alone. I wish I could be there with you."

He grabbed my arms, like he never did before, making me wonder who was this new guy. Where was my cool, collected, expansive, free spirited happy-go-lucky Peter Pan? I guess every man has a dash of control need, even the most liberal ones. He squeezed my body and looked at me a bit lost, and came very close to my lips almost kissing me. His inhalations were heavy and intense, and the exhalations seemed somewhat afflicted, trembling. Air was coming in and out of him fast with a sound that reminded me of the ocean, waves breaking nonstop, one after the other. His breath, for the first time ever, smelled like bitter almond. He came close to a kiss, but instead let out a sad sigh, giving up and banging his forehead on mine.

He bit his lip. I pulled away and tried to understand what was going on, surveyed his now inscrutable face. Whatever he was feeling just a second ago, he was working hard to suppress.

"I'm sorry."

"Sorry for what, Joshers?" I tried to lighten up, to no avail. But now he just seemed sad and irritated.

"Suddenly I became ultra possessive of you. I don't know what to make of it. I don't like this energy, I don't like the way it feels in my body."

"It's ok, we are all human, don't sweat it so much."

"I know. I'm not going to let this take over me. Emotions are like waves: you can't stop them from coming, but you can choose the ones you ride."

"Sounds like a plan."

We kissed finally. A dry, sad, worried kiss. A haunting memory came to my mind: watching a tourist drown among the waves in Kaimu Beach, Hawaii, while his whole family watched desperate and powerless from the warm black sands. But I repressed the thought. I chose to not ride it.

Contradictory as ever, while worried, he would also motivate me to take off. Josh was going to Bolivia for a big food-and-farm tour, then down to Chile to work on some more farms, and finally to Patagonia to explore. He had been planning this trip for years, long before he met me, and he believed that traveling alone was the only way to go.

"It may sound scary, but it's very cool. You're always meeting new people. No need to wait around for anyone; you can change your mind on a whim. It's a nonstop exploration with no room for drama."

So Josh and I parted company—he went to South America, and I went to Italy. Following his advice, I toured Rome and the North before heading to the South.

CHAPTER 3

Benevento

And now here I am at last in Benevento, with my hands dipped in compost again. But this compost is a little messier than the batch that started it all. This one has lots of horse poop, which we volunteers have to collect—even though the horses in question aren't even officially part of the farm. The gypsies who rent this *agriturismo biologico* decided that it was a good idea to board their circus animals here in the farm, and they leave the horses free to roam, eat the tall grasses that nobody has cared to cut for the whole spring, and poop all over the place. No wonder the reservations have dwindled since these guys took over in midwinter, or so Rick tells me. Not until summer arrived, bringing with it Rick, his girlfriend Ila, and a romantic young couple named Ken and Rori, with their cheap energy, willingness to work, and passion for organic farming did any weeding get done.

Now, the swimming pool is back to a swamp. When I remember Rori scrubbing all that green scum and algae, I feel angry. That was her last task before she vanished.

I think back to that day as I shovel the horse poop.

"Now maybe the guests can enjoy the pool!" she puffed in her cute Irish accent, her fair and freckled face all pink from the effort, not to mention sunburn. Her copper tresses were glued to her sweaty neck, back, and shoulder blades, which pointed out like angel's wings. She wore only a lacy cream-colored tank top, olive shorts, and flip-flops. I remember just sitting there, watching her work; already taking my break—I preferred to start working early and be done before the midday heat. The couples, though, stayed up late and didn't start working until 11:00 the next day. Rick has always been the first to come out and drink his *caffè corretto*— which, lately, since Rori's sudden disappearance, has more grappa than coffee.

When I arrived at the farm just outside the Bosco di Melizzano, I couldn't hide my disappointment at the sorry state of the property. I should have taken the hint when I noticed,back in Tuscany, that their website was down.

After telling me such good things about the place, Rick was a bit embarrassed but also confident that things would work out. "We need to bring this place back to what it was! I swear, last summer, it was full of people and lots of fun. I would cook for all the guests. It was awesome. When I first came, I planned to stay for just two weeks and ended up staying for the whole summer. I told you it was one the most beautiful places I'd ever seen. The vegetable patch used to cover this entire spot." He pointed to a sea of tumbleweeds, thistles, nettles, bindweed, ground elder, and couch grass. Since the next town circus gypsies rented out the farm saying they wanted to keep on running the hospitality business, all they've done was ruin the beautiful premises and drive potential guests away. Rumor had it they wanted to buy it in order to build a second circus.

"Well, yes, coming out of New York, this might be a treat. But trust me, you should check out other farms in the program where you could actually learn about agriculture rather than slave away.", I would tell him.

My first stop in Italy, the rolling hills of the Barbapala Fattoria Biologica, another organic farm in Tuscany, had been a dream. What a difference a few degrees of latitude make. And how right Josh was.

As I turned the compost before dawn this morning, I kept wondering why Rick has continued working here even after the police arrested Rori's boyfriend, Ken, along with Kulveer, the illegal Indian immigrant who managed the place. Poor Kulveer had fled India in search of riches, and Ken had thought he would leave Ireland for a romantic Italian holiday with his girlfriend, who is now gone.

Only I know where she is. Well, sort of. And that's why I've stayed, too. Because every now and then, I have the same dream, or at least I dream of the same cabin in the woods where I can see her through the windows. Last night it happened again. And once again, I woke up to find my feet covered in mud and wet grass. This morning, they had something new in them: a huge glass shard stuck in the bottom of my heel. It hurt just a bit. I tried to ignore it, but it was starting to bother me.

After I finished the compost-turning job, I went back to my bungalow, changed from my work boots into sandals, and limped down the path to the guesthouse kitchen. The dogs, which had slept by my door the whole night, followed me. I don't know why those three little mutts have taken a liking to me.

I turned for a moment to look down into the valley, which is gorgeous at dawn. It's a shame that I'm usually the only one who gets to see it.

But this morning, I had unexpected company, Rick's girlfriend.

"Oh, hi, Ila," I greeted her. "What has you up so early? Bed bugs?"

She was sitting by the back door of the kitchen under the sink, gazing out the window at the scattered orange and red sunrise. She never answered me, so I assumed that she wasn't listening or had chosen to ignore me. Ila is part Cherokee, part Mexican, and can be very quiet sometimes, with her huge dark irises and wide, pearly white sclera that made her eyes look like sunny-side-up eggs when she was staring at nothingness like that.

"Amazing, huh?" I said. "That sunrise is one of the rewards of waking up early. The other one is working in the cool of the morning, not in the blistering sun. Of course, you don't get to sleep in late, but . . ."

She didn't respond.

"Well, I'm going to get something to eat," I persisted. "Are you hungry?"

When she still didn't answer, I heated some water for coffee. The whistling kettle woke her from her reverie.

"Oh, hi. Good morning," she said.

"I've never seen you up so early," I said, repeating my earlier greeting. "What happened, bed bugs?"

"Nothing. I woke up in the middle of the night and couldn't get back to sleep."

"Oh." I walked near her to get some coffee grounds.

"What's up with the limping?" she asked.

I grunted; I wasn't ready yet to share the weird dreams with tangible consequences such as wet feet and shards of glass.

"Not sure. I guess I stepped on some broken glass and didn't notice right away. Now it's getting kind of inflamed."

"Wait here."

She sprinted up the stairs and came back with a pair of tweezers. After heating the tips in the stove fire and telling me to remove my sandal, she grabbed my heel and squeezed it while pulling and pinching the skin around the shard of glass. She held my heel tight in an attempt to divert the pain.

"You guys got coffee ready?" Rick asked as he appeared in the doorway.

Ila didn't bother to look up from her task to greet her boyfriend. I felt an icy chill in the air even though the morning sunshine coming through the large kitchen windows had been warming the room for quite a while.

"Morning, Rick," I greeted him. "I've got coffee ready, and Ila is saving my foot from putrefaction."

He didn't answer me, just went straight to the liquor cabinet, grabbed the *grappa* bottle, and took a close look at it; empty. He tossed it in the trash. Finding some brandy, he poured a bit in his mug, filled it up with coffee, and sipped from it while staring out the window.

Meanwhile, Ila had finally managed to pull the brown glass shard out of my foot. After throwing it into some bushes that grow around where the outdoor drainpipe dumps the dishwater, she kept staring mutely at the spot where it had landed.

The gypsies who rent the farm hadn't arrived in the kitchen yet. They're supposed to give us breakfast so we can start working. They don't allow us to cook, but I've been ignoring this rule since I decided to start my workdays early and use my afternoons to accomplish other goals, like exploring. So I wake up before sunrise, work for an hour or so, eat something, work three more hours, pack a lunch from supplies in the kitchen cupboards, and leave; I'm trying to find the log cabin from my dreams. I tell everyone that I go on hikes but, actually, I delve deep into the forest, alone, against the advice of Francesco, the farm owner, who lives up in Naples most of the time now that he's trying to sell his piece of land. When he came visit once, and I told him I was venturing around, he got somber.

"Why do you do that? This forest seems safe, but woods are always woods."

"Back in California I'm a big hiker. I miss it."

"Yes, but a lady like you shouldn't go around alone like that. Your mama never read you the story of Red Riding Hood?

Rick and Ila sometimes break the non-cooking rule too—since Kulveer went to jail they've become sort of informally running things around here, so they don't care.

Thinking about all this, I mixed some cold polenta from the night before with chopped dates and an Italian cream cheese called *mascarpone* and poured hot milk over it. My foot hurt, but at least the shard was out.

Rick was now sitting on a counter by a pile of two-day-old bread, still drinking his *caffè corretto*, when Ila walked up to him, leaning over the counter and crossing her arms. I felt like leaving the kitchen, and I started to gulp from my warm bowl as fast as I could when Ila grabbed one of those rock-hard round loaves and threw it on the floor with a thud. Now she was facing her man with arms crossed again, her bloodshot eyes almost popping out of her skull, the loaf on the floor between them, like a mine waiting to be stepped on. [Rick?] told me that they had met when she was his manager at a Starbucks in Ithaca. That probably set the tone of the relationship.

"Baby, we have flour," Rick said. "Maybe you can try making some of those delicious tortillas you cooked the other day."

Yes, the other day, when Rori was still around, right before she disappeared. She made that nice salad with the greens that she'd managed to forage among the weeds: radicchio, arugula (which she called "rocket," almost crying in glee when she found it), and endive. It was a happy dinner: Ila's warm tortillas and Rori's fresh salad. Now, I couldn't look at food without remembering how she baked a pie for my birthday with the strange berries that her boyfriend Ken had found on the hillside, how she got red stains all over her white cotton top from picking the berries, and how she absentmindedly ate the whole pie and forgot to save a slice for me.

Rori and I used to be the most daring volunteers in the kitchen. We blatantly ignored the gypsies' rules against cooking, partly because we couldn't stand their food and partly because we both had low blood sugar, meaning we couldn't go very long without a meal. Rick was by far the best chef of us all, but he tried to obey the gypsies since he was sort of a senior volunteer. The previous summer, he had befriended the owner, Francesco (but loathed the current tenants running—or ruining—the business), and this year, he had decided to bring along his girlfriend. Unfortunately, Ila wasn't having much fun, especially with Rori gone.

Ila sighs. "Okay, where is this flour?" Her body—strong, muscular, brown, and shiny—relaxes. She reminded me of a mustang that suddenly agrees to let someone else guide its will.

Rick opens a high cabinet and grabs a huge bag of flour. When he opens it and a white cloud burst out, dusting both their faces, they start laughing.

How sweet it is to be in love and only worry about what's for breakfast, I think. Not that they aren't concerned about Rori. They just don't believe my kidnapping theory. They think she might have wandered off since she and Ken had been fighting before she disappeared. Or maybe they're coping by denial. Also, they don't know as much as I do, or think I do, since it's only at night, when I sleep, that I see her. What bothers me is that the visions are so vivid, her presence is so concrete, and they're not like ordinary dreams, which move fast and jump randomly to completely different subject matter. The sensations I have seem real, and the pace is lifelike.

As I finish my warm polenta and drop my dirty bowl into the sink, Ila hands me one of her freshly made tortillas, and I take a bite.

It's warm, but the flour is stale. I thank her and walk away, almost running, back to the compost pile and spit the sour contents of my mouth into it. The aftertaste was almost metallic, reminding me of blood. The last time I tasted blood like that was the incident in the office. What had happened then? I'd been in such whirlwind trying to get out of the country that the whole incident had gone by in a blur. Add to that the fact that nobody seemed to care about or even remember it. Sometimes, I wonder if I was just hallucinating. But, then, I did get the time off. And my skin still recalls feeling the warm, pulsating, viscous fluid pouring out of it. Maybe I'm crazy. Maybe Rori just took off, as Ila and Rick choose to explain her sudden, unforeseeable disappearance, and my dreams are just another symptom of my insanity slowly taking over my mind. But how can I explain the muddy feet? Somnambulism?

And then there was the Florence affair.

CHAPTER 4

Florence

In my first days in Italy, after I had woofed for two weeks in a dream farm in Tuscany and before setting out to my second wwoofing appointment in the south, I spent some time playing tourist on Josh's recommendation. And when it comes to tourism, the city of Florence means business: a non stop dazzling carousel of attractions for the wandering eye. Still dazed from visiting the fabulous Uffizi Gallery, I tried to find a healthy snack, but all I saw around me was either refined grainy carbs or sugar from offerings of pizza, pasta or gelato, so I held out, hoping that the dinner Josh's friend Stefano had invited me to would be more nutritious. Spotting one of those tourist processions in which everyone holds a flag so they know to which group they belong among the many tours crowding the narrow sidewalks of the old town, I thought it would be fun to pretend I was one of them. As I heard the high priest—I mean the tour guide—talking about la Croce, I decided to mingle and check out yet another sight. It was a relief to feel part of something bigger than myself for a while and just be led (so tiring to hold a map and have to choose where to go all the time!), even though I felt a bit worried about not having a flag and the likelihood of being spotted as a crasher

When we finally arrived at the Basilica de la Santa Croce, it was almost closing, and the group decided to quickly climb the stairs, and get inside in a hurry. I followed, but since I was distracted looking at the bell tower, I missed a step and fell, hitting my ankle on the corner of the hard marble stair and my head on the pointed end of a tourist's flag pole. I don't remember anything that happened after my fall until I woke up lying in a hospital bed with a growling stomach, a swollen ankle, and a huge headache.

A few minutes after I woke up, a nurse came in to check on me. "Oh, you're awake," she said. "I'm glad. We were watching you."

"What happened? Where am I?"

"Villa Maria Pia Hospital. Your tour guide left you here. You'll be fine; it's nothing major, but you'll probably need to rest for a couple of days."

I looked at the clock and saw that it was half past eleven. Stefano! The dinner. Oh no. And my cell phone was dead, no battery left.

"Do you have a phone I could use? It's for a local phone call."

The nurse handed me her mobile phone and left the room. I called Stefano, who sounded very worried.

"I don't understand how I could I faint like that," I told him. "I lost consciousness for about four hours after I fell."

"Oh, *cara mia*, I know what happened! You probably had Stendhal syndrome. It causes people to become overwhelmed by great works of art. It happens often in Florence."

Okay, Stefano, I thought. *Whatever you say.* "Have you heard from Josh?" I asked, changing the subject.

"What do you mean, heard? Last time I talked to him, he told me to have dinner with you, which unfortunately isn't happening."

"No, I mean, did he call you after he landed in South America? Do you know if he's already at the farm in Bolivia?"

"Oh. I don't know much about what's going on with Josh right now," Stefano said. "He texted me saying he took a detour into the jungle towards the Brazilian Amazon and was postponing his stop at the Bolivian farm a bit. He mostly asked me to keep an eye on you. I guess he loves you, huh? I never saw Josh caring this much about anyone."

"What do you mean?"

"Well, when Josh is on the road, he rarely contacts anyone. So I was surprised to see him go the distance for you."

Go the distance? A measly text message? Well, live and learn. The Josh I knew was cuddly and cozy, but at that time, he was in settled-down, living-in-the-city-mode. I didn't know his modus operandi when traveling. I could only guess that this relationship was going to be a wild ride, at least for me.

***

Several hours later, I paid my hospital bill of seventy-five Euros and called a cab. They insisted that I stay longer at the hospital for observation, but I didn't have traveler's health insurance and did not want to spend all my traveling money on a hospital bed. Plus, I felt fine, I was going to be okay.

Back in the youth hostel where I was spending the night, I started to take account of my adventures, which mainly amounted to fainting and missing dinner. I'd managed to eat some *osso buco* (veal shank) soup at the hospital, but there was too much pasta in the soup—all that wheat was making me nervous. And my jeans were starting to feel tighter.

Lying in bed, I started thinking that I should take a break from looking at so much art. Stefano was right: The experience was overwhelming, probably because, like most travelers, I tried to squeeze too much into too little time. But I couldn't stop just yet. The next day, I had a date with Michelangelo's David. I had a ticket to see him the next morning, and I was hoping that I could handle a single work of art—nothing to make me faint or go crazy.

But I was wrong. David moved me so much that I had to look at him from every angle, my mind racing. That was the most beautiful male body I had ever seen. And the worried expression on his face, boy turning into man, said more plainly than words, "Good-bye, carefree adolescence. Hello, responsibilities."

I left the Galleria dell'Accademia—David's home—feeling dizzy again. But despite the queasiness, I was starving, so I decided to check out Trattoria Mario in the Mercato Centrale on Stefano's recommendation. It was fairly close to the gallery, and I wouldn't need to cross the overwhelming historical center again. I chose an indirect route where I saw a lot of North Africans and Indians selling fruit, clothing, leather goods, and counterfeits galore. My swollen ankle hurt a bit, but it was bearable.

The plain-looking restaurant was packed with tourists, happily rubbing elbows with strangers at the community tables. Later, I learned that every Florence guidebook ever published recommended the place. Oh well. I was happy to eat at last. I ordered white bean soup, salad, and rabbit. The other guests sharing the table with me were all indulging in a house specialty, *bistecca alla Fiorentina* (T-bone steak). I didn't like my rabbit, it was dry and bland, and everyone around me started offering me pieces of their juicy meat. We sort of connected and started ordering glass after glass of the house red—which was cheaper than Coca-Cola. Across from me sat a Korean family, super polite but quiet. Beside me was a very friendly Mexican brunette about my age. Everyone at the table shared a bowl of cherries, which tasted kind of sour. We talked about how berries from Mexico and California were much sweeter.

"It's the sun," the Mexican girl said. "The sun brings out the flavor. No sunshine, no sugar."

Well, if that was true, I was about to become the sweetest thing on earth. As I said my good-byes to both Korean and Mexican tablemates and made my way out of the *trattoria*, the sun was so strong, I could barely breathe. I felt as if the outside air would burn my nostrils. The breeze was blistering, offering no relief. And I was still working on digesting all that meat and wine. One day, starvation, the next day, gluttony—my blood sugar was becoming manic-depressive. Feeling faint, I glanced at my travel guide looking for the closest point of interest where I could get out of the scorching sun and spotted the Officina Profumo-Farmaceutica di Santa Maria Novella.

Call me crazy, but I find pharmacies fascinating, and this one was among the oldest in the world. I love mixing herbs and coming up with special teas and ointments. My bathroom cabinet resembles an alchemist's cupboard, with all kinds of oils, seeds, and herbs immersed in alcohol, along with other indispensable things like bee propolis, scented sea salt rocks for body scrubbing, and homemade citronella mosquito repellent. So I was looking forward to checking out centuries-old pharmaceuticals and alchemical gadgets in an establishment founded by Dominican friars at the beginning of the eleventh century when they grew their own medicinal herbs and used them to make elixirs and other concoctions.

The museum housed in the old laboratories and storerooms of the pharmacy proved to be a good shelter from the sun. Architecture from times when no air conditioning was available tends to make a building cooler when it's hot outside and warmer when it's cold outside—a lot more organically and ecologically correct than our flimsy modern buildings. The museum wasn't busy, so I could peacefully admire all the machinery that the friars once used, as well the ceramic jars with pictures of flowers and plants on them and the oddly shaped glassware. The most exquisite utensils were the copper and bronze sprinkling can-like devices, with seemingly longer than necessary spouts and the several sizes of crucibles, also made of bronze. Mortars and pestles made of marble, granite, gray china, and glass made me wonder if the material used to crush an herb could make a difference in the final product and its effects.

I travelled back in time, picturing how the friars must have created their concoctions, some of them with interesting names, such as the smelling salts called Aceto dei Sette Ladri—Vinegar of the Seven Thieves. The label claimed that the concoction could ward off the plague, and its ingredients include sage, lavender, thyme, rosemary, garlic, rue, and wormwood—all very powerful heroes of the herbal kingdom. I did a quick web research in my iPhone and found out that one of the many tales behind its invention involves a band of bandits who went around Europe robbing corpses but never became infected with the plague. When the gang was caught and imprisoned, they revealed the secret recipe that protected them in exchange for their freedom.

According to the exhibition pamphlet that covered a bit of the pharmacy's history, some other medicines popular in the friars' heyday were Liquore Mediceo, Alkermes, Elisir di China, and Acqua di Santa Maria Novella—the last praised for controlling hysterics using a local herb with a reputation of calming properties. Nowadays they still sell it, but now they advertise it as having antispasmodic properties. Looking at the venerable manuals inside the display windows, I could read many Latin words and often understand whole sentences. Finally, I'd found a use for that weird class my mom had made me take: It helped me read such old old recipes of the beginnings of Western pharmacology! I was actually shaking with excitement—or maybe I was finally starting a food coma. I couldn't help but remember my grandma's advice against reading after meals.

I heard someone cough and say in a thick accent, "Please do not touch the glass."

"Sorry," I apologized, and the museum security guard nodded. I crossed my hands behind my back to avoid another indiscretion and went on deciphering recipes on the pages decorated with drawings of herbs and fruits or angels holding bows and arrows, jars, or baskets. Another pharmacy staffer, a classy woman wearing glasses almost falling from the tip of her nose and carrying a heavy file, walked over to talk to me. She took off her glasses, which now hung from a golden chain set with semiprecious stones, and studied my face with amused interest.

"So, you appreciate old books? Would you like to see our library?"

I remembered the sign by the front door: "Library closed for repairs. Sorry for the inconvenience," so I didn't know what to say.

Seeing my puzzled reaction, she smiled. "It's closed for visitation now, but you seem to be a book lover, so you're welcome to come inside."

I followed her through a maze of narrow corridors, sudden steps, and quick corners, until we got to an arched doorway, its wooden door barred by two iron gates. She opened the first one with a heavy key and the second one with a combination. Behind them was a door that opened onto a pitch-black room that smelled of mold and dust mites. Thinking of my allergies, I shivered.

"I know it's dark; we're changing our lighting system. Meanwhile, we've been using headlamps. Here, you can borrow mine."

She searched in her pocket and handed me a lamp with a broken elastic band tied together with a knot. The band was greasy with dandruff flakes; white hair stuck out of the knot. I thanked her and she tapped my shoulder with her trembling hands.

"Go ahead, enjoy it." She left me alone, leaving the door cracked open behind her, a sliver of light interrupting the darkness. I turned on the headlamp, but just held it with my right hand.

As I entered deeper into the room, I immediately felt nauseous, but I couldn't turn around and say, "Thanks, but I don't want to do this anymore." Also, I was curious. Here I was, relic book miner for a moment, browsing gold-embossed titles and smelling old leather covers, when something with little cold feet crawled over my foot. A mouse, probably? Argh. My stomach turned over, and I started to leave, but a title in red letters caught my attention: *Malleus Maleficarum, Maleficas & earum hæresim, ut phramea potentissima conterens.* I remember once seeing an English translation of this tome called *The Hammer of the Witches* in the mysticism section of the Russian Hill Bookstore in San Francisco. But this book seemed much closer to the real thing, a compilation of arguments and evidence intended to prove that witches exist.

Right next to it, another small, leather bound book stood, rather unassumingly, but irresistible. Maybe the fact that there was no title embossed in the spine made me want to know more about it? I felt drawn to it, and, even though it seemed rather moldy, I inhaled a deep breath and took it down from the shelf. No title in the cover either. I tried to read it using the light of the headlamp and supporting it on the empty space in the shelf right underneath it , but most of the damp, yellowed pages were stuck together. One section seemed well thumbed, though, and I managed to flip through some of the pages. In the very beginning of it I found a note with an illegible date, and something in Latin that meant "confiscated from witch Alma." It contained lots of spells and recipes for potions and other concoctions, and, alongside them, notes written in blotted ink. My Latin was rather rusty, but I could grasp that someone had consulted some of the spells and recipes and adapted them to their own purposes, just as a cook will substitute olive oil for butter, writing over and modifying the ingredients in a cookbook recipe.

On page after page, I recognized plant drawings from the books exhibited in the showroom. So that was how the friars might have built their pharmaceutical empire: from witches' ancient recipes, the same witches persecuted by their very own Catholic Church. . . .

Standing up, still holding the book, I suddenly sensed how cramped and constricted the library was. I felt short of breath; my allergies, or my rage, made me put the book back on its shelf and run to the door only to find it closed and locked. I knocked and called for help, but it was so thick I doubted that anyone out could hear me. I banged harder, aggravating my tendonitis. Closing my eyes, I tried to inhale deeply, a trick that had always worked to calm me down and help me see more clearly, but the smell of mold and stale air burned my nostrils. I decided to kick the door with my uninjured foot. The impact caused a crack of light to show up in the door, at eye level. A small window! I clawed at the protruding piece of wood with my nails and managed to open the tiny rectangle. Now I could see a bit more light, and the iron bars brought me hope. I screamed, half-crying, half-laughing, "Someone, please open this door for me! Get me out of here, please!"

Nothing.

I screamed louder, in the highest pitch I could reach.

The woman who had invited me in hurried toward me, gasping with the effort. "*Cara mia, che peccato.* I am so sorry. Someone must have closed the door after I left you."

I couldn't reply; I had lost my voice. All I could do was take off the lamp and hand it to her.

She took me to a room overlooking a courtyard with an indoor garden and offered me a seat on a couch embroidered with flowers. I held tightly to a satin pillow and tried my breathing exercises again.

"Would you like some water?"

I nodded yes.

A young fair skinned woman with pitch black hair and rosy cheeks wearing a pharmacy uniform brought a tall glass of water on a silver tray, which I grabbed and gulped greedily. Yuk. It had sugar in it, and it was room temperature. I almost vomited it back into the glass. Managing to hold it back, I returned the empty glass to the tray, the leftover sugar crystals sliding back to the bottom, my hands shaking.

"Do you need anything else?" she asked.

"No, thanks. Can I just rest here for a bit?"

"But of course."

She left me alone in the sober, whitewashed room, uncluttered and spacious, almost empty apart from a second couch and a crystal chandelier. The simplicity, along with the nearby greenery of the indoor garden, helped me to calm down. I felt that I could finally sleep, but I still wanted to keep looking at the light.

***

I'm so tired that I close my eyes, and I see red. My eyeballs move from left to right rapidly like train windows going through a tunnel that has very bright lamps, so these are probably the REM movements. I'm falling fast for I don't know how long. It feels good to rest like I've never rested before, looking at a bright, intense, fierce source of light. I don't know why it didn't prevent my dozing off. Now I'm snoring—oh, how shameful in a public place. Now all the customers passing by me to visit the indoor garden will know that I snore, but I don't know these people, and I probably won't see them ever again, so what the heck, snore away.

In my mind, I go back to a time that I somehow remember as clearly as if it were yesterday. I see a group of women gathered around a big ceramic bowl. Someone is pouring grappa into it. Now, she adds some lemon peels, coffee beans, and three spoons of sugar, at the same time speaking words in Galego that I somehow understand: "*Bruja peido mulher nova casa com home viejo, barriga de mulher solteira.*" Now, she touches the surface of the liquid with a torch, and it kindles with a blue flame. As she scoops the liquid with a ladle and pours it back into the bowl, the fire moves up and down the streaming liquid like ever-increasing blue energy. She drops the ladle onto the table and cups magically appear. The woman pours the blue liquid fire into the cups and passes them among the gathering. I drink mine with gusto. The fire feels cool as it touches my lips, but the drink burns my throat and brings life into my frozen body.

Then, I start dreaming a dream inside a dream. I'm hiding in the dark, inside a barn, crouching among cows, bumping my elbows into restless calves that can't understand the presence of an intruder in their barn; they haven't yet acquired the nonchalance that mature cows usually have. The smell of manure and hay is comforting compared to what waits for me outside. Someone opens the door. I can tell by the red brightness that several men carry torches. All that dry hay could catch fire in a second. The cows grow uneasy and start mooing and fidgeting, and I must move along to avoid being stepped on.

"There. There she is!"

I try running away, but the cows are in the way. Soon, the men surround me. I can't recognize any face. The glare of the torches gives all of them creepy shadows under their eyes. One of them, a man with curly white hair and a dark beard, grabs me by my wrists and pulls me out. The bright sunlight hurts my eyes. How long have I been inside that barn? They tie my arms behind my back and make me march along a road toward the town. A crowd starts following me in a macabre procession. I hear the humming of the voices in Italian.

Once we pass the gates to the city and walk toward the main square, the mob spreads throughout the narrow cobblestone streets. People look down at me from every window, most looking concerned and shocked. Eventually, I come near a blonde woman with a sewn eyelid. The visible eye is emerald green, wide open, and angry. I don't know who she is, but the men pushing me make me stop in front of her. She spits in my face. The crowd goes crazy.

At last, we arrive at the crowded main square. The men make me climb some steps onto a pile of wood with a tall stake in the middle. One man brings more rope, and they tie me tightly to the stake. Someone starts the fire. My long, dark skirt catches fire. I watch it burn up. It just feels warm; the fire isn't touching my skin yet. I feel cold and empty inside, almost indifferent, as I've always known that this would happen someday.

Here at my final destination, I look at the crowd—half of the spectators exulting in a delirious catharsis, the other half quietly observing. Through the corner of my left eye, I see the people in the audience budge a bit until a tiny, skinny, white arm sticks out of the crowd and tries to open the human bodies barrier to come near me. Escaping the crowd, a little girl of eleven or twelve goes down on her knees and crawls toward me, fearlessly approaching the fire, which now burns all the wood below me. An elderly woman grabs her leg and pulls her back into the crowd. She digs the ground with her nails in a useless attempt to continue her intended course. The woman holds the child tightly against her body.

Now the fire is burning my skin; I jerk in pain and bite my lower lip. I look at the little girl, who is crying big, fat tears. My eyes are drawn to a wooden box that she holds squeezing under her armpit. She drops it in the ground and opens the lid. I try to see its contents but to no avail. She is no longer crying; now her fierce hazelnut eyes are inscrutable. She mutters some words. I try to read her lips, but I can't understand. As the flames burn stronger, I can smell my long hair burning, and I remember playing with it as a teenager, singeing the tips on candle flames. The pain is excruciating, I scream louder and louder. The crowd shivers. The girl's lips move faster and faster—

***

"*Signorina?* Are you ill?"

Feeling a cold hand cooling my feverish cheek, I opened my eyes and saw the woman who had brought me the water standing in front of me, looking scared and worried. Behind her, stood the lady who had invited me into the library, with her glasses up her forehead and a very concerned expression. "Miss, you were screaming and convulsing in spasms. What is happening?"

"I . . . I was burning."

"Yes, you have a temperature right now. You're running quite a fever."

"No, I was being burned. At a stake, in public."

"Oh, *signorina, è un incubo.*"

"What?"

"A nightmare, you had a nightmare."

She handed me some Kleenex. I tried to wipe the sweat from my forehead, but the effort was futile. I decided to go back to the hostel, shower, and change.

"Would you like some more water?"

"Oh, no, *grazie mille.* I'm leaving now."

"Take care."

I left the pharmacy. It was still very hot outside. I felt awkward, with my clothes all sticky and passersby staring at me. Their staring reminded me of the crowd in my dream. Once again, I was the odd girl out.

CHAPTER 5

Bosco di Mellizano

Florence seems so far away now. When I left the hot, overwhelming city, I took the train to the South of Italy and watched the green, grassy hills pass by, sprinkled with golden haystacks shaped like half-bitten cannoli and broken here and there by groups of tall, pointy, dark green cypresses. My backpack was open, and I could smell a mixture of dry rosemary, oregano, sage, garlic flakes, and cracked black pepper coming out of it. The family who had hosted me at my first farm had made a batch of Tuscan spice from scratch as a good-bye gift in a mesh bag. Such aromas helped put me in a calmer state, and I'd thought the trouble I'd experienced in Florence would be gone once I got back on a farm.

Unfortunately, being here hasn't helped. Today, I'm just tired of weeding. It's so damn hot and dry—no wonder my ancestors never went back. The winters in New York must have been easier to endure than plowing the land in this scorching summer heat. I'm out of breath and decide to sit in the lounge chair in the shade near the fence. There's no one to check whether I'm working or not. The gypsies aren't coming in today; there are no paying guests whatsoever; Rick is stuck in the office cursing and trying to make the Internet work; and Ila got a ride into town with Luludja, the gypsy circus manager, to visit Ken and Kulveer at the jailhouse and bring them some food. I sneak out, bringing with me a tall glass of elderflower cordial full of ice cubes, and smash in some of the round, red mystery berries that Rori found to give it a kick. Francesco, the farm owner, is supposed to come by tonight. I hope I remember to ask him the name of these berries. And I hope he manages to fix the network. Having no Internet connection makes me feel even more isolated in this godforsaken land.

Still, lying in the shade as I am now, this place isn't so bad. Last night, I managed to sleep well, a dream-free night, courtesy of Tylenol PM. That stuff can sure knock you out. Honestly, I could sleep right now. Maybe Rick and Ila are right that Rori got tired of all this work and just took off. Despite the blight, all around

32

me in this spot is green and relaxing. I stretch my body as I haven't done in a while. I could use some Josh back rubs at some point in this trip; my body aches from all the crouching and plucking.

I turn around and notice a stretch of broken fence. Odd. I see something white caught on the barbed wire. I scratch my eyes, get up, and come closer to it: a familiar piece of pleated silk, ripped by the thorns and now hanging from it like a flag of truce. I remember that fabric; it's from the pleated silk and chiffon blouse that Rori was wearing the night when the gypsies were here; it was translucent and revealing, and we could see her demi-cup plunge bra through it. Sometimes, I wonder if she was absent-minded or just liked to play Lolita, with her lacy black thong sticking out above her low-rise jeans whenever she bent over in the garden. It drove her boyfriend, Ken, crazy, but I noticed that it attracted unwanted attention from the gypsies as well.

I clearly remember the night when Luludja was a bit tipsy from too much wine. She took an avid look at Rori's red curls, and commented, in a pasty voice, "You have such beautiful hair!" and touched it in a longing, lingering manner. Her husband, Joe Pugliese, who wasn't gypsy, just plain Italian, and looked somewhat Greek (Rick told me that he was from Puglia, born and raised in a fishing town by the Adriatic Sea), seemed amused by the sight of his wife coveting the Irish girl who had ended up in their care and management. But Luludja's cousin, Pali, sat smoking a pipe and never taking his gaze away from the unwitting temptress.

Great, now I'm blaming her. If it weren't for my dreams, I would be just fine with the idea that she chose to leave. But the gypsy woman's cousin has dark and hairy arms like the man in my dreams, and that night was the last time we saw Rori.

Did Rori catch her blouse on the fence and leave a piece of it behind? It seems unlikely. I scan the area around the fence, so deceptively quiet. It's almost as the heat makes any living thing, even bugs and lizards, too lazy to move. My mind is racing, though; I take a picture of the fabric stuck in the wire with my serviceless smart phone and jump over the fence to investigate.

A broken branch from a lemon tree farther down the hill is lying on the ground, some rotting lemons still stuck to it. Coming closer, I nudge the fallen leaves around it. Between two pointy rocks, I see a bit of cork. What would a cork be doing here? Besides, all the wine we drink is from huge gallon jugs that we refill at the neighboring winery, and the lids on them are plastic.

I come closer and see that the piece of cork isn't cylindrical like a wine cork; this piece is much larger and roughly angular. And it has metal studs on it . . . I dig it out with my fingernails and pull out the broken sole of Rori's platform sandal! How could I forget it? We teased her all the time for her choice of farming footwear. Now this is evidence!

I don't want to touch it or move it any more than I already have; I take some pictures and get up so fast I feel dizzy; I hold the lemon tree for support and take a deep breath. The heat is taking a toll and I'm getting hungry—it's past lunchtime. As I look at the place where the fallen branch once connected to the trunk, a sharp reminder of its former presence, I see something tiny, shiny, and coppery stuck to it. I try to climb the tree to come closer to it, but the trunk is too thin and the twigs are thorny. I gather rocks and improvise some stair steps. Alas, it's a knotted clump of red hair, a dust bunny with no dust. I take another picture and climb down carefully. I can't wait to bring Rick here and show him; he won't be able to dismiss my theory anymore.

I run back to the main guesthouse where I find Rick lying in the hammock on the veranda, frustrated about being unable to fix our Internet connection yet.

"Rick, she was kidnapped. Now I know for sure."

"What are you talking about?"

"Rori was kidnapped. Now I have proof."

"Are you going to start with this again?"

"Please, you've got to come with me and see this. I've found a piece of her clothes, a broken shoe, and even a clump of her hair, all by the fence near the chaise lounge. She fought her attacker! She didn't want to go. I'm completely sure now."

"Well, *I'm* sure you must be hungry and therefore delirious. Ila just got back, and I have lunch ready, so why don't we all sit down to eat and after dessert, you can show me your evidence? Ila brought tiramisu from town."

Again, he belittles my efforts. I give in since he's right that I'm starving.

Rick has prepared my favorite dish from his wide repertoire: *ragù alla napoletana*, with homemade fusilli instead of ziti or penne. This Neapolitan fusilli has truly gotten the best of me; it's tightly coiled instead of loose like most fusilli with its corkscrew characteristic design, and cooks to al dente perfection. Its shape adds some adventure to the texture and chewing.

We still eat family style despite our suddenly shrunken family. When the summer and the work began, we had six people: Ila, Rick, Rori, Ken, Kulveer, and me. The three who remain are all tired of the usual drama, so we invest in small talk instead.

Rick starts the conversation. "Let's save some sauce. Francesco is coming tonight for dinner."

"Oh, I can't wait to see him," I respond. "I haven't seen him in so long. Have you seen him lately, Ila?"

Before she can answer, Rick snaps, "Ila and I had dinner at his new house in Naples that weekend we took off a while ago."

Rick never lets Ila talk to me. Since she's naturally quiet, anyway, I rarely hear her voice.

But I insist and go into the touchy subject we're all avoiding: "So how are those two jailbirds? Are they starving in their cell?"

"Oh, Ken's family hired a lawyer to work on his case; he may be out soon. He's mostly worried about Rori, though. Kulveer's situation is a lot trickier. He may be deported back to India . . . ." Her voice trails off, and a long moment of silence ensues.

To break the tension, I decide to tell Ila about my discoveries. "You know, today I went out by the fence—"

Rick cuts me off. "Where is that tiramisu you went all the way to town for?" he asks Ila. "Did you manage to find the good kind that uses real mascarpone instead of ricotta?"

I know he means business. He believes in avoiding stressful conversations during a meal. He has a point, and I hold my peace.

"Oh, the *pasticceria* was closed for siesta when I stopped by," Ila responds, "and Luludja couldn't wait for them to open. But we found some woman sitting by the door, selling tiramisu out of a tray, and she told me she made it herself. Sounds promising, doesn't it?"

Rick takes her hand and blows her a kiss, and they go about their lovey-dovey exchanges. I started out in this place as the fifth wheel of the volunteers, and now I'm just the third wheel, but it feels awkward all the same. I miss Josh—and San Francisco. Living there was so much easier.

After dessert (which isn't that big a deal—the woman used ricotta) and coffee, the two of them decide to take one of their noisy "naps." I usually wander around in the afternoons, but I'm determined not to leave until I show them my discoveries. So I wash some dishes, waiting for the building to stop shaking. As usual, they come down from their bedroom holding hands and wearing wide smiles. Irritating.

"Can we go now?" I demand.

Rick sighs and reluctantly agrees to listen.

We all leave, with me leading the way eager to show that I'm not crazy and them lagging behind me at honeymoon speed. I find the fence, still bent and broken, but no sign of the dangling piece of fabric. I run to the lemon tree; the fallen branch is gone, my rocky stairsteps are scattered all over the ground, and her cork-soled platform shoe has vanished, along with the little ball of red hair. I squeeze my forehead as if the effort will make those objects reappear. Where are they?

Rick confronts me. "So, where's your evidence?"

"Here, I have pictures." Or not. Damn iPhone 3G and its useless battery. I need to recharge it. None of the photos was saved, even though I recall snapping each one.

"It was all here before lunch, a ripped piece of clothing, a shoe and some hair."

"But where are them now?", asks Ila, trying to hide a little laugh mixed with compassion and concern.

"Wait. What about the fresh scar on this side of the lemon tree where the branch was pulled off?" I point.

"That's hardly evidence of kidnapping, Cami.", Rick complains. Ila opens her big eyes wide and pitifully.

While they stand there looking at me like grandchildren looking at their Alzheimer's-stricken grandmother, we hear a car arriving.

"That must be Francesco," Ila says.

"Yeah, let's go," Rick responds.

They leave me alone under the lemon tree, not giving me time to point out that the rocks I gathered are still here, but not as I left them; the top ones are now scattered on the ground. Someone intentionally removed the evidence. Unfortunately, that means that same someone saw me finding it, and now that someone knows that I know.

A chill goes down my spine. What if whoever took it all away is watching me? Or, maybe, since the evidence disappeared so fast, it was never there? Were the lock of hair, the piece of shoe, the scrap of silk just my fertile imagination tricking me?

I search the grove anxiously, hoping to prove to myself that I'm not going crazy—now, with that Crying-Wolf moment, my reputation is even more tarnished. As I sit on a stump watching a parade of ants carrying crumbs, I remember elementary school, when we staged "The Boy Who Cried Wolf", one of Aesop's fables, I played the part of the boy's mother. "Nobody will believe you anymore, my dear." I worked hard on achieving the condescending tone even though, secretly, I wanted to be one of the hunters that went after the wolf in our version of the tale, but the teacher reserved those roles for the boys.

As I ask myself why, did I want to be a hunter, I see a spider web in a shady spot with morning dew still clinging to it in spite of the heat. As the sun starts to set in the valley, a ray of light shines right on it, making a rainbowlike effect, I notice a streak of red crossing the rainbow lines. A hair! A long, red hair with a curl on one end. And I can touch it. It's real and concrete. I'm not going mad, and here's the proof.

I decide to save it and not show anybody for fear that it will vanish if I try. And I need it badly—my own anchor to reality—even if, unlike my previous discoveries, it doesn't necessarily prove that she was kidnapped. It could have escaped the bun she usually wore when she was working and ended up in the spider web. Who knows? I'm just happy to have one confirmation that Rori stayed on this farm for a short time since the police took her luggage as their evidence after she disappeared. I roll the hair like a little lasso and save it in the smallest pocket of my jeans.

I press my palm on top of it for a while, sit on the lounge chair, and close my eyes, trying to remember Rori and her ways.

***

"Do you believe in magic?" Rori asked me as she hand-rolled a cigarette using dry herbs instead of tobacco. I opened my eyes wide trying to figure out what was she doing, and she noticed. "This is just mugwort; it helps with cramps."

"Ah, artemisia," I said.

"Oh, is that what they call it here?"

"Yeah, my grandpa was from here, and he was always having some or serving cups of tea to my mom when she had cramps. But isn't the tea better than a cigarette?"

"Well, yeah, but with those gypsies hogging the kitchen, I don't feel like fighting for a cup of tea. And I like smoking it, anyway."

She handed me the cigarette, and I took a drag. The smell reminded me of the acupuncture sessions I had when I was afflicted by tendonitis. The doctor burned a fat cigar and brought the ember very close to the needles, and it made my tensed fists loosen up a little. I tried to inhale the smoke from Rori's cigarette and coughed. I've never been a very good smoker.

"So, do you believe?" she repeated.

"In magic? I never used to, but I'm starting to open up to the idea. I mean, there's magic in everything around us, right? Just think about these herbs—one is good for this, another is good for that. I once had mercury intoxication, and I heard that cilantro chelates mercury out of the body, so I spent a month eating fresh cilantro three times a day. It did the trick! I felt much better afterward."

She stood there silent, her eyes fixed on a dandelion.

That silence sort of bothered me, so I searched for some more small talk to try to break her trance. She was almost becoming one with the little puffy weed, and I felt left out, so I wanted to bring her back.

"And there was also this one time when my boyfriend was getting sick with pollen allergies, and we heard that honey from local bees could provide relief. He was lucky since his neighbor kept been on his rooftop, so he gave us some. It had such a subtle taste, no predominant flavor since the flowers around them were so varied. It was mild and just enough sweet, but never overpowering... and what an exquisite fragrance."

"So your man's *terroir* was subtle and mild then...", she replied, with her eyes still glued in the dandelion, taking another drag of her hand rolled cigarette.

"Excuse me?"

"*Terroir*. It means land in French, and is short for *goût de terroir*, literally, taste of the earth. It's more used for wine."

"Well. I guess the Mission District did have an almost steady micro climate, the temperature never varied too much there, even when it was cold all over the city, he still got a bit of sun and warmth in that spot."

"And your man? Was he mild? How did he taste like?"

I didn't know what to answer, and from the fire in my cheeks I knew I was blushing against my will. Oh, will I ever learn to hold that? I simply hate the fact that I'm so transparent.

She took one more drag, and held it inside for a bit longer, finally deviating her gaze from the dandelion and staring now at me with her still fixed eyes. She let out the smoke and a chuckle. "Oh, I'm sorry, did I embarrass you with my question? I guess you are more like a good girl, uh? Not me, I'm good as well as bad."

I didn't answer her. I got distracted on thinking about Josh and how he had not emailed or communicated since we parted ways. And I don't know if I blushed out of being good or bad. It was more like out of modesty. And Rori was so exuberant; sometimes just her gait and demeanor threw me off.

She went on.

"Don't worry about it, I get red in the face too. We are both fair ladies. Being white means never being able to hide your feelings, unless you are a master of self- control. We are like living walking giant mood rings."

I smiled. I remember having one of those when I was a kid. She smiled back, now less wickedly and displaying a lot more compassion.

After a couple more drags, she offered me her mugwort joint again.

"Thanks, I'll pass."

She blew another cloud of pungent smoke. And changed the subject back to plant power, thank you very much.

"Yeah, the right herb at the right time can do wonders. It also can kill your enemies, and they won't know that the salad they just ate was their last meal. Many a woman who didn't want the baby she was carrying relied on mugwort to get rid of it. But that's just a matter of knowing what nature provides you. The magic I'm talking about manipulates your surroundings and bends the elements to your will."

The bloody scene I'd performed back in my office in San Francisco came to mind. As soon as those images, which I could never explain and therefore tried to ignore, reached my consciousness, she moved her head quickly like a cat that has just heard a big bug crawling nearby.

"What is it?" she asked.

"What is it what?"

"That you're thinking about."

"I'm not thinking about anything."

She chose to stop inquiring and crushed the half-smoked cigarette under the sole of her cork- soled sandals.

"You know, my mother taught me that every woman in Ireland is a bit of a witch. It's our thing."

I nodded, more out of a better thing to do then out of agreement.

One day, I'll teach you some of my tricks if you'll teach me some of yours," she promised.

I smiled. "I'm sorry, but my bag of tricks is empty. At least, I don't know that kind of tricks."

"I see." She opened her pink lips in a slow, mischievous grin, got up, brushed the grass and dirt from the back of her jeans, and gestured toward the lawn that we were supposed to weed that day. "Shall we get back to work, then?"

Those were the last words I ever heard her speak. . I went inside to do some cleaning in the bathrooms, and she disappeared that same evening.

***

I stretch my body from the tips of my toes to the tips of my fingers, gathering strength to spring up from the lounge chair and walk back to join the others and greet the farm owner. I feel a burning sensation in my hip, right under the smallest pocket where I saved the red hair.

In the driveway, Rick is talking to Francesco about this broken truck, so far the sole means of transportation in the farm besides the ATVs—those fun things that only Kulveer was allowed to ride before his arrest.

The truck has been broken for almost a week, and the gypsies couldn't care less that we volunteers are stranded here with no way in or out. The hood is open, and both men have their heads stuck inside, analyzing the intricacies of the internal combustion engine. Leaving it with greasy hands and no immediate solution, they go back to the main guesthouse. To judge from his dramatic gestures, Francesco thinks it's a broken part and he'll buy a replacement. Funny how Italians talk with their whole bodies. I follow them, going a bit faster and eventually catching up.

Hearing me behind him, Francesco turns around. "Oh, the beautiful Carmela. Pure like water. *Ciao, bella, come stai?* I am not going to shake your hands to not make you dirty with grease. And I hope Rick is not making you work too hard, eh?" He shows me that he has grease up to his elbows and tells me that he would shake my hand otherwise. He even has a bit of grease on his receding, balding forehead and spots here and there on his facial stubble. The unshaven style makes him look darker than he really is, and his thick eyebrows, full lips and deep brown eyes help in making that impression. But his neck is fairly white, and a bit red from sunburn. He does have grease up to his elbows indeed, up until his rolled sleeves, so such painted limbs increase my picture of him darker than he really is.

"Io sto benne", I answer in my broken Italian, and both men laugh, Rick leaning to sarcasm as he usually does. Francesco's laugh is more open and good-natured, but somehow finishes with a note of concern.

As we resume walking, Rick is talking nonstop about all the stuff that he's been holding in his chest for so long: how the people renting the farm are not caring, how they've been treating the volunteers, how they bring their mistreated horses here to make it all dirty. . Ila, who was watching them from a short distance away, walks in front of them. Maybe she just can't help being faster, but her head is hanging from her bent neck and I suspect that, like Rick, she's upset about not having a car and not being able to run errands or go to town, but unlike him, she keeps her frustration to herself. Francesco listens until he stops beside his car, a black Ferrari, and takes a clear bucket full of shrimp and other kinds of little creatures from the Bay of Naples from the passenger's seat.

When we get to the kitchen, Ila and I clean the seafood, deveining the shrimp and brushing away sand from cockles and clams. After he and Francesco scrub their arms and hands in the kitchen sink, Rick prepares fresh, homemade pasta with a creamy white herbed sauce. Francesco sits on a high stool drinking white wine and telling us about upcoming reservations and guest lists for the farm. Rick smiles and frowns at the same time.

"It will take a lot of work to prepare this place for hosting guests properly, Francesco…"

"Oh, but, we have all of your beautiful smiles here, that's what it counts.", dismisses Francesco. "And besides…"

"Aaaaarrrgh!" A screech interrupts his sentence.

"Are you okay Ila? Rick runs upstairs to check on his damsel in distress, but she's coming down full throttle and almost runs over him.

"Mice! A full family of mice is living inside the linen closet." She screams, more pissed than scared.

We all look at Francesco, who is scratching his thinning hair.

"Oh well, we shall take a look at them later okay? Let's eat now since the food is warm!"

We help him set up the table, the three of us volunteers exchanging puzzled looks that read something like "now this guy is probably not caring much about the future of this farm". We all sit quietly, but.the pasta is hot and rich, and the seafood is very flavorful and fresh. And the wine he's brought—a new batch from our neighboring winery—is amazing. Slowly we let go of the mice thoughts, and the atmosphere becomes so festive that I almost forget about Rori as I listen to Rick complain about the current management.

"Why won't they let us cook? The other day, they didn't show up to serve breakfast; they just left some stale bread lying around! If we don't break their rules, we'll starve."

"And when they cook, the food is so bad, we can't stand it," Ila adds. "No wonder the reservations are down."

"How could people making reservations know in advance that the food would be bad? It wasn't bad last year. Now that I took over the reservations, and they will be just taking care of the place in general, I'll make sure that when guests are here, mostly weekends, the food will be tasty!" Francesco seemed to have a sunny solution for anything.

"You have a reputation to keep, Ciccio," Rick continues. "If they don't manage to buy this farm after the lease is up and you try to sell it after they leave, it will be devalued by their neglect."

"And they don't even care about poor Kulveer, stuck in jail." puts in Rori. "They used to treat him like an animal, screaming at him and pushing him around. I went to visit the boys in jail and asked Luludja if she wanted to come along. She said, 'No, thanks, got to run some errands.' And when she picked me up again by the police station, she didn't even turn off the engine. She wanted to be out of there as soon as possible and didn't even ask how they were doing."

"I'm sorry to hear that," Francesco says. "My girlfriend warned me that gypsies have no heart, but I didn't listen. Now I'm stuck with them."

I blush listening to such offensive generalization. Now I am glad I hadn't met Francesco's girlfriend yet, a city woman who won't leave Naples and makes the most effort to keep him there as well. I can't resist bringing up the uncomfortable. "And whenever we ask if they know any news about Rori, they dismiss the case like it's no big deal!"

A cloud of silence covers our little dinner party. My obsession with the missing redhead is starting to bother them.

Francesco explains: "You know, Carmela, even though the police did collect Rori's belongings, they closed the case because there's no evidence that she has been kidnapped. She may have just walked away; she had been saying that she wasn't happy here, I am sorry to admit. And the police didn't arrest Ken and Kulveer because Rori disappeared. Kulveer is an illegal immigrant—my fault for having him work here; now I'm in trouble, too. Ken does live in Ireland as a student, but he's a citizen of South Africa and didn't have his *permesso di soggiorno* to work in Italy. Even if he's a volunteer working for food and shelter, not cash, the law still treats it as work. I know that most wwoofers forget to get the *permesso,* but if they're from the European Union, it's no problem. Since he's not from the European Union, he's technically an illegal immigrant. Italy is the only country in the volunteering network that requires extra paperwork, and WOOFF Italy states that clearly on their website, but most people forget."

Ila takes the empty pasta dishes from the table and brings some peaches. Francesco clears his throat.. "You all have your *permessos,* right?

"Yeah, we do.", Rick replies in the name of us all.

So Francesco managed to divert the conversation once again, as he always does when I bring up Rori.

I get up to leave the table. "Thanks, I don't feel like having dessert." I go out for some fresh air and stick my pinkie into my smallest pocket. The hair is still there. I look at the starry valley. I can still see a tiny bit of sun setting in the lower mountains. We had such an early dinner today.

"I'm sorry, Cami. I'm so sorry."

I start and turn around to see who's talking behind me. It's Francesco. How dare he come from behind me like that? He really gave me goose bumps this time.

"I wanted to apologize before I leave. I'm going back to Naples now; that was just a short visit."

"Apologize for what?"

"I'm so sorry that this place is a mess. I'm trying so hard . . . I'll try to come back at the end of the next week and this time stay for the entire weekend."

"Well, it's not your fault that you needed to rent the farm and you're trying to sell it. Maybe you should have taken the farm off the WWOOF volunteering network list since you weren't going to be totally in control of it."

"I know. But what's done is done. Let's try to make things better from now on, okay? Let's forget about the past, about everything that happened."

"Okay ." I don't exactly understand him, but I agree. He's being very emphatic, and I feel that whatever happened, I'd better forget about it.

CHAPTER 6

Caserta

It's Saturday. The bright sun coming through the window wakes me up, hurting my eyes. I've never slept so late here, but it's okay since it's not a workday. I had a night of heavy, uninterrupted sleep, no dreams, and my feet are dry and clean. Good. I'm tired of having to wash the muddy sheets by hand after those vivid dreams. Somehow, something tells me not to throw them into the communal dirty laundry. How could I explain the stains?

One morning, Luludja saw me scrubbing my soiled sheet in the outdoor laundry sink and hanging it on the line (so the midday sun would dry it fast enough that I could use the same one to sleep on). In her broken English, peppered here and there with Italian, she asked why I was doing that since they had a washer and dryer. So much for discretion.

Thinking fast and knowing her curiosity about the strange habits of those weird kids who came to this farm to work for free, I answered in my faulty Italian mixed with English, "It's woman's problems, if you know what I mean." I rubbed my lower belly in a universal gesture that any woman should understand.

"Oh, sorry, okay, okay." She left me alone, walking away smiling letting out almost a blush, closing her eyes and nodding in an embarrassed acknowledgment.

I rub my eyes and realize that I'm late for breakfast, if there's any left. I gather the dirty clothes spread on the floor from last night and wear the same pants but choose another shirt because yesterday's is unbearably stinky. I run out, and the three dogs that always sleep by my door get up and run after me.

In the kitchen, I find only Luludja and her husband, Pugliese. They brought fresh bread—still warm and smelling irresistible—along with ricotta and butter. Too bad that they destroyed the chicken coop that used to exist here according to Rick's past summer stories; I'd love to have eggs for breakfast sometimes. This diet based on bread, pasta, dairy products, and wine is taking its toll on me: I now have to wear my jeans unbuttoned.

I drop the dirty clothes in the communal laundry room, say my good mornings, and start to make myself a macchiato in the espresso machine. Pugliese asks for one, too. I hate the tone they use with us; not even my managers at my short-lived Manhattan waitressing job during High School made me feel so much like a servant.

I decide to ask if they ever buy eggs. "*Uovo?*"

They shake their heads and say something like "next time."

I ask about Rick and learn that he and Ila left with Francesco last night to spend the weekend in Naples.

"Oh, no." I was hoping to hitchhike with them and try to go somewhere, but I missed out.

"Where do you want to go my child?" The gypsy woman asks me.

"Nowhere specific. I just want to get out of here, see something different."

"We are going to Caserta if you want to go there," Luludja says. "We'll take care of business and then come back to Benevento at night. You can take the bus back to Benevento and meet us there to bring you back to the farm."

Okay, anywhere but here sounds good to me. Besides, I hope to get some Internet for e-mail and do some grocery shopping, so any town will do.

I ask them to wait and then run back into my bungalow, brush my teeth, grab my backpack, and come sprinting back to jump into their four-by-four, which is already humming by the gate. The dogs follow me, barking as I get into the car, and follow us out onto the road for a long while.

Pugliese laughs and wonders out loud why the dogs behave like that.

"They've followed me since I arrived," I answer.

"Really?" Luludja turns to me creasing her brows in apparent confusion. And how funny, I can see through the rearview mirror that Pugliese is creasing his brows as well.

I venture an explanation. "Maybe because I shared my salami as soon as I got here."

They laugh out loud. "That will sure give you a loyal friend," Pugliese says, and the ice thaws a bit.

Sitting in the back seat of their car, listening to Hungarian violin solos on their CD player, I realize how transparent I am. I've never really managed to hide my antipathy for the gypsies. But I've never even given them a chance. When I first arrived, before even meeting them, I learned from Rori how horrible they were, mistreating everyone, trashing the place, and serving inedible food. But almost everyone has a good side and a bad side, so I try to give them a second chance. "So, what's good to do in Caserta?" I ask.

"Oh, they have a big palace," Luludja answers, "one of the biggest palaces in the world! Reggia di Caserta. It was built by the French king, when the Bourbons had power in Naples."

"It has more than twelve hundred rooms, adds Pugliese. "They made movies there, *Star Wars, Mission Impossible.*"

Sold! I ask them to drop me off at the palace.

They say they can't, but it's close to the train station and all the buses pass by there, so we go to downtown Caserta instead. They leave me by a supermarket where I buy some essentials to stuff in my backpack: canned tuna, nuts, and a box of popped farro cereal an ancient grain. And—I can't resist—half a dozen eggs and some prosciutto. I ask the cashier, who has a pierced nose (the first piercing I've seen in Campania), where I can use the Web. She leaves her cash register and takes me to the sidewalk. After a lot of gesticulating and pointing, she manages to convey how to find the nearest Internet place. When I get there, all the computers are busy. It's not even 11:00 yet, but I'm already hungry; bread and coffee don't last long in my stomach. And what was I thinking buying eggs before I tour the giant palace? They'll probably go bad in this heat, or break inside my backpack, stored like they are just wrapped in a newspaper. I haven't eaten eggs for so long I wasn't even thinking straight. I definitely should've waited until the end of the day to buy groceries, but I'm ever so compulsive… first things first, no delayed gratification.

The Internet place is half of someone's house; I can see a kitchen behind a cracked door, so I ask the young attendant at the counter if he can find me a way to cook some eggs while I wait. He smiles, opens the door behind him, and calls his mother. She comes out wearing a long black dress that covers most of her arms and legs and a stained white apron with red-and-green embroidery. She raises one eyebrow and looks at me suspiciously. When I hand her the eggs, all six of them, with my best hungry-tourist smile, she grunts, grabs them, and walks back into the kitchen.

Twenty minutes later, my eggs come back, hard-boiled and sitting on a plate. I peel each one, roll the prosciutto around them, and gobble them down, surrounded by a bunch of Italian teenagers pretending to focus on their Web browsing but looking utterly embarrassed for me. Hunger has no shame or regrets. As I wipe the sticky yolk off my chin with the back of my hand, a boy wearing a neatly ironed Eminem T-shirt tucked inside his Diesel skinny jeans gets up and pays. Baggy jeans will never make it in Italy, I suspect.

I jump onto the now free computer and eagerly type in my e-mail username and password only to find a lot of junk mail, along with invitations to Facebook events and requests for photos of the trip from coworkers, but nothing from Josh. I sent him a dozen messages before I arrived in the South, but not a word from him. I check my Sent Mail to make sure the old ones went through. Yep, all there. I open the last one; I don't even remember what I wrote.

Hello there! How are you? I sent you a letter by snail mail. Did you ever receive it? Have you taken the tour of the Amazon yet? I wish I were there with you. I hate to admit it, but you were right. Things in the South of Italy aren't as bucolic as I imagined.

Even though the nature around the farm is beautiful and the kids who work here are cool, the atmosphere is unstable and chaotic (think *Lord of the Flies* meets *The Shining*, set in the Southern Italian countryside). I can't wait to leave this craziness. But I have a hunch I should still hang around; my time isn't up yet. I don't want to go into details, but I think that Rori is somewhere nearby, and I may be able to find her.

Missing you a lot,

Cami

Very frustrating. Maybe I should focus on more sightseeing since he doesn't even care what's happening to me. Is it that hard to find an Internet connection in Bolivia, or Peru, or wherever he is? By now, he should have visited at least two cities, according to his plans. But, then, he told me before he left that failure is part of the plan, and he changes his mind and, consequently, his trajectory as often as he needs to. I log off, get up sadly, and slouch over to pay the boy behind the counter, who asks if I'm all right. "*Tutto bene?*"

I just shrug, sigh, grab my heavy backpack full of groceries, and leave.

Then I remember that I don't know how to get to the Reggia Caserta. I go back inside, and the attendant is happy to see me again. "Yes, of course," he says. "The bus stops right here. You should buy the ticket before. Here, I can sell you."

Ticket in hand, I focus on the future, the fun to be had visiting a new place, I get on the bus, and within fifteen minutes I arrive at the palace. But midday in the middle of Southern Italy means hell on earth, especially with a heavy backpack. I walk through the front garden toward the entrance among people speaking German, French, and Dutch. It's the first time I've seen tourists around here. In the atrium, I pass a dog; it's either sleeping or unconscious from the heat. The flies around it are also quiet, not buzzing in such weather. What a way to encounter a UNESCO World Heritage Site.

I recognize the arches from Queen Amigdala's palace, what fun. But all the art, and room after room filled with elaborate furniture, overwhelms me. I need to sit down but a velvet rope protects every chair. I wonder if I'll ever enjoy a museum again after the gorging that was Florence. Stendhal syndrome, hello again. Peeking through a window, I see people sitting on benches under trees in the garden. I run downstairs and start looking for an empty bench but can't find one. I get into a maze of manicured bushes that are getting brown on the tips. These aren't native plants; I can tell that they're fighting to survive. And they dry up the air around there, making me suffocate. I manage to get out of the maze, but I meet a hungry-eyed kid who asks me for change, the first beggar I've seen in Italy. Other kids see me and come toward us. Not knowing what to do, I dismiss them, walking fast across an emerald-green lawn—the grass feels hard as hay.

In that huge garden, where irrigation works hard to keep the plants and trees somewhat green, I suddenly want to see water. I feel the pull of the sea—salt water, sand, and seashells calling me, stronger than any craving I've ever had. I must go to the sea. I feel like a fish pulled out of its stream. The heat is driving me crazy, and I'm suffocating in that jungle of baroque art, tourists, long spiral staircases, and beggars. I need to get out of there, immediately. I feel like throwing up. Holding a lamppost for support, I force my throat until I feel my face turning red. I drop my backpack, which is open, and a dozen cans of tuna roll out of it. Passersby—burned-out Italians and goal-oriented tourists alike—ignore me or don't even notice my little fit. Nothing comes of my effort, not a single drop of vomit. But I need to get it out of me. I can't stand it anymore, so I scream at the top of my lungs, "I want to get out of the hell of this city! What is this damned place? Take me back to my farm! Take me to the sea!" I keep screaming until someone notices me.

"*Che c'è, signorina?* What's wrong?"

I lift my head—still screaming and still bent over, as if screaming will get something out of me besides angst—a bit of bile would do it—and I see a young, dark haired Italian man, wiry but fit, wearing Ray-Ban sunglasses. Not even in his thirties yet, but dressed in a suit like a businessman.

I compose myself, brushing the hair away from my face, and, when he looks into my eyes, I see that he's scared. And a bit offended, I suppose, since I was cursing his hometown. He holds my arm, somewhat hesitantly, and it feels good. I haven't felt human skin touching mine for weeks. It's hard to be a visitor to Italy these days. However welcoming the place may seem, Italians in the more touristy places seem to have built a wall around themselves, maybe out of self-preservation. Coming from New York by way of San Francisco helps me relate to that, both cities get their fair share of visitor crowds. His holding my arm feels so safe that I burst into tears, the kind with spasmodic hiccups.

"Can I help with anything? Would you like to sit down, drink something?"

Oh yes, please. I hold open my backpack while he collects each can and deposits it inside. I let myself be guided by this man, thinking that if he wants to abduct me or steal my purse, I'll let him do it. He tells me his name: Marco. Marco Sposito. We cross the street, toward one of the palace's many tourist-filled cafés. He keeps holding my arm, firmly yet supportively, and I feel like a frightened little girl whose daddy is walking her to school on her first day of kindergarten.

We sit down at a round marble table under a patio umbrella. Touching the cool marble feels good and reminds me that I need to freshen myself up.

"If you'll excuse me, I need to go to the restroom."

"Oh, sure, no problem, I'll be here waiting." He smiles shyly and very courteously.

In the cramped restroom, I look into the old, stained mirror, and I can see why Marco looked so scared: I have dark-red spots all around my eyes. That happens every time I throw up—or attempt to. My blood vessels just break. It looks just like some kind of contagious disease. I hate it when that happens. In middle school, the kids would call me Chicken Pox Face whenever that happened.

I press the pump under the sink, every time I come into a public restroom I spend a couple of seconds looking for the faucet, still after all this time in Italy I haven't gotten used to it. I fill my cupped hands with cold water, and splash it all over my face. I still want to jump into the sea, but the water on my face suffices for the moment.

When I return to the table, he's drinking an espresso. He offers me a sip, but I tell him that all I can tolerate is water. He orders it, and soon the waiter brings me plain cold water with a drop of lime juice. After drinking it, I feel so much better that I smile and ask my new friend about himself.

"Well, I'm a wine dealer. Pretty boring, eh? What's your story? I'm more interested in that!" He has a broad smile and speaks excellent English, and when he takes off his sunglasses to clean them, I see that he has green eyes. After putting the sunglasses back on, he rests his pale hands on the table with his long, slim fingers interlocked. He seemed to be staring at me even though I can't see his eyes behind the shades, and I see the beginning of a teasing smile.

I still want to vomit, so I blurt out, "Sorry. It's lovely here, but it's as hot as an oven and it's overwhelming for me to be here. All I can think about is the sea."

"Well, the Mediterranean isn't far from here, and there are many beach towns you could visit. Why did you come to Caserta? You don't seem like the usual tourist." He smirks, probably noticing my holey white T-shirt, worn-out jeans, and mud-caked hiking boots.

"I came to Italy to learn organic agriculture. I spent two weeks at a farm in Tuscany, and now I'm staying at another farm here in Campania."

"Oh, how interesting. How long will you be here before going back home to America?"

His questions have a hypnotic energy that makes me answer each one of them without thinking twice. "I don't know yet. I could leave any time since I've already spent the mandatory two weeks, but I feel like staying longer. Even though it's not the best setting . . ."

"Where is the farm where you're staying now?"

"Near a town called Benevento."

"*Ma non è vero!* Really?" His smile grows wider, but now it looks mischievous.

"Do you know the place?"

"*Così così.* Why did you pick that place? Any special reason?"

"Oh, my great-grandfather Raffaele was born there. He left the village when he was just sixteen. He never saw his mother again! So I wanted to know the place where my ancestors came from, get in touch with my roots, that kind of thing."

"You're in for a treat, my dear friend. Do you know anything about Benevento?"

"Not much, only that it was very poor back then. It's bigger now, apparently. Is there anything special I should know about?"

"Not really. Let's just say that what happens in Benevento stays in Benevento."

I look at the clock on the café wall and notice that it's getting late. I don't want to miss the last bus back to Benevento where Luludja and her husband promised to pick me up and take me back to the farm.

"Sorry, but I have to go. I'm late for the bus."

"Are you feeling okay now? Let me walk you to the station, please."

A few minutes ago, I was head over heels for his attentiveness, but now it feels like he's overstaying his welcome. Wondering why I always have such a hard time saying no, especially to good-looking men, I reluctantly accept his offer even though in the small of my lower back, I hear a little voice telling me, "Run as fast as you can, and don't even think of letting him follow you!"

The voice grows louder, and now it's whispering into my ear, so only I can hear it, "Leave. And don't look behind."

I argue silently with the voice and say that it's just plain rude to refuse such a nice fellow. He helped me out and, besides, I won't see him again, anyway.

The voice becomes grumpy. "Okay," it says, "but don't tell me later that you regret it."

Marco carries my backpack, and we walk together out of the palace toward the bus stop across from the entrance. We're standing there waiting, talking about weather and wine, when he asks, "Do you already have your bus ticket? You were supposed to buy it at the *tabaccheria*."

"Huh?"

"The smoke shop. That's where you buy the ticket. The bus driver doesn't sell them. You can't ride the bus unless you already have one."

"Oh, no I don't."

We walk to the smoke shop while I ponder this weird and impractical way to sell a bus ticket. But then, not much in Italy seems practical, especially as you go farther down the peninsula toward Africa. As we enter the shop and I reach into the smallest pocket of my jeans pants looking for change, I find the long red hair that I picked from the spider web the previous afternoon. As I pull it out, stretch it, and start rolling it once again to put it back in there, Marco takes his sunglasses off and opens his eyes wide.

"A red hair!"

"Yes."

"Your hair isn't red." He sounds oddly critical or irritated.

"It's not my hair," I retort.

"Celtic hair. I can smell it." He's shaking now.

I bring it to my nose and close my eyes to sharpen my sense of smell.

"It doesn't smell like anything. . . ." I open my eyes and find Marco gone. Vanished. I buy the ticket and walk out of the store, looking both ways down the street, but he's nowhere in sight. The bus arrives, and I get on. After handing the driver my ticket and telling him my stop, I sit near a window and contemplate Marco's disappearance for a few minutes until I fall asleep.

I'm so exhausted when I arrive back at the farm after Luludja and Pugliese drop me off that I barely register that I'm the only one spending the night there. Rick and Ila are in Naples, and Luludja and Pugliese have gone back to their other home in town. Tonight, it's just me, or rather, the three dogs, faithfully standing by my door, and me. Thank God for them. I pet each one and give them pieces of prosciutto.

Back inside, feeling the quiet safety of solitude, I scan my bedroom and bathroom. What a mess! I clean up before lying down, and the cleaning makes me feel better. My brain slows down while I sweep, scrub, and mop the floor, pick up the scattered clothes, and organize them inside the closet in piles of dirty laundry, not-so-dirty laundry, and still wearable clothes, the last of which I place on a shelf. Traveling as light as I do, my sense of cleanliness has become malleable.

I light a candle and stare for a while at the flickering flame. I consider burning the red hair in my pocket. Maybe that way all the doubt will be gone, and I'll be back to normal. I touch the hair to the flame and it burns a bit at the tip. Now I smelled the unmistakable stench of burned hair. How, I wonder, could Marco smell a plain strand of hair? And why would he freak out and leave like he did? I just want to feel as clean inside as outside, but I resist the urge to burn the hair and tuck it back into my pants pocket. "Not so fast," the tiny voice—now completely settled in the small of my back—directs me. "Your job isn't done yet."

I take a long, warm, foamy shower, finishing off with cold water, just to stay tough, like my mother taught me. I take my time massaging the farm's pressed virgin olive oil over my skin. I need some pampering badly; I have calluses on the palms of my hands, and spreading the rich oil on my thighs makes me feel their roughness amplified. My feet have all sort of cuts and scars, and my back hurts. I fold my jeans and place them on top of the still wearable but somewhat dirty clothes, slide into my silk pajama pants, the one extravagance I allowed myself when I went shopping in Rome—although I had money only for the pants, so as a top I just wear one of my holey white tank tops. I've never liked buttoned pajama shirts, anyway. I sink into bed and sleep the sleep of the just, lulled by the crickets outside.

I wake up even more tired than I was when I went to bed. My legs hurt as if I've just run a marathon. I feel all squeezed and tight. And I'm wearing my jeans under my blanket! My pajama pants are on the floor, and my closet is open. The clothes, once piled up neatly, have fallen off the shelf. The pajamas have muddy footprints all over them. I gasp and look at my feet, which are all muddy again, and the cuffs of my pants are especially dirty. The sheets are dirty, as well. What the ... ?

I open the bungalow door. It's just before dawn, and the dogs, wagging their tails, come to lick my left hand, which has drops of dried, melted wax stuck all over the palm. Surrounded by the dogs, I sit and try to make sense of it all. I recall going to sleep with the candle still lit. I jump up and run to my nightstand. The burned-out candle I forgot to blow out has melted. I pick it up and turn it around to examine it. In the middle of the hardened pool of yellow wax stands the red hair, forming an almost perfect spiral.

I clean it out of the wax, put the hair in a cigar box that serves me a travelling treasure chest, go outside and sit on a log, feeling the first rays of morning sunshine warming up my arms. The smallest dog comes and sniffs the broken pieces of the melted candle in my hands , looking at me inquisitively. The bits of yellow beeswax look like a puzzle to me, the way they somehow connect together to form again a bigger body. I breathe in and out deeply for a long while and try to recall last night's dream.

I remember walking through the woods, careful to not put out the candle, and arriving at the cabin. As usual, I saw Rori being pleased-tortured-teased, but this time she was laughing, complying, accomplice-like, and the sight of it made me angry. In my reminiscence, I clearly see myself taking the hair from my pocket and holding it close to the flame. Immediately, Rori came painfully out of her ecstasy and back to consciousness. She held on tightly to the dirty sheets, covered her body, and started screaming and crying. I heard a man cursing in Italian, and he charged toward her, with his back to me. I couldn't see his face as he grabbed the girl by both arms. She shook her head and cried, "No, no, no!" She had lost weight; her once-plump cheeks were emaciated, and she was pale.

Remembering how much she loved the sun, and used to have her cheeks red from being outside, I cried silently. Just before he grabbed her arms and handcuffed her, the girl and I made a quick eye contact, and I thought she recognized me. I brought my fingers to my lips, silently hushing her. I hid behind the wall by the side of the window. I hear what seems to be a question, and heavy footsteps toward me. Her gaze probably alerted him, making the man come toward the window, and open the sash lock.

I didn't want him to see me, so I ran into the dark woods while he slid the bottom window up. I remember wishing I could take a good look at him, all the while running as fast as I could in the darkness of a waning balsamic moon, the sliver of light showing up here and there teasingly. I told the moon, "I'm not Alice. Please, can you make things more real, right now?"

As I sit and recall what could have been a dream but seems more like a memory of something that really happened, I realize that today is Sunday, and I'm all alone on the farm. I'm so scared; I wish I could leave this place. I feel an urge to go to a church and see a mass, but the truck is still broken. There's the ATV, but only Rick and Kulveer have permission to ride it—or Kulveer did, anyway. Kulveer! I wish I could talk to him about all this mess. I'll bet he would have some wise Hindu advice to offer as he always did when he was here. I'm hungry; the last thing I ate was those eggs back in Caserta.

Locking my bungalow, I find the ATV keys hanging by the laundry room where they always are. I've never driven a machine like that, but I jump on it and start the engine. The dogs bark. I start it, hit the throttle and immediately lose control, going straight into the olive tree by the side of the road. The hit throws me up and out and I fall, hitting my head on a rock.

CHAPTER 7

Naples

"Cami? Are you okay? Cami? Wake up, please. Can you say something? Can you hear me?"

It sounds like Ila's voice. I feel her warm hands lightly stroking my temples. Something, probably a dog, is licking my bare feet. It tickles. I open my eyes and see the purple sky. The last time I looked up it was dawn, and now the sun is already setting? Her breath smells of alcohol. I'll bet they had drinks on the way home.

"Can you stand up? Can you feel your feet?"

Is she kidding? With all this licking, my feet are the only things I feel. Not without effort, I bring my head up and see a dog, the one that has always one ear up and the other one down; apparently, he's the one that was licking my feet. I smile at him, and he seems to smile back. Then I ask myself, *What the hell am I doing lying on the ground?*

"You shouldn't have taken the ATV, Cami," Rick scolds. I follow his voice and see him kneeling beside Ila.

"Take it easy, Rick," Ila returns. "Can we make sure she's okay before you start lecturing?"

"She's fine, and I'm not lecturing; she'd be better off if she'd followed the rules to begin with."

I get up and taste dried blood in my mouth. Something warm and viscous drips out of my nose and reaches my lips. More blood.

"Oh, let me go get a washcloth," Ila says. "Rick, can you stay here with her?"

He sets the ATV back onto its wheels and takes the keys out of the ignition. "I guess I need to find a better hiding place for these, huh?"

I have nothing to say. He's right; I'm wrong. Finally, I break the silence. "I want to leave, Rick."

"Leave? Why? You're not getting your money's worth?" and he glances at me with a mean smile. I know he thinks I don't work much just because I don't follow their schedule. But I do my share, waking up early and minding my own business. Does anyone know much work farming is? It's endless. You can spend hours weeding and cleaning, and the results are barely noticeable. And Rick is clearly drunk.

"Where did you guys go?" I ask, trying to divert him from criticizing me.

"Oh, Naples. We spent last night in a big dump of a hotel, and then we spent the day with Ken. He's out of jail, and today he went to Napoli Centrale to catch the train to Rome and then fly back to Ireland. We had some drinks at bar in the Chiaia district before he took off."

"He's leaving Rori behind?"

"What are you talking about? You really still think she's around here? Ken thinks that come September when their classes start again, she'll be walking around campus like nothing happened."

"But why she would leave without taking any luggage?"

"Ken says she's a very impulsive, fiery, plucky girl, and a decision like that on her part might be puzzling but not improbable."

Poor Rori. Even her man is giving up on her. Rick must have noticed my disapproving frown since he continues, "Oh come on, Cami. Do you think you know the girl better than her boyfriend does? She was fed up with the way these gypsies treated us; you know that. She was always talking about leaving." He mimics Rori's complaining tone. "'What kind of holiday did you bring me on, Ken?'"

"Yes, but that doesn't explain why she disappeared so quickly. No note, nothing." I was on the verge of telling him about my night visions—but what if that just proves to him that I'm crazy? Better not risk it.

"Well, I've had enough of this, Cami. I'm hungry and I'm going to make dinner for Ila and me. I see you're standing up. You're welcome to join us. Or stay here. Whatever. Later."

I stand there, alone, for a while. It's already getting dark; no use trying to get to town. Even if I were lucky enough to find a ride, it would be too late to catch the last bus to Naples and find my way into an airport and out of this country. And what if I didn't catch a ride? I would have to brave the 6.5 miles among dark farms, barking dogs, and unlighted streets, on foot, with my heavy backpack, and then find a hotel in Benevento so I could get to Naples in the morning. I just wanted to leave the *agriturismo* so quickly because I was scared of staying there alone; what if whoever was keeping Rori captive knew where I was staying? They could kidnap me, too. Thanks to the Almighty, those crazy dogs insist on sleeping around my bungalow. They're the only protection I have. I wish Josh were here; he would know what to do. And it's hard to make decisions when it's so dark and I might have a concussion. My head hurts badly in the spot where I hit the rock. At least these guys are back now. Less scary. Where's Ila with that washcloth?

I walk up to the kitchen, where they are probably cooking some dinner. It's dark with a star-peppered new moon sky; fireflies light my way. Sparks of light twinkle on each side of the narrow, olive-tree-lined dirt road that leads to the main guesthouse.

When I get to the kitchen, the strong smell of freshly crushed garlic fills my lungs, and I suddenly feel protected from any evil being that might want to come after me. I remember my mom rubbing garlic on my cousin's ankles and mine when we insisted in exploring the next door jungle during our vacation in Hawaii wearing just shorts, tank tops, and flip-flops. "It's full of snakes out there! Come here! Don't leave without rubbing garlic on your feet." And she would always make me carry a garlic clove in my pocket.

Rick and Ila are making fresh pesto, yum. Rick is toasting the pine nuts; Ila is just coming back in through the side door holding a bunch of basil with dirt falling from the roots.

All my problems go away when I enter a kitchen. Even back in San Francisco, I would leave work stressed out, with back pain, eyestrain—all the typical ailments of a full-time coder. Josh would give me a back rub, pat me on the bottom, and show me his bounty. One memorable day, he had five different kinds of mushrooms from the farmers' market, bunched wild arugula from Rainbow Grocers, snails foraged from a neighbor's backyard for a buttery escargot appetizer, and grass-fed lamb chops from his friend, the Church Street butcher, who always texted Josh when he had something special coming in.

Now, the smell of warm pasta mixed with pesto and freshly grated *parmigiano reggiano* is irresistible although, I must confess, I'm getting a bit burned out on so much wheat in such a short time. In California—thank God for Mexican food—my staple is corn tortillas, beans, and tamales. Even my *nonno* was more into polenta and risotto than pasta, so I hardly ever ate it. Now, I'm living a version of *Super Size Me: The Italian Chapter*. And the more I eat, the more voracious I become. I finish a bowl of pasta only to feel famished less than an hour later, a hungry ghost, never filling my emptiness. And now I'm also hungry for Josh. I got spoiled always having him around me for a bit more than a year. I haven't kissed or hugged a boy since he dropped me off at the airport. And his not answering my e-mails doesn't help. Come to think of it, that guy in Caserta, Marco, was kind of cute. I felt a pull toward him that I've never felt before, and yet the sight of him somehow repelled me, making me feel a tug of war in my guts. After I'd composed myself, I needed to get away from him, and when he vanished, I felt simultaneously hurt and relieved.

After finishing my dinner of spaghetti with pesto sauce, a note of blues pervades my thinking. I'm not sure why. I say my good-byes over protests of "but we brought *babà au rhum* from Naples for dessert!"

No, thanks. I don't need any sugar or booze to bring my mood even lower. I excuse myself and leave. On the way back to my cabin, the number of fireflies seems to have tripled. I lie down in the clearing by the bungalows to watch a meteor shower and remember the last time I saw a shooting star, the first one of that summer, in California's Sierra Nevada. It was also a new moon, and Josh and I could see the Milky Way over our heads. Then I saw a second one. He told me to make a wish.

"True love," I said immediately.

"Is that why you're so eager to go to Italy? I'm not enough?" Josh seemed strange—his eyes lost in the sky, looking for something intangible in the stars.

"Of course not, you silly."

"Then why are you asking for true love?"

"I've always asked for the same thing since I was a little girl. It's just habit."

"Do you think you've found it?"

"Maybe . . . "

I sigh. I miss him so much. I reach for my pocket and find a tiny jar of lip balm that he made for me out of olive and coconut oil mixed with the Hayes Valley beeswax he collected himself and infused with vanilla essence and rosemary oil. I rub my finger inside the almost empty jar until I almost clean it out and rub the balm on my lips. The sweet taste fights with the salt in my tears reaching my lips.

Now I make two wishes: to get Rori out of that cabin, even if the cabin is only in my mind, and to kiss Josh, even though he doesn't answer my e-mails.

I stand up too fast and feel a bit dizzy. My blood is pumping where my neck meets my skull, like a techno beat at a rave I'm dying to leave, only the rave is in my brain, and I can't leave my brain. And it hurts right where I bumped my head earlier today. Funny how we feel more pain when we're quiet or resting; it gets amped up somehow.

Back in my bungalow, I find my pajama pants on the floor, with the muddy footprint now dried to just dirt. I pat it away and get ready for bed. Then, I feel hungry. Again. Damn! I'm not going back to the kitchen, so I grab some tuna from my backpack and devour it straight out of the can with the awkward help of the tiny fork from my Swiss Army Knife. When I finish it, I feel that I could eat another one. I toss the empty can in the bathroom trash and, wondering whether to hold off the hunger or have seconds, decide to empty out my backpack and maybe pile the cans somewhere in the closet. I dump the contents on my bed. In the midst of the cans, the pages of the *Corriere della Sera*, the evening newspaper that was wrapping the eggs, and dried salami, I find a little piece of paper, neatly folded. I open it and read: "Marco. 0824 32 62 47"

Oy vey.

CHAPTER 8

The Meadow

I wake up before sunrise with a huge headache. Probably a side effect of me hitting my head yesterday. Great. I walk up the little hill out of the bungalows and find that the horses have escaped their stable—again. I'm not surprised since the gypsies don't feed them; their ribs are starting to stick out through their skin, and their dull coats are another sign of poor health. I'll bet their owners work them to the bone in the circus.

Nobody is up yet, so I make some coffee and find a basket of eggs and a bunch of day-old *cornetti* left in a basket on the main kitchen island. Cornetti are the Italian answer to the French *croissant*, just sweeter and less buttery. These don't seem very stale, not bad at all. I break an egg, mix it with some milk, sugar, cinnamon, and nutmeg, and—why not?—freshly crushed black pepper. I turn on the oven to preheat it, break the *cornetti* into crumbs, and add them to the mixture. Then, I melt some butter in a cast-iron skillet, sauté the mixture on the stovetop, and finish it in the oven. I guess I just made a *frittata-cornetto*-pudding. While I drink my coffee and wait for the pudding to cool, I wonder how and when Marco managed to put his note in my bag. It was probably before he saw the red hair, freaked out, and vanished. Should I call him? Probably not.

After breakfast, I wander around the vegetable garden looking for something to do, and gravitate toward the tomato patch. Yesterday, Ila finished covering the raised beds with a dark plastic layer that's supposed to keep bugs and other pests away without poisonous pesticides. I start making holes in it with a hoe so we can insert the baby tomato plants, which need just enough space to thrive, and lots of sun to turn the fruit red. *This should be a good spot*, I think.

I walk down to the makeshift nursery that Rick improvised in late spring out of old, ripped sheets from the guesthouse and a bamboo frame. I fill up a wheelbarrow with a dozen baby tomatoes, plant each one in its respective new home, and sprinkle them with the watering can. I feel like cooling off, too.

I go to the kitchen, cut some watermelon slices, and put them in a bowl for a morning snack. As I set the bowl on a large tree stump near the garden to use it as a table, I hear light footsteps breaking the twigs behind me. I turn around. Nothing. I eat a slice and it cools me inside. Just as I bite into the watery flesh of the second slice, a gust of wind shakes the trees that surround me, an icy blow in the midst of such a hot, sunny morning. As I finish eating the fruit, making a sticky mess over my clothes, I look around to see where the blast of air came from. Crazy weather, I guess.

I bend over to grab the wheelbarrow for another trip to the nursery when I hear someone behind me.

"*Buongiorno*, Carmela."

Marco. I step back, surprised, and fall over the wheelbarrow. The bottom is rather rusty and worn out, so my heavy butt makes a hole in it and I get stuck. He takes my hand and helps me out. "What are you doing here?" I ask, baffled. "And how did you find this place?"

"Oh, everybody knows this is the only farm around here that accepts volunteers. The minute you said 'farm' and 'Benevento,' I knew where to find you." He gives me a half-smile. He has changed a lot since the day we met. His pale skin looks tanner and healthier, and I wonder if he went to a tanning booth or something—although in the South of Italy, a person just needs to stay outside for awhile to get darker. He seems to have more life running through his arteries, or his blood has received an extra dose of iron.

"I'm sorry I left so quickly. I was hoping you'd call me, but I was afraid you might never see my note . . . or you might lose it."

"Well, I did see it, but I didn't have time to call, or the inclination."

He's coming closer and closer to me, and I feel a powerful repulsion like the force that keeps two magnets from touching. I sense that he's longing for something, but I can't tell what. All I know is that I'm balking at the sight of him, but the wheelbarrow blocks me from stepping back away from him. I walk around it, positioning myself behind it.

He grabs its handles and half-tosses, half-rolls it down the rocky hill. I gasp. I hadn't expected such strength coming out of that lean body. And why such a drastic move? This guy is definitely trouble. He takes off his Ray-Ban sunglasses, and I realize that I've never seen those eyes before. On Saturday, when we first met, they were green and kind. Today, they're a feverish blue like the root of a flame. His skin color, now almost caramel, makes the blue even more shocking, and I avert my gaze to avoid getting burned—a stupid idea since it instantly puts me in prey mode. He moves confidently toward me, and the bright yellow flyer that Marin Headlands National Park gives to visitors in case they encounter a mountain lion pops into my head:

"STOP! Never run from a lion. Try backing away from it slowly, but only if you can do so safely. Running may stimulate a lion's instinct to chase and attack. Face the lion and stand upright. Make eye contact."

Making eye contact is the hardest part, but I take a deep breath and go for it. He seems surprised, and he stops, seeming to study what to do next. I take a step back, and then another. He insists on coming closer. I tighten my shoulders inward and bring my hands up to my chest. He smiles. I feel short of breath.

The bright yellow flyer from Marin Headlands National Park comes back to my mind, capital letters and all: "DO NOT BEND OR CROUCH OVER; DO ALL YOU CAN TO APPEAR LARGER. A person squatting or bending over looks a lot like a four-legged prey animal. Raise your arms. Open your jacket, if you're wearing one. Throw stones, branches, or whatever you can grab without crouching down or turning your back. Wave your arms slowly and speak firmly in a large voice."

I unzip my cotton hoodie—too bad that I'm wearing just a sports bra under it. He frowns and opens his eyes wide, dumbfounded, making them lose their intense focus.

I manage to scan my surroundings in my memory, and I recall being very close to the tomato beds that I was working on not long ago. I try to remember the flyer; information gets mixed in the stress.

"FIGHT BACK IF ATTACKED. Try to stay on your feet if a lion attacks you. Lions can be driven off by prey that fights back. Some hikers have fought back successfully with sticks, caps, jackets, garden tools, and their bare hands. Since lions usually try to bite the head or neck, try to remain standing and face the attacking animal."

Without turning around, I reach for the tree that stands beside the tomato patch. I stretch my arms as far back as I can while he watches me with amused curiosity. He comes a few steps closer, flashing the brightest smile I've ever seen from a man.

I manage to reach the hoe that I left resting against the tree and, in a move worthy of Luke Skywalker, touch his chest with the blade. He backs away for the first time.

"Can you leave this property, please?"

"Wait, you don't understand . . . ."

"I don't care to. I just want you as far away as possible from me."

"You're making a terrible mistake."

"It doesn't seem so at this moment."

As I relax, confident in the boundary I've managed to build, I feel his pull become stronger. I fall into a trance and start speaking in tongues, with my eyes shut, until finally words I recognize but don't comprehend come out of my mouth: "I already know who you are. You already know who I am."

When I open my eyes, he's gone. He's good at that. I feel relieved for the moment, but very afraid, too. How dare he come here!

I stand for a while near the tomato patch, trying to make sense of whatever has just happened. I dig for a while; making holes in the dirt always calms me down. I go as far down as above my elbow, until my nail hit something hard, and as I remove my hand something comes stuck in my finger. I pull out a silver ring decorated with a pentagram, which has letters around its points and the same letters inside the ring: A, T, L, Y, E, S, A, S, I, V. I hear footsteps; someone is coming. I don't want to share my discovery right now, so I bury it back under a tomato seedling. As I do it, I feel a pull out of my chest, like a heartstring, connecting me to the ring. Like I did not have time to get to know it better, and I already have to let it go, but still some form of attachment has formed. I repeat my aunt's favorite advice "attachment is the source of all suffering", and surrender to the pain of having to hide my newfound treasure so fast.

It's Rick who's coming, coffee cup in hand and wearing just boxers, a pair of blue canvas classic slip-on Toms, and a T-shirt that says, "*Zanini, tutti buona gente pero tutti ladri*" (Zanini, all good people but all thieves). I have to laugh at it, and he tells me it's from his latest family reunion. He's hung over and has a hoarse throat. "What are you doing out here?" he asks.

"Working on the tomato beds." I omit the bit about the visitor—I'll just have to find a good excuse for the hole in the wheelbarrow if he asks about it.

"Well, the gypsies are back, and they have some jobs that they want us to finish before we do anything else. There's a meeting in the kitchen. Can you come?"

I follow him reluctantly since I dislike being bossed around, but I'm glad to have company—especially when the company is a six-foot-tall, short-tempered Italian-American boy from Brooklyn.

The gypsies are here because they've finally managed to book the guest rooms for the weekend, and now they want everything to be shipshape. They assign me to remove all the spider webs from the roofs, corners, and dark spots, and clean the dust from all the bedrooms. I feel sorry for the spiders; I kind of like them. But a job is a job, so I carry on with the arachnid genocide

It's amazing how cleaning gets my brain going. And, of course, I eventually think of Josh, who made cleaning his house a big party, with loud music and dancing. Life around him was always fun because he found the brightness in small things, and just the sunshine filtering through the one and only big window in his Mission studio and the different colors of the Northern California sky in sunrise and sunset made him grateful for being alive. But, then, he enjoyed risking the same life he loved so much. I, on the other hand, am much more contained—I've never broken a leg or an arm, ever. At home, nothing ever happened to me, maybe because I never went close to danger. Now I feel surrounded by danger, and part of me thinks I should just leave. Most of me wants to stay, though, just as it did in the first year in San Francisco, when I started to be a bit more daring.

At lunchtime, we all eat together, tomatoes stuffed with rice and pancetta that the gypsies cooked. The rice isn't thoroughly cooked and the pancetta is limp. Since nothing is more disgusting than bacon that's still a bit soft, I pick it out of the rice and leave it on the plate.

Luludja protests, "You don't like pork?"

I answer that I love it, but it's too hot today for it, which is an acceptable excuse, and I leave the table. I'm eager to do some exploring now that I've finished my assigned chores.

I always take the same road and turn off at one of its many intersections, but I still can't find the cabin from my dreams. Today, I want to take a different path, a crooked, rocky dirt trail that starts behind the abandoned barn. It's so weedy and uneven that it almost doesn't look like a real path, but it seems to lead somewhere, and I see fresh horseshoe prints on it.

At first, I wonder how a horse managed to follow such a narrow and winding path, and the trail becomes still more difficult, winding as it passes over a grassy hill where both the trail and the prints are barely visible. When I reach the valley, the trail picks up again, and so do the hoofprints.

The woods in the valley are the thickest I've ever seen around here. I smile and follow the path, now a bit wet. I can tell by the round rocks and the occasional mud puddle that this section of the trail is actually a seasonal creek now in its midsummer drying stage. Finding that it's a lot more humid in this part of the forest than it is on the farm, I smile again. My skin remembers this moist sensation from my dreams. But the ground is just grass, mud, and rocks with no sign of the moss that my feet would recognize immediately if they touched it again.

I'm tired, so I sit on some cozy roots that look like a mother's lap. The tree trunk is so thick that it must be over a hundred years old, an unusual sight in this land of grapevines and olive trees. This spot feels oddly familiar, making me wonder if any of my ancestors ever sat here. And I feel safe, too, safer than I've ever felt since I came to Campania well over three weeks ago. I doze off in a catnap, but after awhile, I snore and wake myself up. I feel a bit annoyed, but oh so rested as I notice the deep royal blue of the sky above me. Mesmerized, I contemplate the mingling of the green leaves and the blue sky, both colors so bright and saturated that it almost hurts to look at them. It's as if my eyes needed that short but deep sleep to see a fresh, new world.

Far away, I hear the clear, sweet tones of an ocarina. Unbelievable. When I was little and refused to go to bed, my grandfather used to play for me. Instead of lullabies, he played melodies that only he knew. And I'd always fall for it. His father had taught him how to play the ocarina, and his grandfather had taught his father. Nonno tried to teach me, to no avail, and now he's gone. The last time I heard him play, I was eleven, and he was in bed, tired and old, but he still played. That night, he died in his sleep. Now those songs that only he knew are gone, as well.

My after-nap brain is full of empty spaces, like a canyon, and this sound is like a fresh wind blowing through it, filling it with joyful sounds and fragrances. I smell flowers, crushed grapes fermenting in my grandfather's basement, and frangipane. Like a dryad pulled out of her tree by the sound of a satyr's flute, I follow the cheerful sound through the woods, straying off the path and letting the music guide me. The dense tree crowns make it dark around me, even though it's only about two. The sound comes from a bright spot among the trees, and, as I come closer, I see a bright emerald-green meadow in the middle of the forest. I hide behind a tree along the border of the meadow. Something tells me not to step out into the sunlight, not until I know more about this place.

The sound is so close to me now that it feels like the ocarina player is right by my side. I feel sleepy but resist the urge to close my eyes. Is the melody putting me to sleep? Scanning the meadow to find the musician, I see a huge, round rock, the only one in the entire meadow, moving in waves—a rather psychedelic impression—as if the rock is liquid, and it's undulating to the windy sound of the ocarina.

I rub my eyes in disbelief and wonder if eating too many porcini mushrooms could make me have visions. Then, I realize what's actually going on: the rock is covered with snails, and the snails are dancing, stretched out of their shells, moving their gelatinous bodies up and down to the sound. I must be asleep and dreaming. One: Snails don't have ears, so they can't hear. Two: Since when do snails dance?

With my jaw dropped, I watch the hypnotic performance until I notice some honey-colored curls behind and above the rock moving along with the rhythm. I move a bit, changing my spot to hide at the base of a different tree, and from this new perspective, I finally see a boy of fifteen or sixteen playing a gold ochre ocarina. His eyes twinkle with mischief. The instrument has entrancing patterns, mostly spirals, carved all over it.

He stops playing, and I freeze. Does he know that I'm here? I hold my breath for a while, not wanting him to see me. The snails stop moving, too. He smiles, frowns, closes his eyes, and hums another melody as if he's trying to remember its tune. Then he says "Ah!" and begins playing a song that sounds like a march. All the snails immediately tense up their antennae, turn around, and start parading away from the rock, their antennae now moving side to side, almost as if they're whistling to the tune with their bodies. The rock shines with their slime.

They're all coming in my direction. Oh no. The first ones in the line are almost touching my feet. Ick. I climb the tree silently, and they move along into the woods, leaving a slimy trail below me.

The boy stops playing. He takes a brown-and-tan checkered handkerchief from his back pocket and waves it, saying, "*Arrivederci, care signorine.*"

Putting on his fedora hat, he turns around and walks toward a tall, thin sycamore where a white horse is tied. The branch I'm leaning on breaks, and I almost fall, but I manage to grab the tree trunk and stay up.

Startled by the noise, the horse snorts. The boy tenses and turns in my direction, his happy-go-lucky smile replaced by a somber expression that darkens his face like a cloud. The sky has also darkened; a sudden fog has rolled into the valley and now covers the meadow, as if on cue to match the boy's change of mood. He's walking toward me now, and my heart is beating so fast I'm afraid he can hear it.

I hold my breath as if not breathing will somehow make me invisible.

He says something in Italian that I can't understand; I think he's asking who's there. He's angry, and his voice is getting louder. His nostrils are flaring furiously, and he's getting closer to my tree. I don't know what to do. The hand that held the ocarina so gently now has a tight grip that makes his knuckles red; his veins are popping up in his arms, which are very stringy but seemingly strong.

I take a deep breath and try my best to say that I come in peace. "Hello. *Io sono amica.*"

It seems to work; the boy relaxes. "*Ciao.* Do you speak English?"

I show my face through the leaves. "Yes. So do you, it seems?"

"Ah. A spy. What did you see, *signorina?*"

I can't tell what he's up to, but I decide that my best bet is to be as open and honest as I can. I climb down the tree and come closer.

He has both hands by his hips like a mother waiting for her bratty son to explain himself.

"Hi, *mi chiamo* Cami. I'm so sorry. I was walking by and heard your ocarina. It's so beautiful . . . ."

"What have you seen?"

"Well, I saw the snails dance and then go away. How did you do that?"

The kid doesn't answer. Looking rather concerned, he takes off his hat, squeezing it tightly, and scratches his head with the hand that holds it. Still silent, he starts pulling his hair, evidently in self-punishment mode, and his eyes are angry and watery. He's almost crying.

I give him what I hope is a reassuring, gentle look, as if I'm saying, "There's nothing to worry about; I won't share what I've seen with anyone."

It works. The boy calms down, fixes his hat crease, and wipes his eyes. He turns around and rests his body against the rock that, not long ago, was covered in dancing snails, crosses his arms over his chest, and looks at me. I can tell that he's measuring, analyzing, figuring me out. Apparently giving up, he picks up a thick stick from the ground and starts peeling it with a penknife that was hanging from his belt loop. He's carving lines similar to those on the ocarina.

I feel daring and come closer.

He points the knife at me. "Who are you? What are you doing here? How did you find this spot? Not many people come here. Some don't know how to get here. Others know not to."

I retreat, but I'm still relaxed, my arms hanging loose along my body. I breathe deeply. As long as I don't show fear, the opponent is not likely to feel threatened.

"Look, I'm sorry to disturb you. I work at Bosco di Melizzano Agriturismo, and I like to explore the neighborhood in my free time. I followed this path and ended up listening to your beautiful ocarina. *Mio nonno* played the ocarina, too. He played it when I was a little girl so I would fall asleep. I couldn't resist."

The boy opens his eyes wide in disbelief.

"You mean your grandfather was Italian, and he played the ocarina, too?"

"Yes. That ocarina was our family relic and was passed down to him through many generations. He was actually from Benevento, but he left here and moved to New York."

"*Cara, tuo nonno? De Benevento? Ma . . . .*" He seems dumbfounded by this knowledge, but more relaxed and welcoming as well.

As I tell him what brought me here, we get more comfortable with each other. He tells me his name: Andrea.

"So, please tell me, how do you manage to make the snails dance?"

"It's an old snail-charmer trick. They respond to the vibrations."

My jaw drops. What a trip. "Why would anyone on earth want to charm snails?"

"Hey, how do you think we keep things organic around here?" He smiles and winks. "The French eat snails; we charm them away." He giggles.

I look up and see that the sun has moved quite a bit in the sky. It's getting late; I need to go back for dinner. Andrea offers me a ride on his horse.

"Okay. Thanks."

"But I need to let you off around the corner from your gate. I don't want the *zingari* to see me."

I stand on a tree stump and swing a leg over the horse's back after him. "You mean the gypsies? Why not?"

"When the time is right, I'll tell you."

When we're almost at the farm, he stops his horse. I jump off, and, as I blink, the boy and his horse vanish. Damn. Guys around here like to play hide and seek.

As I round the corner, I see a Carabinieri squad car parked by the entrance of the main guesthouse. Through the window, I see Luludja and her husband sitting at the round table in the game room talking to two officers. Her bearded cousin is there as well, looking out the window near the main entrance and smoking his pipe. He looks me deep in the eye as I get closer to the door. I shiver and go around to the back door.

"What's happening?" I ask Rick, who's lying down on the TV room couch watching a cooking show about amaretto cookies. Ila is sitting too, solving crossword puzzles. The recipe looks complicated. He sighs, and I'm already anticipating a minivictory, thinking that he'll say, "They decided to investigate better Rori's case," but no, I just get "The neighbors called the Carabinieri because they found the circus horses eating their grass."

Through the window, I see Luludja outside, standing on the veranda waving good-bye to the Carabinieri. Her cousin is also outside, watching the police leave. I can tell that with each puff of the pipe, he relaxes his tensed muscles a bit more.

She turns back toward the front door, panting and fanning herself with the pink pages of a *Gazzetta dello Sport* magazine. She smiles at him. Seeing me, she smiles even wider and comes into the TV room, talking very fast.

"There they go. We got rid of them. You know, here in Italy, if you have a stupid kid, we say he's going to be either a Carabiniere or a farmer." She laughs at her own joke, but she's the only one in the room laughing.

We all look at each other, perplexed, and she apparently feels it's her cue to leave. The three of us remain in the room, quietly contemplating what we've just witnessed. It seems that we're all thinking the same thoughts.

Ila is the first to speak. "These people have no regard for farmers whatsoever!"

"I can't believe Francesco rented his beautiful property to these slobs." I complain.

"I'm going to talk to him," Rick says. "He's got to drive these people away from here." Rick finishes the discussion by stomping up to their bedroom. Ila follows him.

I turn off the TV and sit by myself, thinking about the amazing things I witnessed this afternoon and about Andrea's last words. He didn't want the gypsies to see him. Why not? What about that creepy Marco coming over in the morning? Some days, it seems that everything happens at the same time. My pulse is pounding, and my thoughts are running fast like water from a broken tap that will soon overflow the sink. I can see the bulging veins in my so tense arms showing up over my tightened tendons. I promise myself that, starting tomorrow, I'll try to drink less coffee.

CHAPTER 9

Galicia

After Marco showed up, not a day went by that I didn't think of him—or, rather, fret about him. I felt a tidal push and pull. Whenever he floated into my mind, I'd shove him away, but back he came, always, constant guardian of my daydreaming. I felt a mixture of curiosity and disgust regarding him, and I had a hunch that he didn't have my best interests in mind. But, slowly, he grew on me. A bouquet of flowers arrived by messenger the day after his unexpected visit, with a card that read "Sorry for my harshness. I can't bear the thought of not seeing you again. Will you forgive my intrusiveness? Please give me a call and let me know." A dozen roses, eleven white and one red.

The guy had style; I couldn't deny it. But his implausible eagerness made me extremely uneasy and suspicious. I decided to text him. After all, flowers are flowers; such a gesture deserves a reply. "I forgive you, but please don't come by without an invitation again."

A shower of text messages followed, three or even five a day. By Wednesday, he had asked me out for a drink. I didn't answer.

Today, Thursday, the invitation is even harder to refuse: "I have a new batch of wine from Sardegna. It's incredible. You've got to taste it. I can come over this weekend with a bottle for you and your friends." He texts me in the morning, first thing, still half sleep, I'm barely thinking straight.

"Okay," I text back.

After all, we'll have a full house this weekend, so he'll have no window of opportunity to threaten or harm me. We'll be surrounded by people the whole time—I hope. Now, sitting on a rock outside of the farm waiting for Andrea, the ocarina boy and watching birds pecking at the grass and lizards slithering around, I even forget about Marco's wine plans. That is, until I feel a buzzing vibration in my pants pocket. My phone.

"When should I come?" he texts again.

I bite my nails. Anyhow, I'm slowing falling for him, at least theoretically. Besides, I've been alone in romantic Italy for more than a month. And Josh is incommunicado. Bottom line, my gut instinct is my only advisor. And my gut tells me to stay away from him. But even so, my thumbs and fingers type, "Saturday around 3:00 works for me."

Immediately afterward as I hear the little whoosh that my smartphone makes every time a text goes out, I regret it, but there's nothing I can do. My message is out there now, ready to cause trouble. I think about writers, wondering what compels them to do what they do. It's heartbreaking: you publish something, and then the whole world can read it and all of them can give their own take on it, misinterpret, misunderstand, create havoc, and even slander the author. It must be just like giving birth. How can you bear to part with a being that was briefly part of your own body and then, suddenly, it's another entity, with its own will and agenda.

This can't possibly be love. I don't know what it is, but it's nothing like the frenzy that I felt when Josh was making me fall for him—unabashedly, urgently, and unapologetically breathless. I still remember the day I realized I was in love: We were running down Valencia Street, late for a movie, when we stopped at a red light and saw a couple on the corner just getting up from their sidewalk table at a ridiculously expensive French restaurant that requires men to wear ties—ties in the Mission, who knew?—and charges around $180 per patron for the weekday prix fixe menu.

Josh called my attention to the unfinished meals still on their plates. "Let's eat it!"

"What?"

"Friends of mine in Davis do it all the time. They're Freegans—a manifesto against waste. They go dumpster diving for groceries, it's the new hunting in our age of excesses. One man's trash is another man's treasure. And it looks delicious."

"You're crazy," I said, but next thing I knew, I was gulping down some stranger's leftovers by the forkful. We even drank their wine! When the waiter came from inside and started insulting us in a mixture of Arabic and French, we ran off giggling until we turned a corner into a dark alley and started making out.

I sigh. I miss him. And I miss kissing. After almost a year of being madly in love, pampered, spoiled, and adored, I've been suffering for more than a month in a self-imposed dry spell. And now Marco is circling me like a shark. At least the dreams with Rori have taken a break for the whole week. Since that last one on

Saturday night, after I met him in Caserta, I haven't had a single one. And I should be very afraid of her captor, but my fear of this Marco outweighs it; it's more useful to be wary of a concrete threat than an imaginary one. I wonder if I'll ever find the damn cabin. And I wish Andrea weren't so late for our rendezvous. Maybe if I'd had company when Marco's text landed in my lap, I could have ignored it or even deleted it.

Now, where's that ocarina-playing boy? He's very late. I look again at the crumpled note that arrived last night tied to a pebble thrown through my bungalow window. It reads, "Meet me where I dropped you last time, *dopo pranzo*." It's already 1:37 p.m. Maybe he eats lunch later than I do. But how did he know which window was mine? The day we met, we said our good-byes here at this corner, but he never saw me enter my bungalow. Weird. And how would he know what time I'm done with lunch? A quarter past one seemed reasonable enough when I arrived.

I watch the lizards circle me. I've never seen lizards like these. They have yellow-and-green heads, and the colors darken as they move toward the tail, which is completely brown at the tip, and they're bold—they come very close to me.

A few days ago, I accidentally cut off a tail with a hoe when I was digging holes for the artichoke beds in the garden. The lizard slithered away and left behind its brown tail, which kept wiggling frantically. I picked up the frenetic tail and tucked it into the front pocket of my overalls, along with the dried lavender buds I'd gathered a while before. It tickled me. Maybe I could save my life for a while by using it, just like Hansel and Gretel did, in the fairy tale showing the witch that kept them captive a lizard tail instead of plump fingers. Only I'm not a captive here. I can walk away any time. The only things that bind me to this place are the dreams and my instinct telling me to stay because I might be the one who can find Rori. Obsessive-compulsive, I know, but I can't stop thinking about her.

I hear a horse and look up. Andrea! Finally. "*Ciao, bella,*" he says. "I'm sorry to be late."

"*No problema, amico.* So, what's your plan?"

"Do you want to jump on the horse with me? I have a special place to show you. But I must cover your eyes." He takes a black handkerchief from his pocket.

Having nothing to lose at this point, I agree to the blindfold. Besides, I trust him blindly, no pun intended. Apart from the mischievous smile he sported when he played the ocarina, he seems pure, almost naive. But I know it was just an impression. I'm definitely not dealing with an amateur here despite his extreme youth.

"Here, let me help you up. Now, let's cover your eyes. Is it too tight? "

"No, it's fine."

"*Andiamo!*" he says, urging his horse to go. He kicks the horse lightly but effectively, and we start trotting down the hill. It's interesting to be riding high atop a horse, in darkness, feeling its movements with my body. After what seems an eternity downhill, the poor animal tenses up his knees to endure the slope. Now we turn sharply left. I hear a trickle of water and guess that we've just passed the Fontana della Madonna, a fountain under a mosaic of the Virgin, whose spring waters are believed to cure any illness. It sits just by the road, the only paved road around here, and for a while, I can tell from the noise of the hoofs that we're still on that road. And then we reach a narrow trail in the woods. The branches come so close that they scratch my arms and face, and I can smell leaves and hear bumblebees humming. The horse trots erratically as if to avoid exposed roots and rocks. This part of the ride takes much longer than the paved stretch, and I know that we must be deep in the woods when we stop. He dismounts and tells me to do the same. I obey without fear.

"Are you ready?" He removes the blindfold, and I see that we're standing right by a very thick oak, with its fat, twisted roots exposed. He grabs one of the roots, which is as flexible as a rubber band. As he raises it above his head, creating a kind of wormhole, his horse steps through the opening and jumps underground. My jaw drops; I rub my eyes and stare at Andrea.

"After you?" He's wearing his mischievous smile again.

I step into the opening. A suction like force pulls me down, and I free-fall slowly through the soft mud that surrounds me. I can feel worms touching my body and gophers sniffing my hair. Somehow, I'm not disgusted. Instead, I feel a deep peace, just like when I started volunteering at the city farm and the compost felt like a magical medicine.

Andrea is just above me. He's moving faster than I am, and sometimes his feet accidentally touch the top of my head. I hear a baffled "*scusi*" every time it happens. It's as if the mud is getting to know me and allowing me to pass through it more slowly than the familiar boy, who gets permission much faster. Unfortunately, I'm in his way. I wonder if I were by myself whether it would even let me in. Something tells me that you have to be invited to this realm and escorted in.

Now, I'm skidding down a slide-shaped rock that eventually spits both of us into a green meadow just like the one where I met Andrea. It actually seems like the same place, only the midafternoon sunlight is subdued here, as if its rays are passing through an amber filter that makes everything soft and fuzzy. I can see the big rock where snails danced to his ocarina that afternoon and the sycamore tree where he tied his white horse. I look at him, puzzled.

"That meadow where you met me is one of the few power spots left on the planet," he explains. "With the right energy and intention, a person can reproduce it in a parallel universe."

"What?"

"Yes, this is the same place. Soon, everything will make more sense."

We cross the grass to the almost perfect circle of trees that surrounds the grassy field. I look behind me, and all I see is an ordinary meadow with no sign of a slide-shaped stone. How, exactly, did we arrive here? I can't make sense of the place. I shiver. What if I want to go back up and I can't? I hate when I can't come and go as I please.

Andrea sees my hesitation and senses my concern. "Don't worry. You'll be back home in no time. Literally." He winks.

I can't help but trust him, and I have no alternative at this point, anyway.

We enter the woods and follow a clearly marked path lined with round rocks on each side. It's well kept but so narrow that I have to walk behind him. The path opens into a wide, fan-shaped piazza, similar to the Piazza del Campo in Siena, Tuscany, with an open market where lots of people are busily trading produce and goods. As we walk, Andrea waves to each one, and they greet him with smiles and happy, kind-sounding words in Italian that I don't understand. I try to hide behind him because whenever people notice me, they frown and look tense. Soon, the whole market is aware of my presence, and its lively atmosphere grows almost sober.

We climb some stairs to a church entrance, but the doors are locked, and from the tarnished brass handles and the peeling paint, I can tell that the church hasn't used for a while. A blind woman, who could be in her seventies or her nineties, I can't quite tell—she seems ancient but full of energy—sits in a rocking chair below the headless statue of a saint. From his long, brown-painted habit, his bare feet, and the baby in his hands, I infer that it's Saint Anthony. His paint is peeling, too. A pet parrot sits at her feet, playing with the ball of yarn.

"I see you brought her here," the old woman says.

Andrea nods. I wonder if that's effective since the woman is clearly blind. But then she also mentioned seeing me.

"The blind often see better than those with eyes, my child."

I suppress a start. If she can hear my thoughts, I'd better be quiet even inside me while I'm here. I remember meditation practice,—every time you catch a thought, you dismiss it saying "thinking."

"It doesn't work; don't even bother," she warns me.

The woman is knitting what seems to be a vest, her fingers moving very fast. Her pet parrot balances atop the ball of yarn like a miniature circus acrobat, going back and forth and sometimes in circles. Now and then, she gives a sunflower seed to the bird, and it says. *"Grazie mille! Grazie mille!"* every time it gets a treat.

The bird's show mesmerizes me, and Andrea wakes me by touching my elbow softly. "You two have a lot to catch up on. I'll pick you up here in an hour, okay?"

"You mean you're leaving me here alone?"

"I'll be around. Don't worry; you're in excellent company." With another of his winks, the elflike boy turns around, unclips his ocarina from his belt, and leaves, playing a tune that brings butterflies from everywhere to follow him away.

"Do you like Andrea? He's a very sweet boy, isn't he?"

"Oh yes, he's lovely. But I haven't got to know much about him yet."

"Oh, you know him better than you think you do."

I stare at her blankly.

"Your blood knows," she continues as if I had expressed my confusion aloud.

I have no idea what to say. As I continue staring at her, she smiles. Her yellow teeth are all there, sound and strong. She may be younger than she seems.

"Oh, I'm much older than I look. We know a few tricks to keep body parts—teeth and feet, spine and hair, tails and nails, hands and knees—all young and strong. We haven't yet mastered the damn neck, though; you'll see a lot of scarves and chokers around here—you've got to hide what you can't provide!"

I chuckle, noticing that she wears a blue-and-white polka-dot silk scarf tied neatly above her collar.

"I just couldn't bother with keeping up with looking young in the surface anymore, you know. It's possible, but also a lot of work. It gets to a point where all you care about is self-maintenance, and you invest so much time on it that you stop living. It's very liberating just to let go and enjoy life as it is and appreciate what it offers. I'd much rather focus on my crafts and play with Verve here, my faithful old old friend. I save most of my spells and potions to keep him young and strong. As for myself, I focus on the functional: working bones, straight back and neck, supple muscles, and of course, strong teeth. Many people take teeth for granted, but the better care you take of them, the longer you'll last."

She's smiling nonstop and broadly now, as if she can finally relax and warm up to me or recognize me from a past encounter. I can't tell, exactly.

"Oh dear child, I know who you are, all right. I've always known. But I've never gotten close enough to tell whether you're good or bad stock."

"Do you know about my friend? The red-haired girl, Rori?"

"See? That's what I'm talking about! Always more concerned with others' well-being and safety than your own. Just like your *nonna*. May the Almighty bless her . . . ."

These last few words sound sarcastic rather than pious. The tone strikes me first, and then I catch the words themselves. "Did you know my grandmother?" I ask, thinking of my mother's mother, the only *nonna* I know.

"Oh no, I'm not talking about that grandmother. I mean your great-grandfather's grandmother."

Oh, I see. The Southern Italian side of my family. Makes sense.

"Yes, those people. But, you know, we're not really from here. A long time ago, we used to live in Spain, in a place called Galicia."

Oh. My father's ancestors were Gallegos, too.

"I know. Why do you think your father felt an immediate attraction for your mama?"

"Well, she was a very attractive and talented woman."

"Yes, that might have been his excuse. We like to stay around our kind."

Our kind? Is she including me in this pronoun?

"Yes, of course. Although it's very diluted in you now, your father's marriage was a good move since your mother also carried some of it."

It? What is it?

"Well, after being persecuted and burned at the stake for centuries, we don't dare say out loud what we are. It's just a matter of precaution."

Stregas. Brujas. *Witches. Of course.*

"Indeed, my child."

My thoughts race as I recall incidents that didn't make sense when they happened, strange habits and gestures that felt familiar at home but which I avoided in public like eating dirt and digging my fingers into potting soil and finding that blue yolk egg by my pillow. Everything falls into place now.

"Whoa," she says. "I can't follow you."

"Tell me more about this *nonna* you mentioned." I say. "How am I like her?"

"Well, you two share the same goatlike gaze, only she had green eyes and yours are dark. But the features, the expression, the way you look at things, it's all goat. The sacrificial goat. I wonder if you have Capricorn rising just like she did."

She looks away like searching for something, turning her head around, sometimes sniffing up the air as a dog would when smelling for clues in a search.

"Come close to me."

She touches my face.

"You do have prominent cheek bones, like she did. And chiseled features. A slightly hooked nose." She goes down with her hands, feeling my hair. "A bit coarse hair. Also a long neck. Just like hers."

She touches my hands.

"I feel calluses and tense muscles. Capable hands. Very Capricorn."

She brings her hands to my shoulders. Her blind, lifeless eyes are now fixed on mine. They move slowly, like a scanner doing its job.

"Dark, wide-set, steady eyes. You are all her."

She seems to look inward now, with a hint of sadness, like she's remembering something sad. She tries to open her blind eyes. I see the opaque pupils—no twinkling, no light—as if she's striving vainly to see something that lives in the past.

"There was a wave of hate. The priests of Spain were talking bad about us again. They called us lovers of evil, murderers, and schemers. Just as our community was growing back to strong. Good people were falling like flies, disappearing. Word got around that the South of Italy was very similar to Spain and there was no persecution there. We hired some sailors and and went on a brutal journey: started in the Atlantic, sailed around Spain, passed through the Straits of Gibraltar, and hugged the Mediterranean, fleeing what could have been a Holy Inquisition revival. When we arrived here, some of us stayed in Naples, near the port, but many of us came to Benevento. Others liked Caserta better, and a few people moved as far south as Santa Agatha sui Due Golfi where you can see both the Bay of Naples and the Bay of Salerno. I have a cousin who still lives there. She has a beautiful lemon grove. Sometimes she sends some lemons for me. Andrea takes care of bringing them to me. Nothing like a lemon that has grown under real sun."

Yes, I noticed that the sun is weak here. I wonder why.

"Well, we had to make this place after what happened to your *nonna*. Or, as some of the elders like to say, this place came to us. We were all running scared. The Benevento group met the Caserta, Naples, and Santa Agatha groups deep in the woods, and like waters from different rivers, we all flooded into that meadow. Once we were all there, we heard gunshots and barking dogs surrounding us, coming through the woods in our direction. That's when Paz—who is now happily living as an oak tree—noticed the meadow's energy, which was stronger than any she'd ever felt before. She wore her long, flaxen hair braided on top of her head in a bun; in a sudden flash of insight, she untied the bun, unbraided her hair, and let it fall, almost touching the grass. I remember like it was yesterday: The grass and her hair connected like magnets and started hissing, and wherever they touched, they bonded, the green grass and the golden hair, tied together like one single organism, forming a half-moon shape around her, and the ground started receding, forming a hole behind her. She pulled some hair to the front until it covered her face, making the circle whole, like a full moon. She started descending into the ground until she was up to her waist. Stretching her arms and opening her fingers wide, she screamed, "Someone, hold my hand.""

Alicia and Giovanna went to her rescue, at least that's what they thought, but Paz continued going down and pulled the two of them with her. More of us came, trying to save the three women, and when the suction was strong enough and the circle, now a wide hole, could fit at least a dozen horses, everybody knew what they had to do. The few men that were with us were the last to jump in. When we were all inside, they said that they could hear the barking close behind them and that the dogs actually saw us going down but didn't dare jump in. Then the hole closed above our heads, and we kept on descending until we found the same meadow but in a different light. Sometime I might tell you the rest. All you need to know now is that the only ones we lost were your *nonna*, and Paz, who couldn't survive the effort. We tried to heal her, but she couldn't live as a woman without real sun after that feat, so now she's the Oak. This place keeps us safe, alive, and more or less thriving."

Phew. I don't know how to process it all, so I sit on the cool marble floor of the porch with my legs crossed in a half-lotus position.

"You can come closer."

I scoot my body near her feet. Verve, the parrot, leaves his yarn and climbs up my arm onto my shoulder. He keeps biting my earlobe, and it tickles, causing a tingling that runs up my neck and my skull to the top of my head, right where yogis locate the Sahasrara, the crown chakra, the seventh one. I sigh. The tingling brings me immense peace and makes me laugh, breaking the tension. I'm getting more and more comfortable around this strange woman.

"See, Verve likes you."

"I like Verve, too. And what's your name, by the way?"

"Caterina."

"Hello, Caterina. I'm Carmela."

"I know. That was your *nonna*'s daughter's name, too. We should call you Carmela the Second. Or Seconda. Yes, let's call you La Seconda!"

"My friends call me Cami."

"Cami. I like that. Cami it will be!

"Please, tell me more about this *nonna* you mentioned. How did you lose her?"

"Well, she was one of those cases of stubbornness meeting compassion. When we arrived in Italy, we tried to be as discreet as possible. We were already foreigners, you see. Not off to a good start. But we came up with a story of a plague and famine back in Galicia and said that we were trying a new place. The farmers needed workers, as they always do as long as you don't ask for much in return, so we worked for food and shelter, and they let us stay."

I smile. It feels familiar. She smiles back, showing a trace of dimples, and then winks. She must have been mischievous when she was a kid.

"Yes, I was! And your *nonna*, too. We used to raise hell around the village. But then she grew up, had a baby with Antonio, and became a rather serious woman."

My body is numb from sitting in the same position for so long. I shift. She picks up her knitting and starts a new row, silently focusing on the pattern.

"And then?"

"Oh. I'm sorry. I got distracted. It's a lot of telling for one day, don't you think?"

"No, please continue."

She smiles sadly. "No, child, you must go now. You can't stay here long." She goes back to her knitting, just a rather ordinary blind woman. Her face loses its light. She seems older, much older now, and her shoulders stoop. Verve picks at the needles.

I feel a light touch on my right shoulder. Andrea. "It's time to go now, *cara. Andiamo.*"

"Okay." I get up. "*Ciao*, Caterina."

"*Ciao, bella*," she mutters without taking her attention away from her knitting.

My eyes feel wet, but I hold back the tears. We walk around the church to find a side door, its handles equally rusty, but this one is open a tiny crack. Andrea forces it inward; the wood sticks to the irregular pink rock flooring. It's dark inside except for the light that comes through the stained glass windows. I follow him over to the white marble holy water font at the entrance of the aisle at knee level. It's a huge basin; a kid could bathe in there. It strikes me as a very unusual size and height for a holy water font.

"*Scusi.*" Andrea grabs me by my waist, picks me up, and places me in the basin. He holds my hands while the marble floor of the basin seems to turn to quicksand. I grab his arms in a fit of desperation as it starts to swallow me.

"There's nothing to worry about. I'm coming with you. Ladies first, that's all." And, as if taking his words as a cue, the sand gets ever so soft and the now familiar suction energy starts pulling me down. Only this time the trip is faster, maybe because after the marble-turned-sand, we pass through water until we reach a muddy spot, and Andrea pushes me out of the Oak roots back into the upper forest.

The sun feels bright now that we're back in the ordinary world. It's comforting to feel the heat on my skin; down there was rather chilly.

Andrea is quiet and seems tired. He sits by the roots, picks up his ocarina, and starts playing. After a while, his horse comes out of the roots.

Andrea hands me the black handkerchief, saying, "You know what to do now, don't you?" and I jump onto the horse after him and tie the handkerchief tighter than he did the first time, as if squeezing my brain this way will help me process all the information that was thrown at me. I abandon my tired body and fall asleep during the ride, waking up as the horse jerks awkwardly up the steep slope.

We stop, and Andrea unties the knot. Seeing the rock where I started this journey, I jump off using the rock as a step. My muscles are tight, so I stretch my arms high to loosen up, closing my eyes for a second. When I open them, my friend and his horse are gone.

"Why am I not surprised?" I ask aloud.

I wonder if he'll get in touch with me again. As for me, after a day of planting, weeding, venturing into subterranean realms, and learning that my great-grandfather's grandmother. might have been a witch, I'm exhausted. Ready for a nap, I head back to the farm. The clock in the kitchen shows that just thirty-two minutes have passed since the time I left to meet Andrea. Rick and Ila, the late risers, are still gardening. I remember from children's stories that in the fairy world, time doesn't pass as it does in ours. Maybe it's the same for those witchy folk.

CHAPTER 10

Benevento

The sun is shining into the huge kitchen this Friday morning, and we three volunteers are scrubbing it clean in preparation for the big weekend. Ila and Rick are on good terms because Francesco brought the truck's missing part and, after some days of toil, the car is finally fixed. Now they can finally wake up again at 4:00 A.M. to go to their *mozzarella di bufala* apprenticeship as they used to do before the truck broke down. "The best mozzarella on the planet comes from Valle di Maddaloni, a small town about ten miles southwest of Melizzano," Rick explained to me as they were arriving back from it. "We came to this farm just to learn how to make it, and after we go back to the States, we're going to buy some land up in Oregon and make it exactly like it's made here, if not better."

I just listened to Rick's plans and smiled to myself, wondering how he could be so naïve. If Campania has the best mozzarella, it's not just a matter of learning how to make it. Even if he manages to buy a water buffalo, does he plan to carry the dirt that produces the dry, crunchy grass that grows here for the buffalo to eat, or the water, with the specific minerals carried around by each creek? Even the sunlight here is brighter than Oregon sunshine. Would he be able to reproduce the exact *terroir*?

I wished him the best of luck with his plan, but I doubted its success. Not that I didn't believe he could one day make mozzarella in the Northwestern United States. I just know that it won't taste the same. But, simultaneously, I secretly hoped that he would prove me wrong, just as California Pinot Noir did with my enjoyment of red wine and my snobby dismissal of any wine not produced in Europe.

As for me, I've just had the best night's sleep ever—heavy as a rock and dream free. And I'm glad to be working in the kitchen now instead of the garden; my back, still stiff from years of web coding, is starting to hurt from so much bending and crouching. And it's fun helping Rick even though he can be such a prima donna in the kitchen. When he really gets into cooking, it's just like watching a show. He's an extremely skilled cook but not humble at all. He flaunts his skill.

For this weekend, when the *agriturismo* will finally have some paying guests staying the entire weekend, he's preparing pumpkin gnocchi dough in advance. The work started early and he's ordering everyone around. Cutting open and peeling a pumpkin with a knife is physically demanding, and I already worked in the vegetable gardens around sunrise. Besides, I'm still awestruck from my visit to the subterranean village and my meeting with Caterina. After that adventure, cooking, eating, and cleaning seem mundane and mortal. Rick, in contrast, is in the zone, so focused on his *osso buco* sauce that his jeans are falling a bit so I can see his boxers and a bit of his butt crack.

"Hey, Rick, your ego is showing."

Ila giggles, but her boyfriend doesn't get the joke. That's me in a nutshell: I like telling jokes that no one gets. Sometimes, it's pathetic: I'll say something to a huge group of people and crack myself up in laughter only to see a bunch of wide-eyed, concerned people wondering what's wrong with me.

Rick gives me his harshest, most disapproving frown. He doesn't appreciate the fine art of sarcasm. And he's holding a huge, sharp butcher knife.

I leave the kitchen with my tail between my legs and go look at the sunset. It's been a long day. The orange-and-red colors taking over the valley move me almost to tears. Where on earth have I ended up? A half moon comes out, and it seems like the sky is laughing at me. My eyes are wet, but I don't want to seem weak in front of the stars, my last connection to reality.

I miss Rori badly; she had a great heart and a wise, mature approach to life, which clashed oddly with her Lolitaesque clothing. I remember sharing with her how hard it is for me to travel because of my pickiness about food—I can't eat much wheat, I miss my brown rice and beans, I have to eat frequent snacks, I need salads and greens—every morsel I put in my body counts and can tip my balance. Worrying so much about what I'm going to eat overwhelms me. She understood. She had low blood sugar like me, but not so much. One day when lunch hadn't been served yet even though it was past two, she caught me shaking. I told her about my blood sugar problem; I can't go that long without food. She helped me scavenge a wilted carrot out of the neglected vegetable garden, and I was so hungry that I ate it in a hurry, barely wiping the dirt off it. When my shaking slowed down, I told her how frustrated I was about being so sensitive. She replied, "Are you going to look at it as an asset or a liability?"

I hear a car engine and then a honk; the mailman has arrived. Ila comes running toward me: "Cami, Cami, it's a letter from Bolivia!"

My heartbeat accelerates. Finally, news from Josh! I grab the envelope eagerly, with Ila next to me, witnessing my excitement like a jumping puppy that's about to get a treat.

I open it and discover my own letter stamped "Return to Sender." Apparently, the Bolivian post office couldn't find Josh on the farm where he was supposed to be working. I rip open the familiar saffron-colored envelope, bought at the stationery store in Stazione Termini, the main train station in Rome. The goofy postcard showing an imaginary Coliseum covered in graffiti falls to the floor, never seen by its intended recipient. I look at the letter written in a coffee shop, the cappuccino stain still showing its broken semicircle in the upper left-hand corner of the verge-textured yellow paper.

He never got it.

I touch the necklace Josh made for me—five teardrop-shaped jade pieces hanging from a braided leather string. There's nothing that boy can't do. Well, maybe there's one thing: he can't keep up a correspondence. Or maybe he can't stay in one place so letters can reach him.

In any event, I'm getting worried. Maybe he caught malaria and died in the jungle. But Josh had all his shots; I double-checked his vaccination schedule before he left. And he's as healthy as an ox.

Wait. Josh is fine. I know it. I just know. But what about me? What's going on with me? Images of the latest bizarre happenings pass through my mind like a very fast slide show. Me, hugging a palm tree and bleeding profusely back at the San Francisco office; the dreams about Rori that end with muddy feet and splinters; Andrea taming a parade of snails with his ocarina; and, last, the subterranean world and Caterina's unfinished story about my supposed great-great-great-grandma, the so-called *nonna*. Whoa. Press pause. Repeat. Pause again. I must look very weird right now, with my eyes wide open and fixated on the postcard on the ground, not so much looking at it as using it to collect my scattered thoughts.

Ila squeezes my hand. "Is everything all right?"

Her warm hand brings me back to the present. She probably thinks I'm concerned about my missing boyfriend. Yes, I am, but not in the way that she might believe. Deep down, I know he's alive. I look into her dark eyes and mutter, "It's all fine," but I sound like I'm trying to hypnotize myself, to make myself believe what I feel. It's all fine, he's doing okay, he's doing okay, he's doing okay. I'm the one who's not—doing—okay.

"*Okay!* Great!" Her emphatic reply takes me out of my trance in a snap. "Let's go think about some dessert for the guests arriving tomorrow! Or would you like to start the dough for the fresh bread? Francesco's coming soon. He'll sleep here tonight and maybe Saturday. The kitchen is in our hands. No gypsies around to spoil our party!"

She pulls my arm, and, boy, that girl is strong. Her energy convinces me to forget my worries. We run together into the kitchen, giggling, to find that Rick has finished the sauce and the knife is out of sight. Ila takes some of the rotten flour from a pillow-sized bag under the main kitchen island and claps her hands between our faces. We all turn white, which makes Rick laugh at last. Now I understand his sense of humor. He's a pie-in-your-face kind of guy.

"What shall we cook?" I ask.

"Let's make the bread dough," Ila says. "And after that, I have a surprise."

Her man spins in a clumsy pirouette, stops, grabs her, imitates Mick Jagger's lips, and gives her a loud smack on the cheek. She pushes him away, laughing. Rick straightens his apron and begins the starter ritual, crumbling the yellowish fresh yeast and dropping it into a glass bowl with some lukewarm water.

I watch as it grows foamy, and the smell takes me back to the Red Vic Movie Theater in San Francisco's Upper Haight district where they used to serve popcorn flavored with brewer's yeast. Josh and I went there on our first movie date; we watched Bernardo Bertolucci's *The Sheltering Sky*. We had our first serious discussion at the bar next door over pisco sours and empanadas, comparing notes and fears about the danger of losing your mind when traveling for too long.

That has always been my most hidden secret: I'm afraid that one day I'll lose my mind. I'm almost sure of it. And I believe that being at home, with familiar things around me—my bed, my fire escape, the view of the Bay, the familiar kitchen—helps me avoid my destiny. But I also have a strange urge to travel, just go to places for the heck of it. Josh told me his belief that you have to lose your way to absorb the diverse riches of our vast planet: If you lose your mind as well as your path, so much the better. He believes in the Zen notion that madness is the ultimate form of enlightenment. After telling me stories about *avadhutas* and *siddhas*, crazy wisdom and holy madness, he finished his lecture with a final gulp of his pisco sour, which gave him an egg white foam mustache over his broad, brave smile. "So, when are you going to loosen up and go . . . crazy?" I remember all of my life being terrified just thinking about the possibility of such a detour, but he was so irresistible that I leaned over the tiny bar table and licked his mustache away. I was much too drunk to be scared.

"Can you do the mixing, Cami?" Ila asks as she takes down the new bag of flour from the cupboard.

Oops. Back to reality. I wish I knew how to whistle. "Can we have some music, please?" I ask, and they comply. Some kind of trance-hop comes out of Rick's iPod. Hypnotic.

First, I make a big mountain on the marble counter with the fresh-milled flour that they just brought in this morning. Then, I open a hole in the middle just like the one at the top of Vesuvius and carefully pour in the activated yeast. I add some pure water that comes from a spring right here on the farm. Kneading works like some kind of yoga for me. Just focusing on the dough, pressing it, watching it come out of my hands when I squeeze it between my fingers, adding more flour as I go and using some lukewarm water to clean off my sticky hands and bring the stubborn pieces that refuse to be part of the whole back into it. I use the heel of my hands to compress the dough and push it away from me. I fold it back, giving it a little turn and putting the weight of my body into the movement. I'm dancing with it now. I go on folding over and compressing the dough until it's smooth and a bit shiny. I press it with my finger, leaving my mark. It's ready to rise. I cover it with a red-and-white checkered cloth and let it rest in a quiet, warm, dark corner. Rising dough doesn't like to be bothered.

"Oh, wait, are you done? Can I steal some?" Not waiting for my answer, Ila grabs a big chunk of it.

I get grumpy.

"It's for a good cause," she says. "Check it out." She takes it to the stove, where a frying pan full of hazelnut oil sits atop a high flame. She makes little balls out of the dough and drops them carefully into the oil. When they're brown and crispy—crunchy on the outside and fluffy on the inside—she drops them onto a plate with a mixture of sugar, cinnamon, and nutmeg. "And a little freshly ground black pepper," she says. "My mom came up with that idea. It makes all the difference!" She waits until they cool off a bit and rolls them around in the sweet and spicy powder.

Now Rick's iPod plays loud hip-hop, and we all dance around the kitchen.

"*Ma que pasticcio!*" A loud knock on the open kitchen door follows this comment on our mess. It's Francesco, arriving with a bang. He pats Rick on the back. We all run to the long wooden table on the side porch where the warm, starry night welcomes us. Sitting around the table nibbling the sweet fried dough balls, we laugh and plan for the upcoming weekend.

There's no need to think about dessert for the guests; Francesco has brought a huge container with *crema sanguinaccio* from Naples. I can smell the strong, dark chocolate even before he opens the carton to give us each a spoonful of the rich pudding. In the midst of enjoying the treat, my sharp nose catches a pungent smell like Munster cheese coming from below me. My eyes follow my nose, and I quickly discover the source under the table: Francesco has taken off his shoes and is getting comfortable, rubbing one foot on the other. It's the first time I've ever seen his feet because he's always wearing boots, along with long sleeves and working gloves that hide his hands and arms. His toenails are long, making me a bit disgusted, and his toes and the tops of his feet are incredibly hairy. Yuck.

He congratulates Rick on fixing the truck and preparing the gnocchi for the weekend.

Rick is elated; we can all see how he loves Francesco. He's also clearly worried about the fate of the farm. "We're not slaves, Ciccio. The gypsies are working us to the bone. Don't they know that volunteers are here for just four hours of work a day for room and board?"

"And the way they talk," Ila adds. "'When we buy the farm, we'll tear down the guesthouse to make room for the new circus.' I mean, it's kind of stupid to think of putting a circus here: this land is mostly rolling hills. But they don't care about farming; they don't even know how to cook! Have you ever eaten their so-called food?"

"How much was their last offer?" Rick asks, sounding anxious.

"Oh, less than half of what I want. Don't worry; I'm actually thinking about evicting them and taking the farm back. But their lease isn't up for two more years."

Silence falls over the once-lively table. In my mind, I see the devastated fields, fallen trees, and decrepit buildings that now mar the farm. If less than six months have brought the place to such disarray, what will happen if they keep it for two more years?

"Well." Francesco breaks the silence, scratching his throat. "What shall we have for dinner?"

"Me, nothing." I get up fast and leave under a wave of complaints. I've eaten only bread and sweets the whole day, so my blood sugar is spiking and I'm getting dizzy. I know that Rick cooked pasta with tomato sauce, and I need something more substantial.

The three dogs follow me to my cabin, and I share my feast with them: canned tuna, salami, and almonds. I save the returned-to-sender letter under my mattress and go to sleep thinking of Josh.

When we parted in San Francisco, the relationship was a bit shaky. Almost every day during the first weeks of my trip, I would remember our last dinner at his house, which haunted me like acid reflux.

"I'm in love with these heirloom tomatoes," I said, complimenting the salad he had prepared. "Eating them is almost like biting into a heart!" He looked sideways into the distance and sighed. He sat silent for a moment, and I wondered why.

"You're going to eat my heart one day, I know it," he resumed, half-joking, half-sad.

"Why me? You could break my heart just as easily."

He got up to wash the dishes and didn't say another word for the remainder of the night. I was restless trying to sleep by his side, and the next morning, he left before I could wake up, just leaving a note complaining that he couldn't sleep well. Later, we met at my place so he would take me to the airport and sent me off in his usual cheerful mood, wishing me an enjoyable trip, but I couldn't brush away the previous night. He kissed me on the forehead and told me I had a hall pass while I was in Italy, but I dismissed the offer. He looked a bit incredulous, hugged me, and nibbled my ear. The biting was wetter than usual; tears were running down his cheek. I could barely recognize my free-spirited boy.

I fall asleep hugging the pillow and wishing he were there with me.

In the middle of the night, at 12:12 to be precise, "*la doppia ora*," the familiar electronic ping of my smart phone wakes me up. It's a text from Marco. "*Buonanotte. A domani!* See you at 3:00!" And a little emoticon winking and throwing kisses followed his words.

Great. I had completely forgotten about that creep arriving after lunch tomorrow.

CHAPTER 11

Pietraroja

Right around 3:15, Marco shows up. He smells like he has sprinkled half a bottle of perfume over his head, and, allergic as I am, I can't help but sneeze and back off a step at each achoo. I try to focus on the aroma of Bolognese gnocchi sauce that previously permeated the kitchen, but synthetic smells seem to always overpower natural ones.

There's no way out; he's already all over the place, mingling with Rick, Ila, and a pair of guests whose names I've already forgotten inside the wood-paneled TV and game room that we've adapted into a dining space to accommodate the weekend crowd. In spite of the bright sunshine brazenly coming through the left side window, they're all sitting around after a long, late lunch. The most adventurous guests have gone out for a hike even though the dry heat begs for cold drinks, fans, or just lying around like boa constrictors digesting a meal.

Rick knows Marco. He told me that he's already bought wine from him, recommended by Francesco, who opened his eyes wide and extended his arms as soon as Marco crossed from the veranda into the darkened room. "Marco! What a surprise!" He hugged the visitor effusively, patting him on the back.

Half a dozen bottles of wine now sit on the round table covered by a checkered red-and-white cloth. Green napkins complete the cliché. Three of the bottles are already open, two whites and a noteworthy red—Cannonau di Sardegna, DOC Riserva 2006—and three of the female guests, in spite of their husbands' presence, are already smiling and flirting with the handsome wine merchant. He keeps pouring more wine whenever he sees a glass becoming empty, and, almost every time, he glances at me with his bright smile, teeth so white that I can almost see a twinkle on the pointy end of his upper right canine. I hold on to my first glass of the Cannonau di Sardegna, still half full, knowing myself too well to get drunk with this dude around.

He has also brought a basket full of Roma tomatoes and *mozzarella di bufala.* He set the basket by the window, and the tomatoes are beautiful, of a deep red I've never seen before. They're also at least five inches long, much longer than the Roma tomatoes we get in NorCal. I'm getting tired of my wine even though it tastes divine. I mean, red wine in this heat—how can I even think? The chilled white that all the others are enjoying would be more appropriate, and I would in theory love to try it if only I didn't despise white wine.

I put down my glass and go outside, not even sure that leaving will help. If the improvised dining room feels like an oven, going outdoors is like bringing it to broil mode. And it's the end of June. I can't imagine this place in August! I sit in the part of the veranda that overlooks the valley. The neighbor below us is practicing his guitar as he does faithfully every Saturday afternoon. Today, he's playing "Sweet Child o' Mine" by Guns N' Roses. It's been ages since I last listened to that song; it feels so out of place here that I have to laugh. I don't know why, but my laughter becomes almost hysterical. I can't help myself; I get to the point of snorting.

I hear Marco's voice and turn around. "*Ciao,*" he says. "What's so funny, *amore mio?* I see you didn't like your wine."

Amore mio? Geez. Get out. "No, it's just a bit hot for red, I guess. And on top of that, Rick prepared gnocchi, such a winter food."

"Oh, *no problema.* Do you grow basil in the garden? Marco here will prepare the *insalata Caprese* of your dreams for dinner!"

Dinner? He's already inviting himself for dinner? Talk about overstaying your welcome. At least the wind is coming from behind me and carrying his unbearable fragrance away. I can breathe near him at last.

"Oh, I already had a great Caprese in Rome, thanks. It's actually one of my favorite salads."

"Rome? Caprese in Rome? *Ma che, signorina,* you have to try the one I make, with the tomatoes from my mama's backyard and the mozzarella from Caserta. Rome doesn't even come close to this mozzarella. The factory here can't keep up with the demand from Campania alone."

"Oh, I think I know this factory. Isn't it the same one where Rick and Ila are doing an apprenticeship?"

"Oh no, I don't think so. They're very secretive about it. Only family members are allowed in the operations."

"Oh. In that case, yeah, I'd love to try it sometime." Oops. I slipped. His spell is already working on me.

"What about dessert? My mother just visited and made me cannoli; it's in my car. Would you like to try one?"

"No, thanks. I know cannoli."

"What do you mean? These are my mama's cannoli. You haven't tasted heaven on earth until you've tried them. Wait right here, *capisce*?"

He leaves, walking fast but not fast enough for my taste. Talk about pushy.

Deciding to get up and walk off the heavy meal, I go down to the shady grove, the only place that isn't too hot right now. Yes, tomatoes should be a good option for dinner tonight. But I wish they were heirloom tomatoes. Right now in San Francisco, the farmers' markets are featuring an abundance of juicy, meaty, funky-looking yellow, orange, and red heirloom tomatoes. I never dared to come close to one until Josh told me they were the best summer offering. He used to make a wonderful salad with heirloom tomatoes and a lemon-basil-honey-truffle dressing that really got me hooked up on them. And it was our last meal together. I feel homesick.

"*Carissima*, you left me!"

I almost jump out of my boots. I turn to see Marco holding a cannoli and looking angry. He has that blue fire in his eyes again. I accept the treat, the fire subsides, and his eyes go from blue to green again. How can he do that?

"*Mangia che ti fa bene!* How do you like it?"

"It's very good!" I wouldn't dare say otherwise even though I'm about to enter a food coma. "Do you want a bite?"

"Oh no, it's all for you. I have a dozen more in the car!"

Oh boy. I decide to divert his attention and maybe save the dessert for later. "Do you know how to find heirloom tomatoes around here?" I ask.

"Oh yes! A good friend of mine grows Cuore de Toro tomatoes. They're incredibly sweet and can be as heavy as two pounds. The name means 'ox heart.' That's how they're shaped."

Of course, he knows. He seems to know everything about this place. I decide to put his knowledge to use. "Have you ever seen a small cabin deep in those woods?"

He seems to stop breathing as he stares at me with his big green eyes. Finally, he replies with a question. "Why?"

"Why what?"

"Well, I mean, you go from tomatoes to cabins so fast. Why do you want to know?"

"Oh, no reason, really. Just curious."

"Well, if you want some privacy, I have a little house in Positano. It's rented now for the summer, but as soon as the vacationers leave, I can take you there. It's small but charming. And what a view!"

Oh boy. Now he thinks I want to get a room with him. Talk about misunderstanding. Should I open up and tell about my dreams—and Rori? Probably not.

"Cami, finally!" Rick's bossy voice has never sounded so good or so timely. "What are you doing here? We have a bunch of dishes to wash."

"I've got to run now, Marco. Thanks for everything." I leave him there and climb the hill back to the kitchen, almost squeezing my cannoli in my tight fist until I throw it in the compost bin. I arrive at the kitchen sink panting but relieved. I'm so thirsty that I drink the cool water straight from the tap, twisting my neck almost into stiffness and soaking my T-shirt. It feels refreshing. As I wash the dishes, going through the motions and touching water sends me into Zen mode. The sound of a car engine interrupts my meditative state. I peek out the window and see Marco's red Maserati convertible leaving along the winding dirt road that leads out of the property. I sigh with relief and finish the dishes.

With the work done, I take a well-deserved siesta after which I wake up invigorated and inspired. There's still quite a bit of daylight left and I have time to kill, so I go exploring again. I'm feeling the call of the wild; maybe today I'll find the cabin where Rori is. The dogs follow me into the woods.

I take off my flip-flops and close my eyes. Walking barefoot on grass and dirt works like magic, and it feels just like it usually does in my dreams since I'm never wearing shoes when I look through the cabin window. I try to feel sleepy, navigating from meditation mode, holding my sandals and hoping that such mindset will help me find that miserable cabin. Or maybe feeling the moist, prickly ground beneath my bare feet will help my body recall the way to get there.

Soon, I regret having left. The darkness falls earlier in the forested valley, and I feel lost and afraid until I find an oak that resembles the one that leads to the witches' underground world. It can't be same oak since I'm now on the opposite side of the valley if my inner compass is right, but it's the tallest tree around. Looking at that mighty oak, I have an idea. If I climb to the top and look around, maybe I can find what I'm looking for.

I climb up, watched by the three concerned dogs. When I can't go any farther without risking breaking the branch I'm clinging to, I scan the territory below me, and soon I distinguish a clearing in the valley with what seems to be a rooftop in its center. The size is right; that must be it!

In my excitement, I fail to notice the first crack in my branch. By the time I notice the second crack, it's too late and down I go, tumbling through the lower branches, which scratch me but cushion my fall, so when I finally drop to the ground among the dogs, I'm not badly hurt. I get up, stretch, and crack a couple of vertebrae. The dogs wag their tails and lick my bare feet, happy to see me back on earth. I manage to find one of my flip-flops. While I'm looking for the second one, lost in the fall, the dogs start barking and howling, tails and ears perked up. As I walk away from the oak and toward the clearing I spotted, the dogs follow me still, but they keep barking and looking behind us. They position themselves in a protective semicircle, the biggest one at my back, the smallest one in front of me, and the one that usually has one floppy ear by my right side. This time, it has both ears up. They calm their barking as we progress, but they never let down their guard.

For a moment, I glimpse a pair of wild feline eyes among the bushes. The dogs bark again, tense and alert. I turn around and make my way back to the main guesthouse. Now that I know where the cabin may be, I want to come back in daylight. After a few minutes, the dogs start barking again, and I see some leaves twitch. I'm not alone in the forest. Again, I see that focused predator gaze, shining against the dark forest. I have no weapon, nothing to help me but the dogs. Still one flip-flop short, I start running through the trees, tripping over roots and getting scratched and snapped in the face by branches. Half-blinded by tears of desperation, I just want to be out of this maze as soon as possible.

The dogs run with me but the burning cat eyes follow until I hit a large rock wall that I've never seen before. Great. Now I'm in new territory and stuck there. I follow the rock wall along. It seems endless. Just as I feel the beast's breath almost on my neck, the dogs stop barking and sit down.

"Come on, you guys," I say to them. "Help me out here. Let's get out of this together."

They don't budge. It's as if some kind of dog whisperer has put them in a trance and there they sit, paralyzed. If it weren't for their tongues out and their usual panting, I would think they were stuffed animals rather than living beings. Feeling defeated, I slide my sore back against the moldy rock and slowly sit down among the stubborn dogs. I cry and wail, feeling that I can put all my energy into it since there's nobody around to hear me. I open my eyes and see a familiar pair of boots near my bare feet. My eyes move up the legs to the torso and then the face. Marco is hovering over me, with his arms crossed tightly across his chest and his eyes blue, fired up, angry.

"What are you doing here?" I ask him. "I thought you went back home."

"I forgot something."

"What?"

"I forgot to tell you that it's not wise to venture into these woods all by yourself."

"That's none of your business."

"Yes, it is. You become responsible for what you have tamed."

"You haven't tamed anyone. And don't Little Prince me! Can't you come up with something more original?" I stand up, incensed. Face to face with him, I watch his eyes shifting rapidly from blue to green and back to blue, driving me crazy. Who is this man? What the hell does he want with me? I can tell that he's wavering between feeling protective and feeling angry.

"I see you like to take lonely walks," he says, his eyes still flickering but now mostly green. "Did you know that this region used to be called Maleventum? The Romans changed the name to Beneventum—after they killed all the witches."

"Romans? There were witches here in Roman times?"

"Yes lots, of them. It's a tragic story, but I'll tell you if you agree have a drink with me. A nightcap. What do you say?"

"But the closest bar that stays open late is at least a two-hour drive from here."

"No, no bars for us. I have a special bottle waiting in my car." His eyes have become steady green again, no more flickering. "What do you say?"

Since I'm lost and he has a car, I really have no choice. I agree, and, as he takes my hand, the dogs get up and follow us. I'm limping; the bare foot is hurt. Marco reaches into his jacket pocket (what kind of person wears a leather jacket in this heat?) and magically produces my missing flip-flop.

"Here you are, my Cinderella."

I grunt and accept the shoe.

Marco immediately starts lecturing me. "Do you know how stupid and risky it is to go wandering around the woods like this? Campania isn't California, and even in California, this wouldn't be a smart thing to do. There are all kinds of criminals roaming around here. I mean, you live with gypsies, my dear. Can't you tell that the world isn't inhabited solely by angels?"

"Wait a minute," I protest. "Those gypsies may be lousy cooks and dreadful farmers, but they're harmless."

"Not in my view. In my opinion, everyone's guilty until proven innocent. I'm Catholic, so it's my prerogative to believe in original sin. Don't you agree?"

"Sin . . . .Yeah, sin is the smartest product ever invented, with the slickest marketing plan. Turn everything delicious and desirable into forbidden fruit and then sell a piece of heaven in trade for repentance. If you're going the Ten Commandments route, I'm sorry, but I'm more inclined to follow the eight limbs of yoga."

"Oh, yes. I forgot that even though you have Italian blood, you've been in California for a while. Those things rub off. I'll bet you eat avocados and make your own granola." He smirks.

"And I'll bet you've spent some time abroad, as well; you're the first Italian I've met who appreciates the fine art of sarcasm."

"Yes, you're right, my dear. I spent a good amount of time in London. In fact, I went to college there. And I go back now and then on business."

We climb some stairs sculpted into the rock wall. They lead to a slope, which we climb grabbing weeds and exposed roots. Soon, we reach the road where Marco parked his car.

"So, selling wine must be a very lucrative business to judge from your ride," I say as we get in the car and he starts the engine.

"Oh no, this car belonged to my father. It's a family relic."

We drive for a while along curvy roads. The wind feels good in my hair and dries my wet face, which I know is still swollen from crying. He stops at a vista point where we can see the lights of a village nestled cozily in a valley, surrounded by a tall and broad mountain range.

He unzips his green army backpack, taking out a bottle and two shot glasses, opens the bottle popping the cork out, and fills both glasses with pale yellow liquid. We touch our glasses softly.

"*Salute.*" He lifts his glass toward the moon, looks at the bright, star-studded sky, and downs the drink in one gulp.

I take a sip, savoring it slowly; I recognize the flavor. "It's Strega, isn't it? I had it not long ago, in Rome. I like the anise flavor, and I've heard that Strega helps with digestion when you eat heavy food."

"Yes. I brought it for you as a gift, so we could have an après-lunch digestive, but you rushed off so fast that we didn't have time. What happened, you didn't like your food?"

I don't want to reveal that what I didn't like was the company even though he seems so mellow now. Even his strong fragrance seems to have faded away. "I'm sorry. I've been a bit overwhelmed. Not the best company these days. . . ." I think about Josh, Rori, and all the mind-bending happenings lately.

Marco keeps quiet for a while and pours himself another shot. This one goes down a little slower, as if he's thinking as he drinks. "What's the matter? The life of a farmer isn't as peaceful as you expected?"

I wonder if I should tell him Rori's story. Can I trust him? But when I open my mouth to say something, he cuts me off.

"See that village down there? It's called Pietraroja."

"What a funny name—*rock* in Italian and *red* in Spanish."

"Exactly. The people there speak a very distinctive dialect. Their word for *witch* isn't *strega*; they call witches *janàre*. I guess keeping different names help them protect their secrets. And I'll bet they still have lots of them."

"Lots of what? Secrets?"

"Yes. And also wizards and witches. Just like Benevento, which had lots of them. After the Walnut Tree Massacre, the ones in Pietraroja disappeared as well. But I'll bet they just went undercover, and they're still practicing their rites and brewing potions." He takes another sip and squints, looking toward the city lights as he wipes his mouth with the back of his hand. I shiver. *A massacre?!* I fear for Caterina, Andrea, and their kin. I fear for myself.

"Are you feeling cold? Here, take my jacket." He's wearing just a white T-shirt underneath, and I can tell that he has a well-defined chest and not much body hair.

I'm not cold, but I accept his kindness out of inertia. "You don't seem to like witches very much," I manage to say.

He points to the bottle, now lying on the car floor. "This is the only witch I like. But we have to give them credit. I don't know if it's just marketing, but the recipe for this delightful concoction may come from witchcraft. It has more than seventy different herbs in its mix, including mint and fennel. Its yellow color comes from saffron. The remaining ingredients are a very well-kept secret."

I change the subject. "You said that the Romans killed witches, and Benevento was called Maleventum. Can you tell me more about that?"

"*La vecchia religione* . . . ."

"'The old religion?'" I translate, mystified.

"Well, there was a time when people didn't worship God, just the Goddess, and the witches were her priestesses, worshiping the Dark Mother. They were also very powerful, and that's why the Romans trapped them all and drowned them in a lake, with the excuse of eliminating evildoers. Nobody dares to go near that place anymore. They say that if you go close enough to the shore, the witches grab your legs and pull you down with them. People around here claim that the lake had plenty of fish before, and now, nothing. No fruit trees grow around it, either."

"You also mentioned a walnut tree."

"Oh yes, that's a different story. The old people say that witches still lived in Benevento for a long, long time after the lake trap. Many different legends mention a walnut tree that the witches used to dance around with the devils on the Sabbath, which managed to stay green throughout the year. Once they tried cutting the tree down. But, according to one tale, a snake carrying a golden cup sprang out of the stump and the tree started growing again. The legend also says that the witches of Benevento used a magic oil to fly at night, letting their long hair float up while they all gathered. They met around the tree, sang, danced, and kidnapped married men to have fun"— and he pauses to make the quote unquote hand gesture and let out a quick malicious smile when he says the word fun— "with them, after which they would turn into wind and blow under the doors."

"Do you think there are still witches around?"

"Well, who knows? Where there's a will, there's a way. Many people have the potential to become witches; the important thing is not to let them have a breeding ground. Otherwise, witchcraft can spread like wildfire."

"Was the goddess Isis? I saw the ruins of her temple in town."

"No, it was older than that. Her name changed many times, but the energy was always the same: Feminine, tricky, sneaky, treacherous . . . ." He's gripping the tiny wooden steering wheel strongly; it looks like it will break apart at any moment. A blue haze surrounds his face; I can't see his eyes, but I'll bet they're turning blue. And his blue eyes are dangerous.

I change the subject. "Well, at least they came up with this great liqueur! Which makes me think that maybe I should drive us back? You've had two of these shot glasses."

"Oh, my dear, I could have drunk the whole bottle, and it would make no difference. I'm almost immune to alcohol. You, on the other hand, seem a bit tipsy." He chuckles and tries to tickle me. I'll never underestimate this man's ability to turn every word I say into an opportunity to touch me. I retreat into my seat, holding the door, about to thrust it open and run away.

"Easy there, cara mia. I'm not going to attack you. Here, let me take you home. Anyway, we have enough time to spare to spend some of it together; hanging out is how you call it in America, uh? Do you know what else they say about Strega liquor?

"No. What?"

"The witches' brew that served as inspiration for its recipe was notorious for eternally uniting couples that drank it."

I smile, remembering the first time I tried it, with Josh, on his way home from his job as kitchen help. I was picking him up and we drank some together at the restaurant's bar. Marco must think that I'm smiling for him since he smiles back with his perfect, shiny white teeth. I close my eyes. So tired.

He makes a U-turn and drives me toward home. I fall asleep in the car.

Later, I wake up lying in my bed, still wearing his leather jacket, and find the Strega bottle, two-thirds full, standing on my bedside table. I don't know whether I'm drunk or just sleepy, but I could swear that I see the little witches on its label dance around their cauldron and wink at me.

CHAPTER 12

Somewhere in the Amazon jungle

After receiving the bowl made from half a gourd, Josh drank the hot ayahuasca tea that the shaman helpers served him. Closing his eyes, he saw Cami walking in a forest and smiled. *My caramel. She always loved hiking,* he thought. But then he realized that it was night and she was barefoot. Crying. Lost. Josh frowned.

The shaman came to him and said something in Quechua, a South American language that Josh didn't understand.

Señor Silva, the guide who had brought him to this tribe in the Peruvian section of the Amazon jungle, translated the shaman's concerns. "Are you having a bad trip? Do you need help? Hang in there." The guide touched Josh's hands, and Josh looked down at his own fists, now tightly clenched, as if that part of his body were angry and ready to attack.

Everything had better be everything all right with Cami, he thought. He didn't know what he would be capable of if she didn't come back safely to San Francisco. Remembering that he had encouraged her to take the trip, he felt guilty. Yes, he was embarking on a bad trip and he couldn't stop the train and get off.

This was his third dose of ayahuasca, and he'd been trying to achieve a visionary state of mind with the herbal hallucinogen. Right now, he had arrived at a stop called sorrow. Not wanting to get off there, he held his breath, as if by not breathing, he could stay on the train. He could feel his face turning purple.

Señor Silva gave him a good shake. "Breathe! What are you doing?"

Josh gasped, taking as much air as possible into his lungs as he did when he went snorkeling and didn't want to leave the fish until almost out of breath. He was panting now. Even if he'd wanted, he could never summon the will to suffocate himself. Lungs beat brains.

CHAPTER 13

Subterranean Heights

The next morning, I wake up feeling so anxious that I even skip coffee. I arrive early at the already familiar rock where Andrea is supposed to pick me up and take me back to his underground world, but he, as usual, is late. I recall my meeting with Caterina and her starting to tell me about this *Nonna* person, supposedly my ancestor.

My eyes follow one of those fearless Campanian lizards that's approaching me. I've never seen such boldness in a small, toothless reptile. Entranced, I wonder if they have some weapon that I'm not aware of. Perhaps they have venom in their tongues, or poisoned claws, which grab you and start to kill you—slowly. At first, you don't even notice; it's just an itch. Then it spreads throughout your body, making your limbs numb and your heart slow down. By the time you realize what's going on, you're about to die. And yet you wonder, panting, nearly fainting, how it happened. You don't even remember the small pinch that a colorful lizard gave you some days ago.

In my trance, I remember the days I spent in Florence and my visit to the *Officina Profumo-Farmaceutica*. The crazy dream I had there comes back to me. I remember the woman burning at the stake and the child running to the center of the circle while almost everyone else was drunk in the lynching, immersed in the catharsis of sacrifice. I remember the child crying and opening a box, keeping the box open and stretching her arms as far as she could to bring the box as close as possible to the poor burning soul.

On the edge of my remembered dream, I hear Andrea's voice. "*Ciao, bella.* Did you wait too long?"

My dream doesn't fade. "Never forget me," it whispers to me. It wants to stay; it doesn't want me to leave it alone.

"Cami, are you ready? Can you hear me?" Andrea waves his left hand in front of my eyes, and I see for the first time that his palm has a big, red half-moon-shaped scar. He snaps his short, strong fingers. As his face comes slowly into focus, the first thing I notice is his mischievous smile.

"Let me guess. You haven't had coffee yet, have you?"

"Uh-uh," I mumble.

"Okay, wait right here. Don't go anywhere. I'll be right back." He leaves his horse near me and goes into the bushes along the road. The horse looks at me with that nonchalant, almost blasé equine face. After a while, Andrea comes back with some dark green leaves, shiny and almost oily. They remind me of bay leaves except that the lines across them are a dark, intense burgundy.

"*Pronto, amore mio*. Chew on these." He hands me some of the leaves.

I look at him, puzzled, and accept the offering, which tastes quite bitter.

"I can't produce a shot of espresso right here, right now, out of thin air, but these leaves have some caffeine to get you started. What were you thinking? You can't just quit cold turkey like that. Soon enough, you would have had a gigantic headache and wouldn't have been able to function. If a heavy coffee drinker like you wants to quit, she must go slowly, decreasing the dose, *piano piano*, skipping every other day, but not in a crucial day like today."

The caffeine kicks in fast, and I jump off the rock and out of my sluggishness. "Crucial? How so?"

"*Andiamo*. One thing at a time. Can you tie this over your eyes?" He hands me the same dark cloth from the previous time. "But first, climb on the horse."

I obey the instructions. After trotting along feeling the same sensations that I felt the first time, we go down the steep slope. The path seems familiar. Somehow, my memories seem stronger when I can't see.

When we arrive at the old oak, he dismounts, unties my blindfold, helps me down, and chooses a different pair of roots, caressing them and tickling them until they start to shake like the limbs of a teenager having a laughter attack. They open wide and a red light comes out of the hole. Andrea takes my hand. "The tree wants you to go first," he says.

I look at him, obviously distressed.

"Don't worry. I'll be right behind you. Here, I'll hold on to your shoelaces." He releases my hand and kneels at my feet, untying and grabbing my shoelaces. Not knowing why, I put my hands together and dive in headfirst with him attached to my feet. I reach a wide space, with very warm, dense air that lets us float rather than fall, and soon we land in a small cave, with a hole in its wall that leads into a hallway lit by candles on each side.

Letting go of my shoelaces, Andrea catches up to me, and his horse follows us. We turn corners and crawl over stairs that go up and down until we reach an arch-shaped wooden door. Andrea sticks his pinky in the keyhole, and the doorknob turns by itself, prompted by the contact with the boy's flesh. He pushes the door open, leading us to an attic. To judge from the weak, colorful light streaming in through some stained glass windows, I figure we're in a church. The attic is full of boxes, trunks, and chests, all covered with dust and interconnected by spider webs. Nobody has been here for a long time.

"I don't use this way in very often," Andrea says, "but I wanted you to see something first thing today."

We go down a wooden spiral staircase that ends right near where the altar in a traditional Catholic church would be. This place has an altar, all right, but it's just a rustic piece of wood, covered with dried plants, animal skins, huge butterfly wings, and all sort of shells and unpolished precious stones. Surrounded by tall, brightly burning candles that don't seem to melt, it's a powerful sight, especially since the rest of the church is unlit.

Led by Andrea, I turn my back to the candles and enter the sacred darkness of the apse. Catholic churches make you feel small and awestruck; that's the goal of the architecture. The large and colorful stained glass windows all over the walls would let in sunlight if this church were above ground, but he feeble light in this underground realm leaves everything but the altar dim. The scenes portrayed in the windows remind me of the *Via Crucis*, the Stations of the Cross that Catholic churches always feature, only instead of the familiar scenes with Jesus carrying the Cross and enduring torment culminating in crucifixion, I see a series of equally tormented women. Some are burning at the stake, others tied to Catherine wheels or buried alive, their eyes and hands begging for rescue under shovel after shovel of dirt. Two of them try to shield themselves with their arms from a rain of stones.

When my eyes get used to the darkness, I notice that there are no pews. Instead, the church is peppered with small altars, reminding me the Day of the Dead celebrated in November back on the West Coast, but these altars don't just celebrate people that have died; they celebrate each witch's own power and individuality, showcasing her strengths and hinting at her weaknesses. It's like walking into a hall of fame. The altars display favorite fruits and flowers, along with paintings of loved ones and drawings, mostly sketched by children before self-consciousness restrains their creativity. Some altars hold little toys, or pieces of embroidery. I see lots of unfinished knitting, some of it with the needles still in, and even pieces of colorful broken china.

Some altars have black ceramic bowls with a ladle inside it, and every ladle holds roasted coffee beans, sugar, and dried lemon rinds. Just like the one I dreamed of at the Florence pharmacy. Every altar but one also holds a round stone placed over the drawings, which usually portray different scenes, most of them by the sea or in a forest, always including a woman. Only one altar doesn't have a stone. The drawing in this one depicts a woman taking care of a sick, bed-ridden man. Oddly, I feel drawn to it.

Mesmerized, I stare at it with my jaw dropped. Suddenly, a sharp, pain stabs my upper neck, sending pins and needles down my arm. My chronic tendonitis has flared up again. I recoil in agony.

"What's going on?"

"I don't know. I wonder how much caffeine those leaves you gave me contain "

"Well, a lot. But you shouldn't feel pain from that."

"Caffeine constrains muscles, and my upper back is my Achilles heel."

He stares at me blankly.

"It's an idiom, just a way of saying that my upper back is my weakest point."

"Oh, I see. Don't be surprised if your strongest point shows up as well. This place is special. Being here does things like that to people."

"Really? Maybe we should get out of here, then. The pain is becoming unbearable."

"Oh no, not yet. We have to stay here. Someone is coming to see you. Let me rub your back and make the pain go away. *Permesso?*"

Before I can say anything, he starts kneading the tightened muscles of my neck and shoulders. The pain melts away, and my heart is melting, too, remembering the first time that Josh kissed me. It all started with a back rub. Where is he? Has he all but forgotten me? Next thing I know, I'm crying.

"*Ma che. . .*? Am I hurting you?"

"No, you're doing perfectly. I just remembered something . . . or rather, someone."

He turns me around, holds up my chin, and looks into my wet eyes. Always blinking, he smiles his most mischievous smile ever, dimples and all, and gives me a hug. I'm flustered, but it works. His warm embrace makes all the pain and doubt go away, like . . . magic?

"*Scusi?* I hope I'm not interrupting anything," says a husky voice coming from the deepest, darkest corner of the church, followed by chuckles. A beautiful woman wearing a snug-fitting purple knit dress that reveals all her voluptuous curves and a hood covering hair and some of her face emerges from the shadows. She strikes a match, lighting a tall candle near her.

Andrea gasps. "Oh, you showed up in full bloom. I can't help but be amazed every time I see you like this."

"Oh, you flirty boy. Respect your elders, please!" She throws back her hood, revealing shiny, completely white hair and diamonds sparkling in a thousand colors in place of eyes. Her face, strikingly beautiful, is oddly familiar. "How are you, Carmela?" she asks.

She knows my name? "Pardon my forgetfulness. Have we met?"

Andrea giggles. "This is Caterina, Cami. I'm sure it's hard to recognize her in this form."

I rub my eyes in disbelief. Is this gorgeous being the ancient woman I met the last time I was here?

"Yes, Cami," she says, "I'm your old friend, the same Caterina you met earlier. When I come in here, my weaknesses show up, along with my strengths, so my hair keeps its true present color. That helps to keep me humble and grounded."

Andrea turns to me, delighted. "Ever since our people left Galicia, Caterina has always been the most beautiful one, anywhere our folk are found."

The woman blushes. *False modesty?* I wonder. She's clearly proud of her looks. I'm puzzled, as usual, but weird things here are the norm. The mere fact that this underground realm exists is a mystery I can't solve.

"Yes. . . .Vanity is my weakness, and keeping my hair white reminds me of the impermanence of bodily treasures."

"What kind of place is this?" I ask. "Why a church?"

"This is our temple. Yes, the irony is not lost in me. We worship in the very church of those who persecuted and burned so many of us during Inquisition. Well, what can I say? What doesn't kill you makes you stronger. Besides, it's an architectural masterpiece; the very shape of the building brings powerful forces together. It simply works."

A long, cold, embarrassing silence ensues as I try to digest all the bizarre new information. I keep looking at my feet and at the red-and-white marble tile that covers the floor.

Caterina breaks the stillness, her voice as grave as a priest's during a sermon. "So, as I told you before, two hundred years ago, in 1809, a group of witches from Galicia fled based on rumors of a revival of the persecution and came here. They swore to act like other people, didn't perform any spells, and didn't grow herbs or prepare potions. They all lived in cities or villages, working on nearby farms, learning Italian, and trying to fit in as much as they could.

One of them befriended a woman whose husband was very sick, and, even though the other witches were against it, she decided to help the ailing man. She gathered herbs from the forest under the villagers' suspicious eyes and started treating the woman's husband. He got better. But since he felt healthier, he started drinking wine again against the witch's orders. He fell sick again, and this time he died. His widow accused the witch of poisoning her husband, and the men of the village hunted her down and burned her at the stake in the main square. The incident grew to a lynching mob going delirious. All the villagers witnessed it, and most were remorseful afterwards, so they never spoke of the incident to their descendants, who knew nothing of it. But during the burning, the witch's daughter collected her soul in a box. If collected properly, every burnt witch's soul can be turned into a stone, and such stones can be very powerful instruments."

I look at the altar that has no stone with its depiction of the woman tending the sick man. A cautionary tale? "How do you collect a burning soul?" I ask.

"During the sacrifice, as the witch is burning and dying, a blood relative must open the box as close as possible to her and say a spell. As the soul leaves her body in pain, it goes into the box seeking refuge. Once it's there, the relative closes the box. After a few days of metamorphosis, the burned soul becomes a rock just as an oyster transforms its pain into a pearl."

A scene from my dream returns to my mind, and I see the girl stretch her arms as close as she can to the burning woman and mumble some words.

"Yes, that girl was your great-great-grandmother, Carmela, your namesake. She managed to collect your *nonna*'s soul. And what a powerful soul it was. Compassion is a very strong trait, especially when it's unconditional like hers was."

I looked at the bowl and the lock of curly golden hair with a purple satin ribbon tied around it, still beautiful despite being cut from a living head so long ago. So, where is my *nonna*'s stone? I ask myself.

"The rock for your great-great-great-grandmother's soul isn't here with us. It got lost when we fled to this place. It's still somewhere in the South of Italy. We just can't figure out where it is or how to retrieve it."

Andrea interrupts us.

"Caterina, I'm sorry, but she must leave now. She's been here for a couple of hours and she told me that her body already felt changed a while ago. It would be dangerous to stay any longer. We don't know what the consequences could be."

"I don't want to leave," I protest. "I want to stay. I want to know more."

"No, you must leave now, my child. Andrea is right. You already know enough. Please leave now." She pulls up her hood, and I can no longer see her eyes. As she turns to leave, Andrea holds my hand tightly and starts to pull me toward the spiral stairs.

"Wait."

Hearing Caterina's voice, we both stop and turn toward her.

She has stopped walking as she remembers something else, and she says without turning toward me, "One last, very important thing: That man, the one whose eyes change color, comes from a witch-killer lineage that dates back to Roman times. Be careful. He may not know or remember it, but his instinct does. And instinct guides action."

"What about my friend Rori? Do you have any idea what happened to her? She's gone now!"

Caterina has stopped in her tracks but still hasn't turned back. She has an old woman's cracked and failing voice now. "Oh, yes. The red-haired girl. Poor thing. Luckily for her, you're as compassionate as your *nonna* was." As she finishes speaking, she vanishes.

Andrea pulls me harder now, almost hurting my wrist. "We must go, Cami. Don't be stubborn, and don't overstay your welcome."

"Why?" I say, noticing that my usual obstinacy has gone up a notch.

"Just come already, now!" He's screaming at me, and I let him drag me up the stairs, across the hallway maze, and out into the woods through the oak roots.

As we ride back to the farm, Andrea seems irritated, almost upset. Even though I'm holding his waist tightly, I almost fall off the horse because he's going so fast.

Finally, he slows down enough to talk. "You shouldn't fight, Cami. If I say it's time to go, just come with me. It's very important that you follow my instructions when we're in Subterranean Heights. I'm the only one who can come and go, and stay in either world as long as I please without having anything happen to me."

"What could happen to me?"

"We don't know. You're the first upper-level, ordinary human to enter our world. But when I sense the energy levels in you change, I can tell that some transformation is starting. Maybe Caterina is right and you really do come from one of us."

"One of us? What are you, exactly? I thought that witches were just human beings who knew some magic tricks."

"Well, it's a bit more complicated than that," he says. "Have you heard of natural selection? We try to choose our consorts among people who have some kind of unusual power, skill, or knowledge. Every culture has shamans, enlightened ones, people who are connected to a spiritual, magical realm. This realm is everywhere, around everything, floating in tiny particles. For thousands of years, we concentrated our powers, and when they reached their height, the reactionary forces noticed and fought back."

"The persecutions."

"Yes. Through your *nonna*'s last sacrifice, and that of Paz—may the sun bless her, as she's now the Oak—somehow, in that last moment of distress, our people managed to create a vortex, which sucked a huge number of magic particles down into the underground. Paz had the box containing your *nonna*'s soul stone in her bag. After that moment, when she created Subterranean Heights, the box disappeared. Paz was inconsolable. She was the one who made your *nonna*'s altar in the temple, alongside the ones that remember the long gone hard years, and it's supposed to be the very last altar, because none of us was ever burned again. But it's also the only altar without a stone. Paz wept nonstop until she finished the memorial, and afterward, she fell terribly sick. She begged for sunshine, and, when the other witches brought her to the surface, she felt happy once again feeling the sun on her skin. She sang one last song, and at the end, she breathed her last sigh. Her limbs started finding their way into the soil, becoming roots, and slowly she turned into the Oak. The few brave witches who stayed watching over her noticed for the first time that while the sun on their skin felt good at first, after a while, it felt excruciating. As long as our kind remains on the surface, they feel constant, unbearable pain."

"What about you? Don't you suffer?"

"I'm half-human, half-witch. That's why I can come and go as I please."

"Oh wow. How did that happen?"

"We also can only reproduce under the sun; it's a rather barren place down below. My mother chose an ordinary man; she wanted to see what could happen. I happened!"

"Nice. Come to think of it, I didn't see many children down there."

"Yes, our population is dwindling. It's a very painful and demanding process for a witch to have a child. First, she has to enter this world and come up with an excuse for staying there. If she's still young—or young looking, since we can change our appearance as we please—she can go to an orphanage and say something like, "My parents died, and I'm hungry." Maybe they take her, maybe a family adopts her, or maybe she finds a job in the village until she spots a good husband, preferably someone connected to the magic realm. She can tell because those men—usually musicians, poets, dreamers—are more romantic than most. She tries to become engaged and then married. All the while, she's enduring tremendous pain. If she wanted to have children with someone from the Underground, they meet in secret, and the unsuspecting husband takes care of the trouble. The pain increases during pregnancy, when she gets very sick, pale, and emaciated. When the child is finally born, she nurses the baby for a few months, as long she can stand it, and then, one day, she dies—at least in your world. When the villagers bury her, she goes back home to Subterranean Heights. There, she needs several years to recover from the effort, and when she feels strong enough, she comes back one night and kidnaps her child, taking it back down with her. After a few years, the child starts to thrive in the lower realm, cultivating her powers and strengths by being there and by performing rituals in the temple."

"Wow. That's amazing. I wouldn't want to go through all that just to have a child. I wonder where my *nonna*'s soul stone is now."

"We know it's around here somewhere. Caterina can feel its presence; your *nonna* was her best friend growing up. And that's one of my tasks; I come up almost every day and try to find it. I'm training the snails to help me."

"Oh, I see. An investigative army of snails. That will take a while."

"Yes, they do things with the speed of glue, but their slowness means they do it very well. They're my only hope. Or they were until you showed up."

"Me?"

"Well, I guess I've said too much. We don't even know even if you're powerful enough. After all, coming from where you come from . . . ."

"What do you mean? Where do I come from?"

"Well, you're made of the same formula as I am: half witch, half ordinary human. At least that's what we think."

"You think? What makes you think that?"

"Well, as I just told you, witches can't have children without sunshine. That's why the first Carmela, the daughter of your *nonna*, had to leave and give up our traditions. She fell in love with an ordinary man from the village. Because she wanted him more than anything else, they turned her back into a child of twelve even though she was already fifteen and able to fall in love, so she could be accepted into Benevento as a lost orphan. Like a mermaid leaving the ocean, she had to give up her magic and her people to have a family. By giving up her power, she could escape the pain. All she could do to maintain her heritage was teach the ocarina to her first-born son. And, apparently, he taught it to his only son.

"My *nonno*."

"*Sí*."

"You're the first woman born from Carmela's blood. We don't know how much of her power she passed on to her children, and we don't know how much of it you may still carry. But the shift of energy is very noticeable whenever you're underground with us, and that's why we fear the consequences. Caterina guesses that the man your grandma fell in love with was no ordinary person after all—otherwise, how a witch could fall in love with him? It takes a lot to sweep people like us off our feet. She thinks your great-great-grandmother didn't want to give up her sons, so she tricked them into believing they were ordinary. If this hypothesis is true, you might as well be one hundred per cent witch stock! And your wine dealer friend probably senses it. Why do you think he's coming after you so hard?"

"My beautiful brown eyes?" I teased.

"More like your big, beautiful witch eyes. Caterina says you have the same eyes as your *nonna*."

"Oh, come on. Big eyes are almost the rule in this part of the country."

"And the rule for witches."

I think about my latest adventures and everything I went through to get to the South of Italy, and, despite its absurdity, Andrea's theory starts to ring true.

"Did Carmela visit Subterranean Heights after she left? How did she meet the man?"

"She already knew him before *Nonna* was burned. She kept coming back up, with the excuse of looking for the stone that carried her mother's soul. Well, she did look for it, but she was keeping an eye on other things as well, including a certain boy."

"I see."

"Actually, she never stopped searching for it until she lost her powers. Now, I'm the only one who can look. It would be very nice if we found it, since the older witches believe its presence nearby keeps things running smoothly in the underground realm. If the rock leaves this region, their world might crumble."

Speaking of rocks, we have almost reached the rock where I usually sit to wait for Andrea and where he drops me off.

"What about your father? How was he?", Andrea asks.

"He died when my mom was still pregnant. He was a musician, and partied a bit harder than he should… ." I lower my eyes as usually when this subject comes up.

"I'm sorry to hear."

"Would you like to come in for coffee or cake?" I ask him as he touches my arms warmly. "Let's continue this conversation."

"Why not?" He sounds uncharacteristically sarcastic. "Let's have the sheep come for supper in the wolf's cave."

"What do you mean?"

"Well, I don't dare come close to these *zingari*, the gypsies from Campania. They're the oldest enemies of my people around here."

"What do you mean?! They are a persecuted minority just as you are. How can they be your enemies?"

"It takes one to know one. When the Galician witches moved here, they gypsies soon sensed we were not just hungry immigrants. They used to spy on the young witches gathering herbs in the woods, kidnap them, and sell the virgins to places as far away as Arabia and China. Many a witch ended up in a harem and never saw her people again. These *zingari* have their ways of making the young girls forget who they are and embrace such a twisted destiny." He stops his horse abruptly. "That's why I leave you here."

I get off his horse. Again someone around here brings up discrimination against gypsies. Only this time is sweet Andrea. Instead of blushing now I feel angry and annoyed. You just need an other to blame, when we are all human beings? Andrea disappoints me, and I feel frustrated. Nobody is perfect, I guess, not even him.

"But this was a long time ago, and these people here have been long assimilated. They don't dress like typical gypsies, and they run their businesses in the circus and the hosting of people in the farm's guesthouse," I protest.

"Really? And how these businesses are going?" He arches one eye brown with a touch of cynicism, like he knew the answer before he asked the question. "Do you know the story of the farmer and the viper?"

"About the man who finds a frozen snake on his way home?"

"Yes. And he brings it by his fireplace, helps it warm up and when the viper is healthy again, it bites the very man who saved her life. That's why I don't trust them; they may seem adjusted and imbibed in this country's fabric, but once a snake, always a snake."

I look at him with clear disapproval in my eyes, but he holds his own. He seems so defiantly sure that I start to suspect that I might be the one wrong to see injustice in his prejudice.

He diverts his fierce, defiant eyes from confrontation with me, looks at a tree by his side, touches its bark caressing it, almost like someone asking for inspiration or advice, he sighs, a deep, giving-up-letting-go sigh. Then at first hesitating, he blurts out, "You know, they used to be particularly fond of red-haired girls."

My heart almost stops. "Do you think they . . . were the ones?"

"I'm just telling you what I know." He raises his eyebrows inquisitively.

I close my eyes for a split second, trying to recompose myself. That's his cue to vanish. I sigh—why does it always have to be like that?—and take a deep breath. I have a lot to process. Then, it dawns on me; he was so distressed when we left the underground realm that he forgot to blindfold me. And even I notice it only this very moment, after he's gone.

Now I know the way that leads to the Oak.

CHAPTER 14

Here Now

I come back and it's still early in the Sunday morning, just in time to help in the kitchen, even though I'm exhausted from my latest underground excursion. According to the kitchen clock, only seventeen minutes have passed since I've left to meet up with Andrea, but I know that I spent a couple of hours down there.

Rick's apron is inside out. Maybe he hasn't noticed because the inside looks just like the outside, and I can tell that he has already enjoyed one *café corretto* too many before midday. Now he has to prepare lunch, and the pressure is on. Twenty-seven guests arrived last night, in addition to the nine already here, and more will come just before midday, just in time for a big Sunday dinner. Ila is just back from cleaning up all the remaining guest cabins that were closed for so long, changing bedding and checking for spider webs and such.

Rick grabs his favorite wooden spoon, the one he uses indiscriminately to prepare every dish. It doesn't matter that he's making sweet cannoli cream filling on the front burner and Bolognese sauce is simmering on the back burner. Everything on the stove always ends up having a bit of everything else combined with it just like yin and yang with a dot of black in the white part and vice versa. I can see a squid tentacle floating atop the sweet *panna cotta* mix.

He chooses the biggest cast iron skillet, informing me that he's going to heat it up in order to braise some of the calamari that Francesco brought and add it to the *tagliatelle al frutti di mare* sauce for the egg pasta that he's been making from scratch all morning. Ila cuts thin strips out of the rolled dough while Rick boils some mussels in another tall pot, and in a little saucepan he prepares the white wine and herbs broth for the shellfish. I watch him cook and wonder when he's going to ask for my help. He likes to order people around, so I don't dare take any initiative when he's at the stove. He doesn't seem to need help today.

Everything is under control until he grabs the olive oil bottle and, as usual, sticks it in the front pocket of his apron—which isn't available. The bottle shatters and the oil spreads all over the floor. He swears and takes a false step, sliding in the oil, and, as he falls, he reaches for support from the now very hot skillet, which burns his hand and flies from the stove, hitting his knee.

At first, I stand paralyzed, not knowing how to help the screaming man. Then, using a potholder, I pick up the pan from the floor and put it back on the stove. Holding onto the counter to avoid sliding, I take his hand and help him up. Looking nervous, his pride obviously shattered along with the oil bottle, he leaves the kitchen and enters the adjacent yard to run cold water over his burned hand. I go along to pick up a broom and mop from the service room outside, trying to remain aloof. Through the corner of my eye, I watch him run his oily fingers through his hair, grabbing his skull and squeezing it as if trying to pull hard enough to peel his scalp off.

"Oh, *porca miseria*," moans Francesco, looking at the mess on the floor as I reenter the kitchen. He must have come in while I was looking for the cleaning supplies. "Here, Rick. I'll give you a hand!" he calls.

"At least the pasta didn't fall," adds Ila from the doorway. "That's what you get for breaking traditions! Who ever heard of *tagliatelle* with seafood?" She's clearly in war mode with her boyfriend, who is still outside, ignoring us all and talking on his cell phone. He seems to have recovered from his mishap, so I go out to enlist his help in cleaning up the mess he made, and I overhear him end the phone call: "Okay, I'll be there. Later." As he closes the phone and turns around, he looks surprised, almost as if I'd caught him doing something wrong.

"Hi! Were you here long?"

"No, I just arrived." It's a white lie, but it works. He seems relieved, and we go back inside.

But as soon as he enters the kitchen, he starts arguing with Ila. I tell them that too many people in the kitchen will be counterproductive. "I'll take care of the mess. You guys go find something else to do. In ten minutes, this place will be squeaky clean." Once I'm alone—Francesco has already joined the guests in the fancy dining room reserved for such occasions—I kneel on the greasy floor and manage to pick up all the broken glass down to the smallest shards and throw it away. Then I take a good look at all that precious, greenish-golden extra virgin olive oil. The smell inspires me, and, moved by something other than my own will, I take off all my clothes except my bra and panties, and rub my whole body on the floor, trying to soak up the last drop of that precious, viscous, moisturizing treasure. I massage my legs, chest, arms, hair . . .

"Carmela?"

Francesco, Ila, and three guests that have just arrived stand above me, jaws dropped. I blush, collect my clothes, and leave embarrassed, mumbling something like "I couldn't bear to see such a treasure go to waste . . . ."

As I leave the kitchen, I hear Francesco calling me "*la ragazza americana*," the American girl, trying to explain my apparent insanity through culture. I'm mortified, but deep down I feel justified: my skin was getting dry, and the oil felt wonderful. Taking off my clothes to bathe in it might have been out of place, but—I smell my arm and smile—totally worth it. I'm beginning to see method in my madness. Or maybe I'm just plain going crazy and reaching that phase in which lunatics no longer notice their own delusion. In the next stage, I'll probably be accusing everyone else but me of dementia.

The day goes on without any more incidents, despite my not being present in the moment. I manage to pretend well even though all I can think about is the siesta time when I plan to venture out again, now that I have a concrete sense of direction, and reach the cabin that I finally spotted in daytime. When I'm not thinking about the cabin, my mind is with Andrea and the weird places he takes me.

"Click!"

Some thick, hairy, tan fingers snap in front of my eyes. "Are you daydreaming, *bella* Cami?"

"Huh?" I wake from my trance and realize that I've been holding the empty fork for a while, letting my pasta get cold while all the others have almost finished their first course.

"Time to bring the mussels. Rick? Ila?" Francesco is directing the show this weekend. He's a lot more energetic but also more high-strung than the gypsies, who don't seem cut out for the hospitality business, anyway. He makes everyone swirl around his orders, but in a less irritating, more fatherly way than Rick does, sweet, yet firm That's probably why everyone around town calls him Don Francesco.

Rick's marinara mussels mesmerize the guests; the bread goes fast, absorbing every last bit of sauce. "Can you take care of the dessert, my sweet Carmela?" asks Francesco, charming as usual. "Please brew some fresh coffee and bring in also the limoncello and the tall aperitif glasses to serve it." He really knows how to handle being a host. It's a shame he wants to sell the property.

But as I serve the *culurgiones de mendula*—a smallish almond ravioli covered with a shiny, sticky honey glaze that some friend of his brought from Sardegna—I take a good look at him. He is happily sipping his limoncello, but I can't help but notice the slight hunch in his neck. The tiredness from being on top of things the whole weekend is starting to wear him out, and a passing shadow makes his face go dark for a moment, a cloud passing over the sun. This man is clearly ready to retire; I can't blame him for trying to sell his business. Too bad the only interested people are those circus gypsies, who couldn't care less about the land. Gypsies are by definition nomads who don't lay down roots, at least not for long.

As soon as everyone has finished eating, I announce that I'm going to my bungalow to take a nap. I remember Marco's advice against roaming the woods. This time, the dogs don't follow me because the kids of the guests staying over the weekend are playing with them and giving them treats. Maybe it's for the best; this way, I can be more discreet in my explorations.

Despite my perfect plan, it takes me a while to find the cabin. As usual, it gets dark faster from within the thick woods, but this time, I'm prepared: I have a flashlight and a much better sense of direction.

When I finally see the cabin, I understand why it took so long to find it again. The usually candlelit bedroom is in darkness. The only light I can see is a very fickle one coming out of the front door, which is ajar. I freeze for a second, not liking this unexpected change. I've never seen it open before.

I come as close as I dare, hiding behind trees and rocks all the way. If I'm really a somnambulist, as I've come to suspect, someone chased me away the last time I was here. But now, aware and awake, I can be more careful. Gluing my body to the wooden wall, I manage to peek inside. I can see only an empty room with no furniture, but the weak kerosene lamp is lit.

Crouching like a ninja, I circle the house until I reach the window through which I usually see Rori and her tormentor. Pressing my face very close to the glass, I blink as my eyes adjust to the darkness. The bedsheets are gone, and the room is empty except for a worn-out pink-and-blue striped mattress on top of the metal bed frame. A pair of handcuffs still hangs from one of the bars. I shiver. From the size of the small front room, I can tell that it and this small bedroom are all there is to this cabin. Taking a deep breath I summon up the courage to return to the door and slip inside. It smells like sweat and mold. The windows haven't been opened for a while. All the previous furnishings—the pillows, feathers, whip, and chains that used to hang from the walls—are all gone. So is Rori.

A chill runs up my spine and I hold a tear. Where can they have taken her? I feel that my time here is up, and I leave as soon as possible.

Halfway home, the failing battery of my small flashlight dies, leaving me with no light except the stars. Remembering Marco's advice—don't roam the woods—I feel a need to make myself invisible and realize that the loss of light may actually be an advantage. True, I can't hide myself completely, but I can at least try to hide my fear. I read somewhere that fear generates a rush of adrenaline in your blood, and beasts can smell adrenaline like a kid can smell fresh-baked cookies. Let that feeling stay in a place so deep that not even you can access. *Don't allow predators to perceive you as prey,* I remind myself. *Once they do, they'll follow you around until they can attack you.*

I see a movement in the bushes, followed by the shadow of someone walking quickly and a glint of shiny metal. A pistol?

I crouch close to the ground, trying to hide, but ready to sprint away. Slowly getting away from here. This way, whoever is here with me may mistake me for a wildcat or a baby deer. Wait! What if it's hunting season? I don't know how long I can keep moving crouching like this. My legs are getting sore and my heartbeat fast. I guess I have more adrenaline running in my blood than a—

Whoosh!

Suddenly, I'm up in the air, caught in a net and hanging from a tree like ripe fruit. Damn! Before I can rip a hole in the net to escape, I feel cold steel touching the back of my neck. I freeze.

"Don't worry; I'm not going to hurt you." A man is speaking in a falsetto voice, with a slight accent. He uses the barrel of his pistol to turn the net around and when I face him he then places the tip of the barrel in the middle of my forehead. If I really had a third eye like my yoga teacher aunt claims I do, right now it could only see darkness. He's wearing a mask improvised from several pairs of women's stockings squeezing his face and features, so all I can see is generic eyes, nose, and mouth. I'm sweating cold; he's holding the net and sizing me up as a hunter would his latest catch.

"You never know what you're going to find in these woods, that's why I carry a gun. I wouldn't use it on you, Carmela."

Whoever he is, he knows my name.

"But I must warn you: if you continue this nasty habit of minding other people's business, I might have to break some of my gentlemanly rules. You like to take too many risks for a woman. Not good for your own safety or the safety of others, you know." I listen paralyzed, and wonder who the others are. Rori, who might be anywhere now? Kulveer, who's still in jail? My eyes scan him rapidly, trying to make sense of his silhouette, the minimalist, blurred features under the pantyhose squeezing his nose down. He's wearing leather gloves and a turtleneck, despite the heat.

"So, what do you say? Maybe it's time to go enjoy another part of the country, or perhaps go back home. You've already had your taste of farming in the South of Italy. Maybe you're staying for a little bit too long around here."

Should I answer him? Words fail me. I can only keep looking at him, and I decide to pray. I remember Marco telling me that the witches used to worship a goddess around here, and I remember Caterina saying, "Your blood knows." I breathe fast and deep; I feel a stream of energy shoot from my intestines straight into the ground like a jet of warm piss; I connect with the woods around me and ask for help.

"So, what do you say? Do we have a deal? Are you going to leave me alone so I don't need to use this baby on you?" He shakes his gun, and it seems light; I have a feeling it's not loaded.

I breathe deeply, thinking, *This guy's not a professional; he's scary, but he's an amateur*. Dogs bark from a short distance away, and he turns around. I wonder if I should try to kick him in some vital part, but before I can decide, the three dogs jump on him, biting and growling, sending his gun flying into some bushes. The dogs are furious, ignoring his attempts to calm them down: "Allegra, Fido, Pepe, *che stai a fa*? Stop, now!" They keep attacking him until he runs away. I stretch up inside the net and try to untie something, anything that can make me free. I'm so focused on the ropes that I almost don't notice the knife and the hand. As fast as a movie director can say, "Cut!" I'm free.

Andrea is here.

"Oh my, I'm so glad to see you!"

"You're getting into trouble, huh?"

"Yes. Do you know who that was?"

"Who? I didn't see anyone."

"The man with the gun. The dogs chased him away."

"Oh yes, I heard the barking. So that was it. Someone's after you?"

"You didn't bring the dogs?"

"No, they must have heard you scream like I did."

"But I never screamed."

"Yes, you did. It was a gut scream. Clear as crystal, and loud as thunder."

"A gut scream?"

"*Sí*. One day you'll understand. It's the kind of thing that you can feel but not put into words. But you're starting to get it. *Brava!*"

"What do you mean? I don't really understand."

"Listen, I don't have much time now. I'll escort you just to the edge of the woods, and you can find your way from there, okay?" His horse shows up, we mount it, and before I can even say thank you, I catch a glimpse of the main guesthouse.

"I'll leave you here."

"Wow, that was fast. I didn't even feel us move."

He patted his horse's side. "It's magic. I don't use it much with him because it makes him extra tired—and grumpy. Horses like to roam around, and he gets dizzy and confused when I use magic. I have to run now. Be careful, okay? Please stay out of trouble."

As I walk to my cabin, I pass Rick, who is leaving in the ATV; I wave, but he's so focused on his own thoughts that he doesn't seem to see me. I notice his bloodshot eyes, and I wonder if he's been crying. I've never seen him cry, only get angry, but today he was weird all day.

Whatever, I think, echoing Ila's words whenever her boyfriend is having a fit. *Just ignore him. He'll work through it and come back sweet as a lamb.* She's a very grounded, present-in-her-body person. It must be the Cherokee blood. I'm learning how to be more in my body as the years go by. Developing my gut wisdom, as Andrea would put it. Right now, my mind is racing, but at least my body is sending clear messages that it needs to rest.

When I finally arrive at my cabin, I notice that the dogs aren't there as usual. And then I remember: the masked man. Whoever he was, he knew each dog's name! I didn't even know that they had names; they don't even wear collars. Rori's kidnapping is definitely an inside job.

After my shower, I put on a fresh set of cotton pajamas—after drying under the strong sun, they now have a different energy. I lie in bed thinking about the usual suspects, recalling every reverie. I realize that I've only seen Rori in the cabin when I was dreaming. I've never seen any solid evidence in that cabin except the handcuffs. All that I have is one hair, saved in my cigar box-treasure chest. I did see more evidence the same day I found the hair, but the broken shoe and the scrap of silk vanished quickly. Was I delirious when I saw them? And what about the handcuffs in the cabin? Did I imagine them, too? Have I been away from my routine, my city, my aunt's house, so long that I'm losing my grip on reality?

I recall the story of my father's crazy aunt, his father's sister, who never left her bedroom after she decided to walk naked around the neighborhood on her nineteenth birthday—she lived her subsequent thirty-one years as a recluse. A chill goes up my spine. They say that every family has a crazy person; some talk about it, some don't. Those subterranean people are telling me I have witch blood. What if that's also just the product of my dementia-infused imagination?

After tossing and turning for an hour or so, I try a trick my aunt once taught me: find a spot on the ceiling and fix your eyes on it. Look at the spot intensely and intentionally. It starts working fast. When I'm almost asleep, the noise of an engine struggling to go up a hill wakes me up. I look the time: it's almost midnight, and someone is trying to leave in the ATV. Nobody used it after I crashed; it hasn't worked well since then. I hear a voice cursing in a language I don't understand. I peek through my window and see someone kneeling, trying to fix the broken engine. Kulveer!

I run out the door wearing just my pajamas, barefoot. What if he manages to fix it before I can reach him? I climb the hill wanting to scream his name but, obviously, that isn't a good idea since he seems to be on the run. When I come closer, panting, he's cleaning his greasy hands and jumping back onto the ATV. He smiles at the sight of me and then looks immediately concerned.

"Kulveer, what are you doing here? Did they finally set you free?"

"No. I set myself free, with the help of a friend."

He doesn't need to tell me names. Now I understand Rick's odd behavior the previous day.

"What are you going to do, become a fugitive?"

"I'm already an illegal immigrant, and one of the officer's in the jailhouse told me they were about to deport me back to India. I can't afford to be deported. That way my sister will never marry."

"What does your sister have to do with it?"

"I was the only one in my family who made it out of India. The day I left, my younger sister told me that she was in love with my best friend. They want to marry, but she needs a dowry. I promised her I would help them."

"But if you escape like that, you'll become an outlaw."

"I have nothing to lose. It was so complicated to leave India that I prefer to stay in Italy, no matter what the cost. I'm going to the North. They have factories there that need workers; they pay cash and don't ask questions. I've never managed to save a cent here in the South, anyway. All I got was an accusation of a crime that I would never think of committing . . . ." For the first time I see the sweet, light-spirited Kulveer with a spark of anger in his eyes.

"I have to go now, sweet Cami. Stay well and be careful, okay?" He frowns.

"Be careful of what, Veer? Do you know anything that I don't?

"He did it, Cami."

"Who did what?"

"The gypsy. He took Rori. I saw them taking her. It was Luludja's cousin, the gypsy. He brought another man to help him." Tears run down his dark, oily, sunken cheeks—he has lost weight in jail.

"Are you sure?"

"Yes, I saw everything, and I wanted to help her, to save her, but I didn't think I could fight them. I was afraid. There were two of them and they were much bigger than me. He's the cousin of the new boss. I wish Francesco had never rented the farm to those people."

The words burst out of him, and he's getting a bit too loud.

"Shhh," I warn, trying to calm him down.

"It's the first time I've said this to anyone. I couldn't admit it. I'm so ashamed that I did nothing to help her. She was fighting hard when they were taking her away until the other man whose face I couldn't see took a syringe and injected her with something that knocked her out right away."

"Does Ken know it? Or Rick?"

"No, Ken thinks she just left. I couldn't bring myself to tell him, or anyone else. Please don't tell anyone I told you this."

"Why not?"

"I'm afraid the gypsies will come after me."

"Okay, Veer."

"I'm so sorry, Cami, to leave you like this. But something tells me you'll be just fine."

He's so scared that I take off the jade necklace that Josh made for me and give it to him. He holds it, wipes his wet face with it, kisses the tear-shaped stones, and hands it back to me. "You'll be okay; but you still need this more than I do."

He turns on the ATV and rides off without looking back.

The dogs show up, running after him, barking loudly.

"Shush!" I run after them and touch each one lightly, and they quiet down. They follow me back to the cabin.

Now, I'm happier than ever to have their company.

CHAPTER 15

Still in the Amazon Jungle

Josh kept braving the leaves and branches, slashing the vines that grabbed his limbs. For the first time in his life, he felt like he had something to lose, not his life—he knew he would die old after telling all his stories—but Cami. Carmela, his caramel, was lost, and he desperately needed to get out of the jungle and help her. So he kept walking even though his GPS battery was dead and the compass didn't work anymore after falling into a river. But then he saw a hummingbird the size of a beetle, and thought, *I wish I could take a picture of this amazing creature*. He recalled shopping for cameras and Cami's teasing him for deciding on the most expensive one even though he was broke. She had laughed and pinched him, and said, "What in the world is the use of a camera with a built-in GPS?"

Aha! He turned on his camera, its battery full of life, and started taking pictures, checking his position, and then looking at the maps and guides in his backpack. There was light at the end of that green, humid, tree-and-animal-filled tunnel. He was going to escape and rescue her from whatever she had gotten into. And he had pictures to tell the story!

CHAPTER 16

The Oak

I wake up with a stiff neck, my body screaming in pain from the stress of getting caught and lifted up in a net. Some kind of muscle memory, some kind of body chemistry makes my bones burn and my tissues tight. I try to do some stretching and yoga poses, but I can't stop thinking that what I really need is for Josh to show up right now and give me a massage. Maybe that could take me back in time, before this all started, and I could change my plans. Paris, anyone? Because a massage from Josh led me to a relationship with someone that convinced me I could go anywhere, which led to my hanging above the ground in a net trap with a man wearing a woman's nylon stocking over his face holding his gun barrel against my forehead.

I remember telling Josh about my chronic neck pain. We were still getting to know each other, working a late afternoon shift at the urban farm. It was shortly after he asked for my number. He laughed at the idea that someone in her twenties could have chronic neck pain. I told him I had hunched over laptops for the past ten years, so there you go.

He replied by telling me that, besides a wanderer-farmer-surfer-cook, he was a licensed masseur. I wondered, *What doesn't this kid know how to do?* While he rubbed my back and worked through the knots in my neck like he was kneading bread, I could smell a mixture of underarm funk and Dr. Bronner's hemp peppermint soap. Then I heard his hoarse, soft, laid-back voice close to my ear lobe. I could feel the warmth of his breath: "I'm a Sagittarius. I never stop moving. I don't have my own space, but I make house calls, and I bring my massage table to people's home." Yes, a sag, indeed, he had this fiery power. As this thought went through my mind, he said, "I've got a lot of *chi*; that's why I'm good at manipulating the body." Chi, the Chinese concept of vital energy, life force. An old friend who was studying acupuncture once told me the Chinese believe that a child conceived in an act of love full of desire and passion is likely to be born with a lot of chi. I imagined Josh's parents making love in the mid-eighties and made a note to self to fact-check that concept. But how do you check the validity of Chinese medicine, a practice that's almost like a concrete, bodily woven poem?

His massage made me feel very relaxed; I turned around to say thanks, and my lips accidentally brushed his chin.

He grinned and showed his large, white, horselike teeth. So close I could see in detail the freckles on his nose, and his surfer-blond sun-bleached hair growing in curls that he tucked behind his ears. We were too close. Feeling awkward and needing some space, I took a couple of steps backward and tripped over a stump I hadn't noticed. He caught me to prevent a fall. With my eyes at the level of his chest, I noticed his T-shirt. Its white fabric was thinning and it had tiny holes; it featured a stooping Charlie Brown sitting on a rock by Lucy at her stand with signs that announced "Psychiatric help 5 cents" and "The doctor is IN." He noticed me noticing the shirt, and said, "Do you like it? I found at the Salvation Army for ninety-nine cents!" He grinned even wider, and we both laughed. I let him kiss me, and he gave me a hug, lifting me from the ground and planting me on the top of the stump.

"Your highness, what else can I do for you today? Will you allow me to cook you supper tonight?"

I smiled and said yes. That was probably when my life started changing at unbearable speed.

Now I'm here, in the freaking South of Italy. Whoever my ancestors were, whether they were witches or farmers, they had good reason to leave this harsh, hot, dry place. It's also a beautiful place full of grapes, lemon groves, and mozzarella, but now, it feels rather dangerous. Looking back at the last two weeks, I I pick up pen and paper make a list of the odd happenings:

1. Rori disappears, kidnapped by gypsy cousin of current farm manager who wants to destroy farm and establish a circus in this hilly place

2. Actual farm owner and other volunteers are oblivious to her disappearance

3. Her boyfriend thinks she just took off and will show up when college starts

4. Witches live underground in the area and claim I'm one of them

5. Elflike boy Andrea shows up and takes me down to visit witch land—a place he calls Subterranean Heights

6. Josh is nowhere to be found

7. Angry, armed masked man catches me in a trap and tells me to take off

8. Kulveer is threatened with deportation and runs away from jail

9. I'm getting fatter by the minute on this dairy-pasta-coffee diet

That's it. I sigh, feeling that something is missing. What's the tenth item? But before I can answer my own question, my phone buzzes, indicating a text message.

"*Ciao, bella, come stai?*" And a little yellow emoticon keeps winking and sending kisses. Marco is asking how I'm doing. I get back to the list and add the tenth item:

10. Weirdo Italian witch-hater dude stalking me

Okay, I'm getting the hell out of here. I gather my toiletries and stuff them in my backpack, along with the remaining tuna cans, salami, and nuts. Then I add all the clothes that will fit.

I dress quickly and go outside to see if anyone can give me a ride into town. It's Monday morning, but the farm is empty. The guests have gone, Francesco's car isn't here, and both the truck and the ATV that Kulveer took are missing. Maybe Rick and Ila took the truck to go to their apprenticeship at the cheese factory?

I feel trapped and alone. It's getting close to midday, and soon it will be unbearably hot. At least the three dogs are still here. My chest full of angst, I have only one goal in mind. If I start walking the five miles into town now, maybe I'll get lucky and catch a ride. Ken and Rori often hitchhiked; they visited a bunch of places on their farm holiday with the power of their thumbs.

I prop my huge backpack against my spine and leave. The dogs come after me. I beg them to go back and even resort to throwing rocks, but they ignore my pleas and surround me every step of the way. Not many cars show up, and whenever someone does slow down and look at me walking with those dogs, they step on the gas and leave me standing by the side of the road. My backpack is heavy and I've forgotten to bring some water.

By 10:30, I've managed to walk just about a mile and a half on a dirt road that has just farms, vineyards, and walls on each side. Soon, I'm glad that the dogs came with me: six or seven Dobermans jump a fence and come after us. I run as fast as I can, and the barking dogs somehow fend off the ferocious Dobermans.

The running has made me even thirstier, but I'm close to the Fontana de la Madonna, and I walk a little faster until I get there. Making a cup with my hands, I drink the fresh spring water, which the locals believe will miraculously heal any ailment. I sit by the fountain and look at the beautiful mosaic above the running water. The Madonna seems to be looking at me no matter where I am. I stand up and she's still looking at me. I lie down, using my backpack as a pillow, and there she is, with her eyes on me. God's mother? I don't know what to believe anymore. I'm just happy that I got a drink of water.

A car shows up and stops. "Where do you want to go?" an old, balding Italian man asks me.

"Benevento, to catch the bus to Naples."

"What about the dogs?"

"They belong to the farm where I'm staying. I'll leave them here, and, hopefully, they'll go back home."

"Okay. I can take you just a mile. Then you get out and continue on foot, or find someone else?"

"Deal."

As I start to get into the car, a rusty white Fiat with no backseat and boxes of vegetables and a couple of chickens in the amplified trunk, the dogs protest and try to follow me into the car. Leaving my backpack in the trunk, I kiss each of them and push them away. As I climb into the front seat and close the door, they jump, scratching the doors and trying to climb through the open window. As the old man turns the ignition with a knife instead of a key, we take off. They bark and run after us until they give up, howling in protest and lying down in shady spot beside the road. We turn a corner and I can't see them anymore. I feel guilty about leaving the dogs behind like that, but I'm in survival mode.

The driver stops at an intersection to let me out. "Okay, I have to make some deliveries here, but in an hour or so, I'll go to Benevento. If you're still on the road, I can take you there."

"*Grazie mille!*" I leave the old car and sit by the road watching him take a left turn and disappear. I wait for about ten minutes but no car shows up, so despite the blistering heat, I decide to keep walking; I just want to be as far away as possible from that crazy farm. I walk a bit, regretting not having a bottle of water. I'm getting hungry, as well. I stop and take off my heavy backpack. Sighing, I decide that it's better to lie down here and wait until the old Fiat shows up again.

At a point when I'm not sure whether I'm resting or I've fainted, a red car shows up. The Maserati. He has his top up. Marco rolls down his window, looks down at me through his Ray-Bans and I can hear the dogs barking from inside the car. Paws, noses, and tongues show up in the rear window, fogging the glass.

"Are you crazy? What the hell are you doing here? Get in the car, right now!"

126

Out of better options and afraid to upset him any further since I can't see under his shades to tell whether his eyes are blue or green, I say, "Oh, no worries. I've got a ride. I'm just waiting for a nice old man who'll come back to pick me up and take me to Benevento so I can take the bus to Naples."

"Giuseppe? The chicken guy? Don't count on him. I already told him I'd be taking care of you."

"What?"

"Well, once I got a couple of phone calls from the neighbors telling me that *la ragazza Americana* from Francesco's farm was trying to hitchhike around followed by three dogs and carrying a huge backpack, I quickly learned that Giuseppe had not taken you far. That's why I'm here. Why such a hurry?"

"Lots of things have been happening lately, and I just don't feel comfortable anymore. I want to go somewhere else. I want to see the Mediterranean."

"Oh yes, you've been talking about that for a while." He takes off his Ray-Bans, and his eyes are a hopeless green. In my thirst for the ocean, I imagine jumping into one of those pools of sorrow and desire. I snap myself out of it when I notice his snarky grin.

"Look, why don't you get in? It's almost lunchtime. I can take you somewhere, and then we think about where to go next, okay?"

"Listen, it's all right, really. I'll find a lift and eat something in town. I just have this feeling; I need to go to the ocean."

"Not yet, Cami. Wait a bit more. My little cabin in Positano will be vacant soon, and you can go there."

"I don't want to go to Positano! What am I going to do there, rub elbows with New York honeymooners? No thanks! I want to jump into the sea, not into a hillside Manhattan."

"Geez, be polite, *signorina*. Someone offers you a treat and you spit on the plate like that?"

"Okay, I'm sorry. I'm just hungry. That's why I'm grumpy."

"Oh, now we're talking. Let me take you home and get something in your stomach before you die. *D'accordo?*" He opens the door and the dogs jump and celebrate. I throw my backpack inside and sit in the passenger's seat, cross my arms over my chest, and sigh.

He drives away in the opposite direction from the farm.

"Wait, where are you going? I thought you said you were taking me home."

"Yes, to my house. It's my turn to cook for you."

I hold my breath for a long while and think about it. Seems tempting, but no.

"Uh-uh, I don't think that's a good idea."

"Too late, we're already here."

He stops in front of a large red-painted wrought-iron gate, lowers the car top and jumps out of it without opening the door. Unlocking the gate, he pushes it open to reveal a long, winding dirt road lined on both sides by lemon trees bursting with fruit.

Great. I'm running from one trap just to fall into another one. My good-girl sense of danger is blinking red alert, and I remember the park's mountain lion brochure warning: predators can smell adrenaline. So I swallow my fear, put on a huge smile as he jumps back into the car, and pretend that everything is fine while he drives me slowly into his huge estate. A golden retriever comes running and barking, its shiny, healthy fur gleaming in the sun. The dogs in the car bark back and jump out to greet the retriever. The usual butt-smelling and nipping ensues.

Marco parks the car in the driveway near a surprisingly quaint yellow house. On that large piece of land, it looks almost small, but if you placed the same house on a San Francisco street, you'd have a mansion—size is so relative. He runs into the house leaving the door open for me. Surprised by his lack of formality, I enter his territory slowly, lingering by the door.

He shouts from what I guess is the kitchen, "Come on in, I don't bite!"

As I come close to the kitchen entrance, I can tell that he, too, enjoys cooking. Beautiful iron skillets hang above the central gas stove; a second wood-burning stove sits inside a huge and ancient fireplace in a corner; lots of spices are tied upside-down on a line to dry: I recognize rosemary, bay leaves, and oregano.

"This used to be a sharecropper's house inside a bigger property, I restored the fireplace but don't use it much except sometimes in the winter just for fun. It's nice to have a fire burning inside the house."

I smile and nod.

"What would you like to eat?"

"Anything but pasta," I blurt, thinking about my emergency tuna cans in my backpack.

128

"Just name it."

"Um, steak?"

"How would you like it cooked?"

"Rare?"

"You've got it!"

He opens his fridge to produce a huge *bistecca*, making me wonder if he isn't as capable of magic as Andrea.

Almost as if he read my mind, he says, "You're lucky. My friend who has a cattle farm just delivered this steak not long ago. It's the freshest steak you'll ever find in all Campania. Do you mind making some salad? Just go out in the garden and pick anything you want."

I pass through a red iron door into a small but flourishing vegetable garden. He has beautiful endives, arugulas, and radicchios. I pick up a small, purple head of radicchio, which reminds me of a cashier at Whole Foods, who remarked with surprise, "Oh my! You managed to get the smallest vegetables. Look at this tiny cabbage!" "Oh no," I responded. "This is radicchio." And then I got the receipt, looked through it and added, "And this isn't a tiny ginger; it's a sunchoke." It was her first day on the job. I miss San Francisco and its newcomers learning the lay of the land.

I also gather some red-leafed lettuce and cherry tomatoes. It's going to be a rather red plate.

A few minutes later, Marco serves my lunch, complete with a white linen napkin. As I cut the steak, which is cooked to perfection (at least to my kind of perfection, with blood running all over the white china), Marco sits across from me, wide eyed, watching me eat voraciously and barely touching his own food.

"Boy, you like meat, huh?"

"Well, I haven't had anything like this since Florence. I eat at least three steaks a week back home."

"I like to watch a woman who enjoys her food. That tells me a lot about her personality."

"I see," I answer, not thinking much, just washing down the beef with some Chianti. When I'm done, I wipe my mouth with the napkin, which now has red stains all over it, and close my eyes in the familiar ecstasy of a full belly. When I open them, I see a pair of eyes, the right one blue, the left one green, too close to my face. I try to back up, but I'm stuck between the chair back and the tall bar table where my empty plate lies. Cornered, I can smell his skin. Finally, he forgot to wear cologne. There's nothing like the scent of a real man. His lips are full, and his skin is tan. Now both eyes are green, I relax a bit. I let him kiss me lightly, with a soft finish that makes me shiver with fun and guilt at the same time.

"Would you like some dessert?"

The red light of danger is blinking wildly in my brain, and I feel a pain in the small of my back.

"No, thanks." I get up and ask where the *gabinetto* is.

"You have to go into my room. It will be one of the closet doors." He starts cleaning up, clearly upset but keeping a poker face.

The rooms are all so tiny that the house seems bigger on the outside than the inside, but I finally find the bedroom with an attached bathroom. I wash my hands and face with cool water, dismissing the temptation that is standing in the kitchen washing dishes. Looking at my reflection, I can't resist opening his mirror cabinet atop the sink. Nothing very revealing: aspirin, Q-tips, shaving cream, shaving brush, razor, and blades. He doesn't use anything automatic or disposable. But on the uppermost glass shelf, sticking out of the wall, I see a brass doorknob. A doorknob inside a medicine cabinet?

Once more unable to resist my curiosity, I turn the doorknob, and the whole wall, sink and all, opens wide, leading me into a dark room, every wall covered with books. When my eyes get used to the darkness, I look into the books, one of them very familiar: The *Malleus Maleficarum*. Most of the books are about witchery, wizardry, magic, and other esoteric subjects. On top of a desk, I see a laptop. Hanging on the wall, a couple of ancient-looking pistols and rifles, some darts, a bow, and some arrows. Colorful ropes made out of sometimes smooth other times rough fibers and a dream catcher hang from the ceiling above the headrest of a couch like the chaise longue I imagine Freud might have had in his first office. A maze of papers clutters the floor in front of the couch. I kneel to look at them and see lots of handwriting in a language that seems to be Celtic, and a small, thin photo album. Curious, I open the photo album. A red-haired baby talks on a phone in the first photo. I chuckle at the classic image and silently bet all my money that the next one will be the same baby smiling and sitting on the potty. But the pages are stuck together, the photos possibly melted, and I can open only the last page. It's Rori, in all the glory of her red mane, her full pink lips smiling. I recognize he cute freckles and the dimple in her left cheek.

Now what? Who is this man? Maybe he's the other one who kidnapped Rori!

I leave the room in a rush, forgetting the first rule of spying: leave everything as you found it. As I run away, I realize that I left the photo album open to that last, revealing image. But I'm already beside his Maserati, picking up my backpack. As I run along the seemingly endless lemon-tree-lined road, slowed by a stomach full of steak, I pray that the gate will be open. The dogs bark and come running to me: my three and his golden retriever. I hear the car starting. Luckily, the gate is closed but not locked. Looking over my shoulder as I open it, I see the red convertible at a distance, coming toward me. After closing it again, hoping to slow him down a little, I run along the main road. The three dogs from the farm catch up to me as I reach the Fontana de la Madonna where a short white haired older man wearing a pink polo shirt is filling bottles of water. He has a little red rusty Vespa scooter. I ask him for a ride to Benevento, and he agrees, as long as I wait for him to finish.

Marco arrives, but with another man around, he doesn't dare get out of it. "What are you doing here?" he demands. "Why did you leave so soon?" I can see streaks of blue in the green ocean of his gaze. He's angry—surprise, surprise.

"I'm sorry, but I have to go to Benevento."

"Oh, but it's not polite to eat and run away."

"Ah, yes, thanks for lunch. Thanks for everything, but I've got to go."

He leaves the car and grasps my hand, firmly but gently. "What are you doing? You say you want to see water. Why don't you wait? In two days, I'm going to go clean up my cabin in Positano. My guests will have left, and you can stay there free. I won't stay there with you if you're afraid of me."

"Wow. Wine dealing must be a very lucrative business for you to have all these assets. What else do you sell, my friend?" I tried to hold in my anger, but he can clearly feel it.

"I have no idea what you're talking about. I just know how to manage my money well, that's all." He's lying, I can tell. But deep inside, I can't believe that such a good kisser could be also a kidnapper. I just hope that the kiss wasn't part of his tricks, making me fall for him and lose all my discernment.

He says something in Italian to the man at the spring, who looks at me apprehensively. "Now what?" I ask in a low but concerned voice. "You're ruining my ride! Can you get out of my way, please?" Even though the other man doesn't seem to speak much English, I don't want him to see how angry I am.

"Listen, I'll take you back home, and you can stay a little longer at the farm. Soon, you can go with me to Positano. I don't want you to go to Naples all by yourself. Do you even have a hotel?"

"I was going to find one when I got there."

"Ha! Don't you know Naples's reputation?"

"Well, I was born and raised in New York, so I think I can handle Naples."

"Well, if someone told you they were going to New York and they were just going to figure out where to sleep after they arrived there in the middle of the night, what would you think?"

I say nothing, imagining myself in that predicament.

"Yes, that's exactly what I mean. *Andiamo*, Let me take you back home. In two days, you'll see the Mediterranean."

As if I'm under a spell, I agree to get back in his car, and the dogs follow me inside. Admittedly, the South of Italy is not a place where women can come and go as they please. I go along in a trance, biting my nails, an old bad habit that my mom cured before I became a teenager by applying hot pepper oil to my fingertips day and night until I stopped. With no pepper to stop me this time, I nibble my nails until my fingers hurt. Along the way, I wonder why he has a photo album of Rori. How did he get hold of it? Is he a stalker? And why does my mind react to him suspiciously when my body and soul trust him enough to enter his car? My brain is on maximum speed now, but, apart from my nails and teeth, I feel ultra relaxed. Even my neck pain is gone.

We arrive at the farm, and he says, "*Ciao, bella.* I'll see you in two days, okay? I'll take you to my cabin. *Mi casa es su casa!*"

I say good-bye and walk back to my cabin like a zombie.

"Why the backpack, Bel?" Rick asks. He and Ila are making out under the dark shadow of the big fig tree by the entrance.

I barely notice them. "Long story."

Inside my cabin, I fall like a log onto my bed, forgetting to brush my teeth or take off my jeans—no time for bedtime rituals. I doze off until someone bangs on my door. I wake up sweating and panicking, wondering who it is. I see through the tiny window that the sun is starting to set. Deciding not to open the door just yet, I look through the large keyhole and see a hairy, tan male arm. There is a smell of pipe tobacco in the air. I shiver. He knocks again, louder this time. I climb onto the toilet to escape through the tiny side window and peek around the corner of the building: it's exactly who I thought it was, the gypsy pipe smoker, Luludja's cousin. He's after me. It was probably him back in the woods with the gun and the stocking on his face, and yet, he seems taller than the man with the trap was. But I'm not coming closer to measure. I sneak out through the back side of the cabin, stepping in some horse poop.

Once I read somewhere that in Brazil, stepping in cow's poop means good luck. What about starving horse's poop? Hopefully, double good luck. I run up the hill until I reach the rock where I usually meet Andrea. The sky is deep red. Panting and breathless, I try to evoke the same energy I sent out when he last showed up. I close my eyes, breathe deeply, and scream inside my head, "Please come help me; I need you here more than ever." I squeeze my eyes shut as if doing that will dissolve the material world around me into pure energy that I can swim across until I'm in a safer place. *Okay, if I open my eyes now, will you be there for me?*

Nope. Nobody. Sitting on this rock, I've never felt so alone. I can't trust anyone around me, and maybe this elf boy, Andrea, is just some byproduct of my craziness, a hallucination of some sort.

"No."

Someone is talking, but nobody is even close to me.

"You know it's real."

Oh, it's just the soft voice in the small of my back. I don't even know if I can trust that anymore. If I'm going crazy, that voice must also be the invention of my malfunctioning synapses.

"You know you can trust me." Josh used to say that to me a lot. Funny, somehow I feel like he's right here with me. Wait, I know the way to the Oak. The last time we went there, I learned it on the way back. If the mountain won't come to Mohammed, I'll go to it.

Even though the sun has set, the rising almost full moon lights the horse trail that leads to the Oak. I recognize the ancient tree easily and pull its roots, but they're as stiff as any ordinary oak root would be. The soil under them is dense and packed—nothing like the first time I came here. But now I'm alone.

I talk to the tree. "Please let me in. I really need help. I must find Caterina."

It doesn't budge.

I stroke it lightly and pour all my intentions into my hands, my sore, bitten-away nails red, almost bleeding. I keep on stroking it, like caressing a newborn, ever so gently. How do you make a tree open itself? Some gardeners talk to their plants, and scientific evidence shows that plants that are talked to tend to thrive.

It trembles. Or maybe I'm hallucinating. In my desperation, I take the trembling as a sign and try to pry the roots open. Nope. They remain as stubborn as a donkey that refuses to move. I start crying. What am I supposed to do now? Soon it'll be too late. God knows where they're taking Rori now, if she isn't already far away. But something in my gut tells me that she's still around; my legs feel that they could walk to her if I wanted them to. I rest my head on a root shaped like a loosely coiled snake; it fits my skull just like one of those basins where the hairdresser washes your hair. Maybe I feel that way because my tears are running down my temples and soaking my hair. I turn sideways and curl up into a fetal position, sobbing loudly, but nobody can hear me so deep in the forest. My tears drop in a torrent into the soil between the roots. I bite my knuckles hard as I always did as a child when I felt that I'd cried enough, but my tears won't stop.

The last time I had to bite myself this hard was at the aftermath of the bee-slaying at Hayes Valley Farm. Some lunatic trespassed one night and sprayed pesticide at the entrance of each hive, killing more than two hundred thousand bees. One day, they were buzzing happily around us; the next, they were just piles of sadness. The sight of all those black-and-yellow bits covering the ground brought me to the brink of a breakdown. I sobbed so hard that my throat became hoarse, and I fell to my knees, grabbing the dead bees and rubbing them all over my wet face. When I saw the other volunteers staring at me wide eyed, I decided I had to stop, so I bit my knuckles.

I never cry over dead people, and I've never been to a funeral. When I think of the way my father died—a drug overdose after a concert in which he played the meanest guitar ever, according to my mom—I always get sad since he didn't take care of himself well enough to be around when I came to this world. It seemed to me he never really wanted to be alive.

The bees, on the other hand, were minding their own business, bringing more life and sweetness to being. And now bees all over the planet are in crisis, whole colonies dying mysteriously. In China, the dying of bees is so rampant that now thousands of farmers must painstakingly pollinate their trees by hand. I get terrified just imagining a world without bees. We just take them for granted like we do the loved ones who are so close to us that we stop saying I love you. And then they leave us because we took them for granted.

I think about Josh. I tried to connect with him, but he's unreachable; and yet, I feel so close to him now. Marco, what a sneak. What's he up to? And Andrea. I call him as hard as I can, but he doesn't show up. Can he be upset with me?

I give up on the inexorable tree and decide to leave. As I press my hands against the tear-drenched soil to leverage myself, my fingers go deep into it; it's as soft as pancake batter! Now I'm up to my elbow in the ground, and I feel a mild suction pulling me into it. "Yes!" I cry in joy, and more tears drop. Now the roots start to open up, contracting and dilating inward and downward as if the tree is giving birth to me in reverse, and I'm up to my shoulders. It's as if the ground is breathing me back into it. Now the opening is as large as my upper body and I dive in.

I fall smack in the middle of the town's main square. The market is crowded with some kind of gibbous moon celebration and everyone pulls away from me, clearing a path that leads to the church. They all know who I'm looking for. I run to the church and find Caterina on the porch in her rocking chair, her blind eyes looking into emptiness as she knits at full speed.

"I see you made it through the Oak. Congratulations. I knew you could do it."

"Oh, really? What else do you know about me? Why can't you tell me everything now and be done with it?"

"Oh, I don't know that much. And we'll only know if it's all possible when you discover it. You must conquer everything that comes to you, learning to swim as you drown. If I give it away, it's not fun—or effective."

"It seems that everyone around here has an agenda, even you. Why didn't Andrea hear my plea for help?"

A voice behind me answers. "I knew that you knew the way. I just wanted to see if you would remember it and have the courage to try. I'm happy to see I was right!" His sardonic smile gives him away; even he has plans for me.

"Can I spend the night here? I want to leave the farm. I tried today, but someone got in the way of my plans. And I don't want to go back again."

"I understand," Caterina says, "but I can't allow it. You're well aware of the risks you would be taking if you spent too much time down here with us." Caterina stops her knitting and Verve the parrot grabs one of the needles and starts playing with it. She rests her hands on her lap now, just a bit tense.

"I'd rather take the risks here than take the risk of staying there," I say, not recognizing my own voice.

The blind woman squeezes and twists her skirt, lifting it just above her bony knees. "See, you're changing already. The effects may be cumulative; we don't know. Andrea, will you please escort her out?"

He reaches for my hand; I pull it away abruptly.

His jaw drops. "Easy there. You look like a wild buffalo."

"I'll take full responsibility. Whatever happens to me, it'll be my own fault since I chose to stay."

Caterina gets up; she's very sharp and quick for an ancient blind woman. She rubs her needles with her dry, gnarled fingers, obviously annoyed. "Stubborn, just like your *nonna*. Let's just hope your determination won't be your death. History tends to repeat itself, but the ones who know it can avoid falling into the same traps."

"I've been already taken in a trap recently, as you may know. I don't want to wait to see what the criminals do to me next. They know that I know they took Rori. What would they lose by eliminating me?"

"The people in the village have been talking about the missing redhead," Andrea says. "If another girl goes missing . . . I don't think the gypsies would dare touch you."

"I understand. But I have a feeling. . . . Well, I just want to go near some sea water."

Caterina creases her brow, looking inward, and smiles.

"Really? What else do you feel?"

"I've been craving water. I want to look at the sea. And my body knows that if I sleep in my farm cabin tonight, that won't be possible. I don't know if the criminals will kill me or send me away, but my thirst for the sea won't be quenched."

"In that case, I'll allow you to stay. Andrea, can you host her?"

"But . . . ."

"It's okay, Andrea. If something weird happens to her at night, having you close by is her best chance of surviving it."

He scratches his head and agrees.

As Caterina sits back down in her rocking chair, Verve jumps onto her lap holding the knitting, which he has completely unraveled, in his beak.

This way, she'll never finish whatever she's making, I think.

She pets the green bird and resumes her knitting. "Now off you go, you two. You young things make me exhausted."

Andrea takes me to his cottage, which looks like a summer home for Snow White's Seven Dwarfs. It has only one room, with a woodstove in the middle. He makes me some tea and asks if I'm hungry, gesturing for me to sit down on a sort of large sofa.

"No, I had a huge steak not too long ago, but thanks."

"You're welcome. Maybe it's better this way. We don't know what might happen to you if you ate our food."

I smile. My scalp itches, and I scratch it as discreetly as I can.

"Are you all right? Do you need anything?"

"I need to get some sleep," I say, yawning. "Where's the bed?"

"You're sitting on it."

"Good. Off I go." I drop my head onto an orange pillow that smells like sweat. Apparently, Andrea needs to do some laundry. I sleep like a corpse, and I don't care if I ever wake up again. I've never slept so deeply in my whole life. The only time I almost wake up, not sure if I'm dreaming, I find Andrea cuddling me and holding my hands in a brotherly way. I feel his cool palm on my forehead and hear him whisper, "Carmela, you're burning with fever. Would you like some water?"

I don't answer him, but I know instinctively that he won't sleep tonight. He'll lie awake by my side the whole night, watching over me.

CHAPTER 17

Andrea's Well

I wake up feeling rested and as strong as I've ever felt. Apart from my itchy scalp, I'd say I've never felt better.

I look around me; I'm alone in a tiny, single-room home. Where is Andrea? I'm so thirsty that I reach for a mug of water by the bed, and as I extend my arm, I see my fingernails—long, pointy, thick, shiny, and purple. I drop the mug, screaming, and it breaks into many pieces, spilling the water. I touch my nails and find that they're as sharp as an iron knife. I wouldn't want them close to my skin, anyone's skin, ever. My scalp is itching like hell, but I'm afraid to scratch it with these scary claws.

"Andrea? Are you here? Do you have any more water?" My voice is raspy and hoarse. My throat is itchy, as well. I need to drink something. I grab a bowl from a table and notice that there's no sink anywhere in the cabin. And then I remember seeing a well in front of the house when we arrived last night. The feeble morning daylight is weaker than sunlight on a foggy San Francisco day. In spite of the haze, I squint. My eyes can't handle the light.

I look into the well and I see a woman with long dreadlocks and shiny, red-streaked hazel eyes staring at me wide eyed. Wait. She looks a lot like me. I touch my hair and pull a long, thick dreadlock. Wow. My skin is very tan now, and my teeth are ridiculously white, like they've been photoshopped to a pearly shine. The dreadlock is dark blonde, just like my natural hair color, but there are red and purple threads mixed with it now.

My thirst is unbearable. I pull the bucket from the well and, ignoring the frogs that come up along with the water, I fill a bowl that was sitting by the edge and drink greedily.

As I put down the bowl, I notice my toned arms. Where are my feeble computer-programmer limbs? A few weeks of farming alone can't have done that. My whole body is different. I feel a lot more energy running through my core, but I'm still thirsty.

"Yes, I'm so glad you survived your night here. It was fun to watch you change." Andrea comes from behind me, sporting his mischievous grin. "Let's see how you fare in the upper world now." And his grin gives way to a frown.

"I'm so thirsty that no matter how much water I drink, it can never be enough."

"Are you still thinking about the sea?"

"Yes, I just feel the need to jump in some water."

"Let's go show the new you to Caterina."

"What for? She's blind; she's not going to see anything." I blurt it out, surprised at my own defiant tone.

"You know very well that she can see better than most of us. She can see beyond the ordinary world. She probably knows about you already. I just thought of going to her to acknowledge the fact."

"You don't need to come to me," Caterina's voice says. "I'm right here."

We look around, but we don't see her.

"You look stunning and powerful," she continues. "I hope that you didn't lose your sweetness in the exchange."

Andrea cries out, half-laughing and half-angry, "Where are you, you old witch? Don't play tricks on us!" And he looks behind bushes and trees, even under rocks and mushrooms.

"I'm here in the well."

"In the well?"

"Yes. To be precise, inside the bucket."

We both look at the bucket. It holds some water and three frogs. One of them is blind, its eyes white and lifeless. "Yes, I'm the frog," it says.

We all laugh. The frog seems to giggle, too.

"So, tell me more about this wish of yours for water," the frog says.

"I don't know. I've been having this craving for a while now. Since I went to Caserta, since I found Rori's—oh no, Rori's hair! I left it in my bungalow. I left everything behind me, but that—I shouldn't have forgotten her hair."

"You can pick it up anytime. It'll still be there waiting for you. After all, you hid it so well . . . ."

I look at the frog, dumbfounded. "You know everything, don't you?"

"Not really. Tell me more about your wish for water."

"It isn't just thirst. I need to be surrounded by water, like a fetus floating in amniotic fluid."

"Let your cravings be your guide."

Andrea frowns, evidently disliking this advice.

I ignore him. "Where should my cravings take me?"

Andrea holds my arm, but his grasp seems weaker than usual. Or am I the one who has changed?

The frog blinks and points with its froggy hands to the bottom of the well. "Down here, for example, there's plenty of water. You'd be surrounded by it in a second."

Andrea holds me tighter. "Caterina, I'm sure you know where this well leads!"

I free myself from his grip and climb onto the well's edge. I've never felt so sure of myself in my life. "Where to?"

I can see the frog smiling.

"No, Cami," the boy cries. "This will take you to the Doomed Witches' Lake. Nobody dares to go there, not even our kind. You'll never return!"

"We'll see about that." And I jump. The well is long; it takes forever to reach the water.

Andrea jumps in after me. Soon the cold water turns into leaves at the top of a walnut tree full of ripe nuts. It was if they'd matured and sun dried still in the branches; they were ready to be savored.

"Oh, wow, these are beautiful." I pick one and I'm about to crack it open with my bare hands, I so want to eat it, but Andrea grabs my hand before I can break the shell. "Don't even think about it! This is the Damned Walnut Tree, the

140

one that bears fruit year round. No one should eat from it; the consequences could be disastrous."

Some kind of white viscous milk starts dripping profusely from the branch I broke picking the nut. Recalling Marco's stories the night he gave me the Strega liquor, I drop the nut. When it hits the ground, it turns into an albino mouse that runs for shelter inside some exposed roots.

Nearby, a clear, placid lake reflects the tree, the clouds, some birds crossing the sky, and the two of us perched in the highest branches.

"Look, Andrea! That's what I've needed. That's the answer to my cravings. I'm going to jump into that water." I pull off my T-shirt and unzip my jeans, preparing to jump straight out of the tree into the lake.

"Not so fast, my friend. Do you know what lies beneath that mirror surface? Your worst nightmare! In the Roman times, hundreds of witches were killed in a trap in this very lake, and after that, no one who went near it ever came back to tell the story."

"But what about Caterina's advice to follow my cravings?" I ask as I somehow manage to slide out of my jeans and hang them in a branch beside my shirt.

"I don't know exactly what she meant by that; she's been acting so weird these last few days that I can hardly recognize her. She doesn't usually tell people to take risks."

"Maybe she saw how strong I've become and decided to let me give everything a try!"

"Okay, but please be cautious. Why don't you climb down the tree and test the water with your toes before jumping in headfirst?"

"Okay." I climb down like a monkey, jumping from branch to branch.

As I reach the grass-covered ground, an icy breeze gives me goose bumps, in spite of the strong sunshine and the blazing heat. When I step out of the tree's shade, I have to squint. "The sun burns my eyes!" I scream back to Andrea.

"I'll throw you my hat; it should help." The elflike boy takes off his green felt Fedora hat and tosses it down to me; now it's his turn to squint.

I catch the hat and put it on.

"How does that feel now?" he asks.

"Better, thanks!" I smile at him and walk backwards toward the lake five feet away.

"Cami, watch out!" calls Andrea, pointing behind me. "The water in the lake, it's moving!"

I turn back toward the water, fighting an energy that's pulling me toward the rippling water. I see a muddy, greenish arm with a wounded hand rise out of the water and several similar hands surface around it. The snakelike arm is long and undulating. The other hands rise higher, followed by their respective snakelike arms. I stare at them, fascinated by their malleability. They don't seem to have bones inside, maybe a very soft cartilage. The open wounds ooze dark blood as they move closer to me. Even an ant would be smart enough to get the hell of there, but I can't move. I seem to have grown roots. The arms leave the water and slither in my direction, leaving a glossy, gooey trail behind them that works like acid, killing all the grass it touches. I can tell by the noise that Andrea is coming down through the tree branches, but I can't turn my head to look at him.

"Cami, what are you doing? Get out of there!"

"I can't move!"

"I'm coming to help you!"

"Don't! You might get stuck, too. Think of something else. Do you have a rope?"

"No."

"It's all right. I don't think I could move my arms to grab it, anyway."

The first arm is about thirty inches away from my feet, moving very slowly. Only a fallen log separates it from me. The others are close behind their leader. I close my eyes. So this is how I'm going to die . . . .

With my eyes closed, I hear drums beating and the frail yet powerful voice of an elderly woman singing in a language that sounds strangely familiar even though I can't understand it. I open my eyes. The drums stop beating. The first arm is now inching across the log, which melts at its touch, hissing and releasing a burnt smell. As I close my eyes again, I can hear the drums louder than before. They're trying to tell me something.

"Andrea, can you hear the drums?"

"Which drums? What are you talking about? I can't hear anything."

"Close your eyes and pay attention."

A second later, he responds, "Yes, I can hear them. But where are they coming from? Wait, the sound stops when I open my eyes."

"Yes, for me too. But I think these drums are trying to tell us something. Can you try to understand them?"

The first arm is now about fifteen inches from my feet. It stinks exactly like some pork chops that I once accidentally put in the recycle bin instead of the refrigerator. Three days later, the whole kitchen smelled putrid.

"I know!" Andrea says. "My ocarina!" And I hear him playing, jamming with the drums, evidently keeping his eyes closed.

I open my eyes. "It's working, Andrea! The arms are backing off!"

He stops playing to look, and the arms inch toward me again.

"Oops!" Andrea closes his eyes tightly and plays his ocarina along with the drums once again. The arms back ever so slowly toward the water. After ten minutes or so of music, they're back inside the water.

"Don't stop Andrea, please. I'm thawing. Soon, I'll be able to move again."

Poised like leprosy-infected cobras, the arms seem to watch me attentively as I approach the lake. I feel that they need just one false step on my part to attack me, but Andrea's frenzied playing seems to be keeping them at bay—or maybe it's the drums. I close my eyes. Yes, the drums are going wild.

I touch the water, which feels lukewarm, and most of the arms move away as if they're now afraid of me. But the first arm—the largest and grossest—doesn't budge. The water in the middle of the lake forms a swirling funnel like a tornado, and something comes up in its center, floating above the water—a stone. It's an ordinary, dull gray stone, but the attraction is irresistible. I must have it.

I walk around the lake, away from the arms, which follow my movements as if they had tiny eyes in each of their pustules, but they remain where they are. As I stretch my arms, preparing to dive, Andrea sends out a higher-pitched note, at which all the all the arms except the biggest one jump as if startled. I dive in and swim underwater for a while then coming up to breath and aiming toward the stone, which is still suspended in the air above the funnel of water. I close my eyes to listen to the drums, opening them when I reach the stone. It feels warm in my hands, and I feel like I've finally come home. But I see the biggest arm undulating, swimming toward me. I try to swim fast as I can, but the stone, which fits in the palm of my hand, is much heavier than it looks and weighs me down.

As I reach the water's edge, my free hand touches some exposed tree roots that help me reach the shore, but the slithering arm grabs one of my dreadlocks. I smell burning hair and remember Rori's little red hair hidden in my cigar box treasure chest back in my bungalow. I throw the rock onto the grass, and, still holding to the roots in the edge, dig my nails deep into the decomposing flesh of the hand gripping my hair. My nails melt fast, leaving purple liquefied metal dripping like wax down the stalking arm, but, at least, the thing releases its grip. I climb out of the water, grab the warm, heavy rock, and try to run. The snakelike arm ignores Andrea's ocarina, coming after me much faster than before.

I hug the tree trunk with my arms and legs, but it's hard to climb holding such a heavy weight.

"Andrea, I need help."

"Do you think it's okay if I stop playing?"

"Yes, please come down. This thing is ignoring your music, anyway."

The arm is now close to the tree's roots. Andrea clips his ocarina to his belt and comes down to me.

"Here, hold this rock while I climb up a little higher."

"Sure." He takes it with one hand. "What's the matter with you? It's not much heavier than an egg!"

I climb fast, concentrating too much on escaping the slithering arm to make sense of Andrea's comment about the rock's weight.

Once I reach the top branches of the walnut tree, I put my clothes back on, take the rock from him and almost fall out of the tree.

"How strange," I say, more to myself than to him. "It seems to have a different weight depending on who's carrying it." I hold it in my lap where it feels warm and cozy, and no heavier than a baby would. The arm is now writhing around the lowest branch like a snake. Its scaly body is so long that its end is still inside the lake. Unlike my hair and the log, the tree seems impervious to its corrosive slime.

Yielding to an impulse, I rub the rock. I see Caterina's face, the younger version, with fully functioning eyes, strikingly deep-set and violet.

"Congratulations, my child; you've found your *nonna*'s soul."

"Oh!"

"Oh, so that's why you let her come here," Andrea snaps.

"I know. I'm sorry to put you at risk like that," Caterina continues, addressing me, "but something in my heart knew that her stone would be instinctively attracted to you."

Unfortunately, so is the hand that once kept it. The slimy thing has almost reached my feet.

"Now what should we do?"

"Go back down. Let's take a look at it!"

Her face fades, and the rock turns into an ordinary lump of stone again except that it's still very heavy. Andrea ties two young branches into a loop and holds them open for me. He grabs my clothes hung in the tree and throws them through the loop, and they disappear as soon as they cross into it. "Step through this. It's our passage to the other side." I clutch the heavy rock close to my chest, but the hand grabs my ankle. The pain is so intense that I almost drop the rock.

"Ouch! Andrea, help!"

He takes the rock from me, ever so easily, and climbs down to the hand holding his silver-bladed penknife in his mouth. The thing is stuck to me like it has suction cups and I smell my own flesh burning. I puncture the hand between its knuckles with my fingernail. The nail melts fast, but at least the thing lets go and backs off for a while.

"Fast, climb up there, cross the loop fast!" Andrea screams while he stabs the oblivious hand, which keeps on coming toward us. "I'm going to cut it off it's wrist, that should stop it!" He yells. I go up and pass through the loop backwards so that I'm still facing Andrea, keeping my free hand on a branch to keep the loop from closing. "Give me the rock!" I yell to him.

He gives it to me, but the sudden weight forces me to let go of the branch, closing the temporary gate between realms, and start a free fall that's dizzyingly fast since I'm heavier than ever.

Andrea doesn't come after me.

I land in a meadow. From here, I can see the steeple of the Subterranean Heights church. I rest the rock in my lap, the only place where its weight isn't unbearable. My hair drips and my underwear is soaked, and even though the soft light of this place barely bothers my eyes, I realize that I'm also missing Andrea's hat, which must have fallen off when I jumped in the water. Will he come back safely?

My clothes lie on a heap a few feet way. I get up to go pick them and get dressed, and my leg hurts. I look at my ankle. A purple bruise where the hand grabbed me looks almost like a snake-scale tattoo circling my ankle. I look back at the rock now resting in the grass and remember my dream of the girl opening a box as her mother burned to death at the stake.

I stand up gingerly and limp toward the church. Should I deposit the stone on *nonna*'s altar, the only shrine without one?

145

When I reach the porch, the rocking chair is moving back and forth, but no one is sitting in it. Only Verve the parrot is still there, balancing on the ball of yarn.

The church is quiet and dark, lit only by some candles here and there. My eyes feel comfortable in the dim light. I make a note to myself: Must retrieve sunglasses. I tie my dreadlocks in a bun above my head, and look at my shadow on the floor. It looks like I have two heads, one on top of the other. I walk around the altars, trying to remember which one belongs to *Nonna*.

"*Ciao*, Cami. What are you looking for?"

"Andrea!" I want to run to meet him, but I hesitate. His voice sounds different, and he's walking funny, like a puppet manipulated by a master. His once lively, twinkly eyes are empty; he seems to be staring at nothing.

"Come here, my darling!"

"Huh?" Darling? What the hell? That doesn't sound like Andrea. His legs wobble; he's coming toward me but definitely not of his own free will.

"Come here and bring the stone. Let me see her!"

It's definitely Andrea, but he's acting weird. Maybe he bumped his head trying to get here after he crossed the loop. He extends his arms, coming close to me, hesitating, almost as if someone is pushing him toward me. But he's alone; there's nobody here but the two of us.

I walk slowly to meet him, not sure that I should but not knowing what else to do.

I see Caterina step out of the darkness right behind him. I smile, and I'm about to greet her, but she brings her finger to her lips, shushing me.

Too late. Andrea blinks and frowns; he's noticed my changed expression.

Caterina raises her knitting needles high, about to pierce the boy's neck.

My jaw drops in horror.

He turns around, grabs her arms, and tries to redirect the needles into the ancient woman's face.

Now I see the purulent hand, dripping wine-colored goo from its mangled wrist, grabbing Andrea's neck and controlling the boy's movements.

"Help, Carmela. Help me," Caterina pleads.

I'm afraid to come close, but the needles are inches from her cheeks and she can't hold them back.

"Use the rock. It wants the rock."

I lift the heavy rock with both hands in front of my face and blow some wind toward the fight.

It works. Andrea slowly lowers his hands, releasing Caterina. As I come closer, he turns around, pushed by the hand on his neck, and starts walking in my direction, but his feet fight the movement; the hand doesn't have the situation completely under control. I look at my right hand; I have two long nails left. I try to hold the rock with just my left hand, but it's nearly impossible.

Noticing my efforts, Caterina starts to sing an old Italian lullaby, and the rock feels lighter. I come close to zombie-Andrea and kiss the rock in front of his wide eyes: "Is this what you want?"

As he lifts his arms to grab it, I move my right hand as if to embrace him and pierce the wounded flesh of the hand holding his neck, using my pinky fingernail like a skewer. My nail is melting fast, but it sticks to the putrid flesh like a tick.

Andrea grabs my left arm and tries to take the rock away from me, but Caterina, still singing the lullaby, sticks her needles sideways into the hand, which curls up like a dying tarantula. Andrea falls to the floor with a thud, bleeding profusely from the back of his neck.

Caterina runs out of the church with her prey like a housewife that has just caught a gigantic rat.

"Help him; don't let him bleed away!"

I kneel on the floor beside the boy. He's losing a lot of blood. I try to stop the flow with my hair, which soaks up the blood but does nothing to slow the bleeding. My tears fall on the rock, which is now heavy again with no lullaby to lighten it. Seeing the image of Andrea's ocarina show up in the rock, I unclip the instrument from his belt and play the only song I know. He closes his brown eyes.

"*Grazie*, Cami. . . ." He's leaving me; his breathing is getting weaker by the second.

I play it faster, frantically. I'm losing my breath, but I don't want to stop playing, hoping that the sound will extend his life a little. My crying and sobbing make it so hard to play that I'm ready to give up when I see the first snail coming close to his wounded neck, closely followed by a second one. I look to my right and see a procession of snails entering the dark church. They cover his wound and then his whole body except his face. He looks like a chrysalis, a pupa made out of snails. He opens his eyes and closes them again.

"Is that it, my beautiful boy? Is this the requiem you wished for?" I touch his plump lips, so quiet now.

The snails keep moving, enveloping his body in a slow but steady rhythm.

Suddenly, I see something move against that pattern. It's his chest. He giggles. "Ouch, that tickles. Stop, *signorine!*" He grins, opens his eyes again, and winks at me.

I've never seen a snail smile. But now I see hundreds of them chuckle silently in unison.

CHAPTER 18

Il Bagni

After finding my *nonna*'s altar, I deposit the rock there, among the many other mementos and souvenirs, and improvise a prayer:

"*Ciao, Nonna.* I wish I had met you. You sound like an amazing person. I wonder if my obsession with finding Rori will lead me to a doom like yours. I can never forget the friend that I barely knew. I feel that we connected at a very deep level, and all I can think about is saving her from those people. Please guide me in this quest. I wish I had someone to hold my hand right now."

I kiss Andrea on the forehead and leave the church to find someone who can help him. When I'm a few yards from the door, I hear a clatter as if a heavy object is rolling across the marble floor of the quiet temple. I turn around, but I can't see a thing; I resume walking toward the door, and I hear the rolling sound again. It's clearly coming after me. I stop as I reach the door, but I don't turn around until the rolling is very close behind me. I look down and there, right by my feet, is the rock. It came after me.

I pick it up with both hands. Even though spending the night at Subterranean Heights has made me much stronger, the rock is still incredibly heavy. I leave the church hunched over with the weight.

Such awkwardness attracts attention. A girl of what it seems about fourteen—but who knows how old anyone around here really is?— offers to help me. She grabs the rock and starts juggling with it. "Why, it seemed so heavy!" she says, and she goes on doing tricks.

I don't have time to play. "Do you know where Caterina is?"

"Oh, she's at Andrea's well."

"Can you help me carry this rock over there?"

"Sure. What's wrong with Andrea? Why was he acting so weird earlier?"

"Oh yes, that. He needs a doctor right away. To make a long story short, he's at the church covered in snails that are stopping the bleeding from a nasty wound on his neck."

"Oh." She sticks two fingers in her mouth and whistles. A little purple-haired boy carrying a black-and-white polka-dot cat shows up almost immediately.

"Can you call Alexis? She must come see Andrea at the church."

The boy vanishes in a puff, and we go on toward the well. "Alexis is very good with herbs and healing," the girl explains. "Besides, she's Andrea's sweetheart, and nothing like love to cure anything." She winks at me.

"Oh, I didn't know Andrea had a girlfriend."

"Oh yes. Several of them, actually." And she half smiles, one corner of her lips turning up and the other down. I wonder if she's one of his minor girlfriends. I don't know what to say next, so I change the subject: "And you, what's your name?"

"Gabi."

"And what do you like to do?"

"I like to juggle. I also like singing and taking care of chickens." And she does a trick with the rock, which is so heavy for me but for no one else.

"I see."

Luckily, we reach Andrea's cottage before I run out of small talk. Caterina is looking down the well, holding her knitting needles. A dark purple, viscous liquid drips from their tips. Gabi gives me back the stone and leaves, nodding with deference to the older witch.

"That one was hard to defeat. I wonder if we should put a lid on this well so the creatures won't come back searching for the rock."

"Why do they want this rock so badly?" I ask, resting my heavy load on the edge of the well. Caterina looks at me with her blind eyes as if she wants to see something behind my eyes, somewhere between the retina and the optic nerve to be precise.

"Compassion is a powerful weapon."

I look down the well, and I can see some bubbling and smoke coming out of the water. "That sounds beautiful, but it doesn't say much," I respond after a moment.

"Your *nonna*'s heart was the most compassionate of all the witches. That makes her rock capable of great feats. These people in the lake had none. They need it desperately; they think that if they ever learn how to be compassionate, or how to extract the essence of compassion from the rock, they'll be free from their purgatory."

"Why did they end up there?"

"When they were in power, they were ruthless, resorting to sacrificing animals and children to their gods; and that's why the Romans decided to do what they did. I'm not defending either side, just wishing such harsh measure had never been necessary. If they were more compassionate, they would probably not have ended that way."

"I see. But they don't seem to making much progress...the way they took Andrea over to recover their prized object wasn't very kind."

"Yes. That's why they'll never leave that place. They just don't understand. Compassion at the highest level is a gift. You have to be born with it. It can be cultivated but never acquired through force or indoctrination. And another secret: you must be able to let things go and work with resignation toward how things are. Patience and persistence." Her knitting needles start moving; the purple liquid floats in the air and stretches itself toward the rock in a puny little obsessive effort to seize it. "Now I have to bring up some water from down there to clean these needles. This water is so pure that it's the only way to keep their realm away from invading ours. I hope they don't find a way to come back and claim it again." She lowers the bucket.

"How preposterous."

"Well, they're entitled to it. This rock actually belongs to them. We just stole it thanks to you."

"What? You made me a thief?"

"Your great-great-grandmother Carmela decided to leave us forever and move to the upper level for good because she was madly in love with your great-great-grandfather. Love can blind us and make us do stupid things. She gave away her most prized possession, her mother's soul rock, so these creatures could grant her wish for humanity. She lost all her power, too. No man on earth deserves so much."

"I was told my grandfather was a very special man."

"I'm sure that he was, but even so . . . ."

I don't know what to say, so I change the subject. "So, now, do you want to keep this rock? I tried to leave it at the church, on my *nonna*'s altar, but it keeps following me. And it's almost as heavy as I am. I can't carry it."

"I know. It's your fate to carry your great-great-grandmother's misdeed. But if you sing her favorite lullaby, it will be lighter. It goes like this:

"*Ninna nanna di pace che invento*

"*Pensando a un bambino*

"*Che è arrivato stanotte dal mare col freddo che fa*

"*Trasportato sulle ali del vento*

"*Da un paese lontano, fin qua*

"*Con in tasca il ricordo più dolce di un'altra città.*"

I ask her to provide a rough translation and she says, "It's a lullaby of peace about a child that came from the sea carried on the wings of the wind from a far country. You'll understand it more clearly when you sing it."

I spend half an hour or so learning to sing it. And when I finally get it right, I can lift the rock effortlessly.

"But what if I stop singing it?" My answer comes to me as I speak and the rock grows heavier by the second. I settle it on the edge of the well again.

"I guess you'll have to find someone that you trust to help you carry it. Or you can try to convince it to stay here."

"How do I do that?"

"I wouldn't know. That's something you'll have to find out."

"How do I find out?"

"The answer might come to you. The lullaby trick came to me as an insight in the face of danger. Or it may come during a prayer or in a moment of ecstasy. Stay with the rock for a while. You'll get to know it more as you live with it." She looks at me with watery eyes, which seem to tell me that it's time to leave. I get the message and leave slowly, singing my lullaby and waving good-bye to her with my free hand. A few curious passersby who have gathered around to watch us end up helping her lift a heavy round wooden lid and close the well with it.

I wander until I reach a cozy bit of woods and follow a trail that leads me to a small creek. Tired of singing, I sit down for a while and enjoy the quiet, just listening to the trickling water. After a while, I curl up with the rock and fall asleep.

I wake from my nap to the sound of waves crashing onto rocks, and I find that I'm sweating. When I lick my sweat, it tastes like salt, but not like the usual saltiness of sweat. Instead, it tastes like ocean water that dries in the hairs of your arms when you go to the beach, leaving them a bit white, crispy, and salty. The rock is moving by my side, and I can see a little movie inside it. I see the emerald-colored waters of an enclosed tiny beach surrounded by a rock wall. A triangular crack in the wall lets in the noise and some of the foam of the sea waves crashing outside , but the water in the small beach keeps still. Some kind of seaweed is floating, spreading on the surface in a corner of the pool. As I look closer, I can see that it's hair. Red hair.

I get up in a rush, and, singing the lullaby, I pick up my rock and go to look for Caterina. She's no longer at the well, so I go to the church, and there I find her, kneeling beside Andrea and helping a girl with blue hair apply compresses to his neck wound. He's sleeping but smiling. I drop the rock near him. The boy trembles a little.

"Oh no," the girl says. "I guess that hand infected him with a bit of its own desire for the rock. This is going to be more complicated than I thought. He'll need a cleanse."

Caterina replies, "Whatever you say, Alexis. I trust your advice." She looks up at me. "Hello again, Cami. Tired of caring for it?"

"Well, yes, but that's not why I'm here. I want you to see something." I pick up the rock, singing again—oh, how tired I am of singing to it—and show them the little movie.

"Oh, what a beautiful place," says Alexis.

"What do you think it means?" I ask. "Do you see the red hair floating here in this corner?"

"Well, I'm blind, my dear; have you forgotten?" Caterina replies, with a sad but mischievous smile. "But if the rock is showing this scene to you, it's trying to tell you something. Does it remind you of any familiar place or situation?"

"No. It reminds me that I've been craving the sea."

"You should listen to your cravings."

I look for a while at the image, which is now flickering and fading. I grab my phone from my jeans pocket and take a picture just before it vanishes. I put the phone back in my pocket and wander around the altars, carrying the stone and humming the lullaby. On one of the altars, a blue aquamarine lies besides a green topaz, each stone shaped like an eye. I feel an impulse to push one away from the other.

"These are displayed there to remind us of the commander who led the Romans in the lake massacre—" Caterina's story is interrupted by my phone buzzing in my jeans pocket. A text message: "*Ciao, cara.* Are we still up for Positano? I'll pick you up at your farm in three hours. Pack your swimsuit!"

Wow. The coverage reaches here?! I hold my breath, type "OK," and hit Send.

"Now hold on there. I told you to listen to the cravings, not to follow them," Caterina warns.

"I need to go back to the upper world. How can I do it without Andrea?"

"You can use the holy water basin. It will take you back just outside the Oak."

I pick up the rock and jump into the cold water inside the basin that Andrea and I used earlier. Good thing my phone is always in its waterproof case. Soon, I feel squeezed as if I'm passing through a funnel. Luckily, the rock is weightless in the swift current. When I reach the meadow, the bright daylight, even in the shade of the Oak, hurts my eyes, and I regret leaving Andrea's hat back at the walnut tree. Using my right hand as a visor, I put the rock in my jeans left pocket and start singing. In my new body I walk so fast that it takes me very little time to get to the farm. The gypsies are all there, drinking tea in the gazebo, including the pipe-smoking cousin.

"*Ma che*, Cami, have you been working out?" asks Luludja? "Or is it all the farming? Are we putting you to work that hard? And what have you done with your hair?"

She and her husband laugh, but the one smoking the pipe keeps quiet and goes on puffing and squinting at me.

I excuse myself and rush into my bungalow.

Taking the rock out of my pocket and putting it on my end table for the moment, I change into overalls for my journey—I hate carrying bags, and the overalls are full of pockets. Then, I open the closet and grab the cigar box where I keep some small treasures. I open it and search frantically among the shells and feathers that I've collected since I came to Italy until I finally spot the red hair rolled around the tail feather of a red-rumped swallow.

Rori's hair clings to the feather as if doesn't want to part from it, but I'm determined and soon I have it. I tuck it deep into a front pocket of my overalls, making sure I choose one that doesn't have any holes yet. In the holey one, I shove a swimsuit and a change of underwear. My wallet and cell phone go in the back pockets, closed up with buttons, and a can of tuna and a bag of trail mix go in the large front pocket under my chest. I fill a Tupperware container with water and drop the rock inside. It does the trick—no need to sing endlessly anymore. I tuck the container into the big front pocket, along with the food.

I hear a honk; it's Marco in his car. The dogs bark at him angrily.

"It's okay," I tell them, but if I don't believe it myself, how am I supposed to convince the dogs of it?

He smiles at me and to the dogs, his hypnotic green eyes commanding obedience, and they calm down immediately. And so do I. What a charmer. Even so, the dogs follow us until Marco hits the paved road and steps on the gas pedal with gusto.

I keep my hands over my eyes; the bright sun is making me cry.

"Are you okay?" he asks.

"Yes, it's just the sun hurting my eyes a bit."

"Here, take these." He hands me his Ray-Bans.

"Thanks!" I put them on gratefully.

"What happened to you? You look . . . different."

"Long story. When I have a chance, I'll tell you all about it."

"I have a feeling that I know this story already." And he gives me a glance, smiling and frowning at the same time, before turning his attention back to the road.

He likes to drive fast, and as his focus on speed frees me from his influence, I remember why I decided to accept his invitation to the sea. "I need your help to find a place," I tell him.

"Oh, don't worry, *cara*. I told you already: you can stay in my cabin. If you don't feel comfortable, I can get a hotel room for myself."

"No, that's not what I'm talking about. Can you stop for a second so I can explain it to you?"

"*Perfecto*. I need some coffee, anyway. Let's stop right now."

He parks beside a bakery and coffee shop in the tiny town we're passing through, and we go inside. Marco orders an espresso and asks me what I want.

"A cappuccino, thanks."

The man behind the counter laughs. "*Cappuccio? A questa l'ora?*"

"*Ragazza americana,*" Marco replies with the smirk of an accomplice.

"What's the matter?" I ask him.

"Well, it's past noon, and it's unusual to order drinks with milk after lunch. In Italy, milk is for breakfast only."

"Hey, guess what? I haven't eaten anything yet, so this is actually my breakfast." As I blurt out these words, I realize that it's been a long while since I've had any food, and yet, I'm not hungry. Me, the low-blood-sugar-all-day-snacking kind of girl.

"I'm just explaining my culture. Here, have a *cornetto* with chocolate along with your coffee."

We sit down at a tiny marble table tucked into a corner, the only table in the bakery. I find the picture of the beach with emerald-colored waters on my phone and leave it on the table while I devour my pastry and drink my coffee.

"Nice, where is it?"

"I don't know. That's why I need your help; I need to find this place."

"Why?"

I pick up the phone and enlarge the image down to the detail of the floating red hair.

His eyes grow wide, and I see blue streaks showing up in his irises. He calms down and puts on a poker face, but I notice a tiny drop of sweat rolling down his temple.

"What's this, some kind of rusty seaweed?" he asks.

"Listen, I know about your interest in my red-headed friend. I've been trying to find her, and I know she was kidnapped. I even know who did it, and I have strong reasons to believe that she might be near that pool we're looking at right now."

"Really? How can you know that?"

"I'll tell you, but only if you tell me why you have her photos in your office."

"*Ma—?* So you've found my office?"

"Yes, pardon my curiosity, but I have a bad habit of snooping into people's bathroom cabinets."

"I know; you can learn a lot from them." He squints, looking past my shoulder into nothing, and downs his last sip of coffee.

We sit there for a while in silence, and I can tell that he's thinking what I'm thinking: Whatever we've been hiding from each other is so obvious now that it has to be said. Or maybe there's no need to talk about it anymore.

I decide to open the discussion. "Let me guess: You've only been so keen on me because I know something about Rori's disappearance. I can't forget how strongly you reacted to a red hair the day we met."

"No, that's not true." He holds my hand tightly on top of the table and squeezes it hard. "But, yes, I'm looking for her, and I had a hunch that you were on the same quest. With much better results than I've had. But then, who can compete with witchery?"

His eyes turn to blue fire, and he presses my hand and pulls it toward him, his face coming closer and closer to mine.

I have to close my eyes. "I don't know what you're talking about. Let go of me, please, or I'll scream."

He loosens his grip until I can free my hand, and as his eyes fade back to green, he lowers his gaze so that it looks like he's having a conversation with his shirt buttons. Finally, he looks up at me again, speaking in a low voice. "Okay, here's the deal. All I can tell you is that Rori comes from a very old, traditional, and rich Irish family, and I was assigned to find her. My wine dealing is a cover; I actually work for the British Secret Intelligence Service."

"But why would the British care about an Irish girl?"

"You leave no stone unturned, do you? But, okay, I think I can trust you. The British are actually investigating a group of white-slave dealers, and we have strong reasons to believe that they abducted Rori."

"Slave dealers? In this day and age?"

"It's more common than you think, and nowadays they have new tricks. Once they get hold of a girl, they brainwash her, making her believe that she wants to have sex for fun, or for the experience."

"I see." And I remember what happened in the cabin where she was held captive.

"They surround the girls with an atmosphere of lust and drugs until they actually choose to do it and sign a contract. After that, it seems like it was their option. Ours are loose times, and with so many girls travelling to exotic lands on their own, it's been easier than ever. Hundreds of British women have been abducted this way."

At this point, the bakery owner comes up to our table to ask if we need anything else.

"No thanks, we're good," I say.

"Oh, what is this picture?" he asks. "Can I see?"

"Sure." I hand him the phone.

"Oh, yes, long time I haven't been there. When I was young, I go there many times. Bagni Regina Giovanna . . . *mamma mia!*" He brings his fingertips to his lips, kissing them with a loud smack. "Good times!"

"Do you know this place?" I ask. "Where is it?"

"On the outskirts of Sorrento, just off the coast on the way to Massa Lubrense, along the Via Capo. You walk down a narrow path to a rocky beach in the ruins of the Roman Villa Pollio Felix. The beach in your picture is enclosed by rocky walls. Giovanna, the Queen of Naples liked to bathe there in the nude." He winks and gives me back my phone. "Are you two planning to go there? It's very romantic!"

Marco gives him a noncommittal smile. "Maybe. This tourist"—he indicates me—"wants to spend some time by the sea. Which reminds me. We should get going, right, Cami?"

I get up fast and feel immediately dizzy. The pastry hit hard on my empty stomach and I feel like I'm about to faint.

"Are you okay?" Marco asks.

"Yes, let's go."

As we walk out into the bright sun, I put on Marco's sunglasses, a bit big for my face, and follow my nose to the side of the café.

"Where are you going? The car is right here."

Tiny, sweet-smelling succulents cover the ground next to the building. Kneeling, I start picking them and filling my mouth with them, dirt still dangling from their delicate roots. I like the taste so much that I bury my head in the plants and start grazing like a cow would. Only cows are a bit more placid, zen and contained in their eating manners. I'm more like desperate famished now.

"Wow, you like *portulaca* a lot, don't you? I'll remember that the next time you come over for lunch. And remind me to lock my medicine cabinet."

"*Portulaca*, is that what you call purslane in Italian?" I ask, ignoring the remark about the medicine cabinet. "I'm sorry, but back home I eat two salads a

158

day, and here it's so hard to do that," I say with my mouth still full, dropping bits of leaves onto the ground as I speak. I sit up, wipe my chin with the back of my hand, and take a moment to breathe deeply. The nourishing potency of the plants streams through my body, and I stand up feeling renewed. "Okay, let's go."

Marco looks at me suspiciously. "You're really one of them, aren't you?"

"One of who? You believe what you want to be true. Now let's go. I've got a feeling we're running out of time."

CHAPTER 19

Sorrento

After driving through the town of Sorrento as fast as we can and managing not to hit any tourists, we arrive at the entrance to the villa ruins that guard the Queen's Bath. Marco parks in a lot nearby since the passageway that leads down to the beach is very steep and narrow. We walk quietly, paying close attention to avoid stumbling on the rocky path, which winds down like a maze with its high walls that block our view of its twists and turns. After the third left turn, we reach a plateau with a dirt ground and vegetation. We can see a shiny, silver Vespa half-hidden among some bushes. We can hear laughing and splashing a little farther away.

Marco stops and scans the scene. "It must be around here somewhere."

"Yes, you're right. I can smell the salty water."

"Well, that's the most obvious thing you ever said to me. We're right by the sea. Of course, you can smell salt water."

"Oh boy, someone is grumpy today."

"I'm not grumpy. I'm just speaking the truth."

After walking a bit more, we find a short vine-covered rock wall. The laughter is louder here. We look over it and find the small enclosed beach surrounded all around by a tall rock wall that keeps it separated from the sea water, apart from the triangular crack that lets water in an out. Below us, a bunch of British kids are swimming toward a flat boulder where two topless girls are lying down, sunbathing. A rowboat is tied to some branches close to the surface. I wave to one of them.

"Hey, hi there. How do we get down?"

"Turn to your right. There's a trail that leads to these stairs." The girl points to a stairwell with steps improvised out of rocks right below us.

When we reach the place, the water is deep blue and very calm, much different from the image that my *nonna*'s soul rock showed me. Nevertheless, as I approach the sand, the rock inside the Tupperware container tucked in my front overall pocket starts moving frantically, as if it wants to jump out of the box.

Marco frowns and opens his eyes wide. "What is it? Is your heart trying to get out of your chest?"

"Kind of. Let me see." I pull the container out of my pocket, taking out the rock while I sing the lullaby.

"What, are you trying to put it to sleep?"

I hand it to him. "I have to sing. Otherwise, the rock is too heavy to carry."

He looks surprised but takes the rock, anyway. "Let's look for our redhead," he says. He turns to the group of kids, all of whom are now sitting or lying on the rock smoking hand-rolled cigarettes. "Have any of you seen a red-haired girl around here?"

"No," a bunch of them answer in unison, but one, a short, scrawny and curly-haired boy holding a snorkel and a pair of goggles, answers, "Yes."

Everyone turns to look at him.

"Funny you mention it," he continues. "I'd almost forgotten. Early this morning, I came here to dive—it's the best time to see the fish, you know—and I found this red-haired girl lying on the sand. It was trippy; she was white as a ghost and covered in bruises, shivering and feverish. She was so weak that she couldn't even get up. All she could do was hold my hand and say 'help.' I tried to carry her up the stairs, but she was too heavy, so I told her, 'Stay here. I'll come back with more people.' I left her here and found this family fishing on the other side of the beach, but when I came back with the father and the son to help me, she was gone. Vanished. The two of them thought I was on drugs or something, but it's true; she was here."

"Where?"

"Right there, under that flowering tree."

Marco and I walk to a small hibiscus tree growing in the ground bordering the sand at the water's edge across from the opening crack in the rocky wall that separates the swimming hole from the sea..

"Aha!" Marco says.

"What?" I ask.

"Here, look." Marco shows me a red hair caught on one of the branches. He pulls it off; meanwhile, the rock in his other hand is slowly turning amber.

"Ouch!" He drops the rock onto the sand less than a foot from the shore and loses the hair, which falls into the water. "Oh no, let's not lose our one piece of evidence!" He strips to his Speedos (what is it with European men and Speedos?) and steps into the water, leaving his clothes on the shore.

Meanwhile, the rock is rolling toward the water as if it's aiming for the hair as well. I grab it, but as soon as it touches the water, it speeds up immensely and I can't let go; it's as if my left hand is glued to it. My water-soaked overalls and tennis shoes are getting heavy, and the rock quickly drags me underwater toward the crack in the rock that leads to the open sea.

"Wait, Cami, are you crazy?" Marco screams, swimming right behind me, but his protest is futile. I'm not in charge here.

Once I pass through the crack, I rise to the surface and can breathe again. I can see Vesuvius in the distance but I don't have time to appreciate it. The rock starts going berserk, as if it doesn't know where to go or what to do. To my left, I hear a boat engine start, and then I see a motorboat coming out of some ruins shaped like a dock. It starts out going north, but then it makes a U-turn to the south. The rock is pulling me toward it as if it, too, has a powerful engine.

Marco, who jumped on the rowboat, is coming up behind me. "They must be going to North Africa," he yells. "Once they hit a place like North Africa, it will be almost impossible to find her. Can you stop swimming, Cami, and climb inside with me?"

"I can't! Do you think I chose to do this?" I'm actually moving much faster than Marco is, but I'm terrified to be so far from the shore in the open sea. I'm very close to them. I can even see the man steering the boat. He's wearing the same mask as he did on the evening when he trapped me. I can see Rori's hair flying in the wind; her arms and legs are tied. Another man in a mask is sitting near her, a pipe sticks out of his back pocket. The gypsy!

My wet clothes are making me extra heavy. I kick off my shoes. As I wonder if I should try to take off my overalls, too, I remember some stuff in my pocket. I search inside and find the lizard tail, all dried out and stiff. It grows in my hand until it becomes a fishing spear; I throw it and manage to hit the masked man in the arm.

He falls to the deck, bleeding, and the gypsy grabs the steering wheel, dropping his pipe. He takes off his mask and with one hand on the wheel, he slips the other one into his pocket, takes out a pistol, and starts shooting at us. The bullets are coming closer and closer when Marco starts shooting back from his boat.

With my free hand, I rummage in my front pocket again and pull out Rori's hair—the one I brought with me—which grows in my hand until it becomes a copper lasso. I throw it and manage to catch her. She's unconscious and heavy, but I still manage to pull her out of the motorboat. I'm trying to bring her closer when the gypsy shoots the rock, which falls from my grip. I feel immediately weaker. I'm drowning, and so is Rori, but I won't let go of the lasso. As I struggle to swim one-handed toward the falling rock, a bleeding hand comes out of the darkness and snatches it down to the bottom of the sea. I grasp the lasso tightly with both hands as everything becomes pitch-black in front of my eyes, and I feel very, very sleepy.

CHAPTER 20

The Mediterranean Sea

I wake up with Marco's mouth on mine. He's resuscitating me, and I spit salt water and gasp and scream, "Rori, where's Rori? You've got to go get her!"

He presses my forehead as if trying to suppress any anxiety and looks deep into my eyes. "Stop. Everything is fine. Rori's here in the boat. She's fine and safe."

His touch and the soft rocking of the drifting rowboat soothe me. I look behind him and see Rori curled up in fetal position. She's unbelievably pale and skinny. Through the improvised blanket made from a fishing net, I can see how badly her captors have abused her. Behind her, the turquoise water of the Mediterranean Sea makes me wonder if we're all dead and are meeting up in heaven now.

"I like that lasso trick of yours," Marco says. "How did you do it?"

"Do what?"

"Well, after you pulled Rori from the motorboat with it, and both of you were drowning, I managed to rescue you, but the gypsy kept on shooting back. The lasso came out of the water, knocked the gun from his hand, and tied the two scoundrels together. They're still there, as you can see."

I look toward the drifting motorboat and see the two masked men tied up like cartoon villains. The masked one is bleeding profusely from his arm where my spear hit him while the gypsy is huddled in pain and clutching his hand.

I close my eyes and sigh with relief. It feels just like I'm waking up from a very long nightmare.

Marco takes the oars and rows closer to their boat and ties it to ours. "Maybe you should stay here while I check on them. I'm going to use their radio to call the Marina Militare." He climbs up the rope ladder with his pistol tucked inside the elastic waistband of his Speedos, and the grip is covering his belly button. I wonder if he's an innie or an outie. Josh is an outie, and I remember telling him that his navel was the only feature of his that creeped me out. I close my eyes and take a deep breath. Somehow, I don't feel that Josh is so far away anymore. He feels very close now, actually.

"*Ma porca miseria!*" Marco cries out, rousing me from my thoughts of Josh.

"What happened?" I call back.

I look up and can see only Marco's back and bottom blocking my view of the men. He's holding the stocking mask in one hand.

I climb aboard and find to my astonishment that the man sharing the lasso with the gypsy is Francesco.

Marco is still staring at him in wide-eyed disbelief. "*Ma que*—What do you have to do with all this, Ciccio?"

Francesco doesn't answer his neighbor's question. Instead, he looks at me. He's drooling, his eyes are red, and his white linen shirt is soaked in blood. "If it wasn't for you, I would be out of debt now and would've gotten those gypsies off my land!"

"Me? What do I have to do with it?"

"Why did you have to snoop around and worry about that little red-haired whore? She was my ticket to riches! But you had to get in my way. . . ."

"Francesco, you were the brains behind all this?" I ask.

"Sure, why not? All these little sluts want these days is some adventure, isn't it? So, I provided her with what she secretly desired so I could get out of debt and not have to rent or sell my land to the family of this loser here!"

His helper, who has been holding his injured hand tightly, opens his eyes wide as he hears these words. He turns around, bringing his face closer to Francesco's, and, without saying a word, squints and spits in Francesco's face, a mixture of saliva and blood.

CHAPTER 21

Positano

After the police came and took the two criminals away and Marco got dressed again, we drop Rori off at the hospital nearby and go to Positano. I'm not hurt, just rather shaken and exhausted, so Marco suggests that I rest in his cabin.

I don't have enough energy to protest. In fact, it sounds like an excellent idea.

He parks his car on the road below the cabin, but we still have to climb very steep stairs to reach the place, which is perched on a slope overlooking the Mediterranean. When we finally get inside, I'm so tired that I fall asleep as soon as he shows me my bedroom and lets me borrow a shirt and a pair of boxers.

When I wake up, I see a pink sky outside, but I can't tell whether the sun is rising or setting.

Marco is sitting in an armchair across from my bed looking at me. "*Brava,* good morning. I'm glad you're okay. I was wondering if I should take you to the hospital as well as Rori. You howled the whole night."

I scratch my head and sit up.

"No, don't move," he orders. "You should rest still. Here, let me bring you breakfast."

He leaves me wondering again if I've died and gone to heaven. Someone bringing me breakfast in bed? I start stretching but have to stop because I'm so sore. I notice a purple stain shaped like a Crescent moon in the palm of the hand that was holding the rock. I'm still looking at it when he comes back inside, bringing a tray.

"Here you go, latte, eggs, brioche, and—"

He takes off the lid of a little china bowl to reveal a huge purslane salad and some carpaccio!

"Oh my! And eggs, too!"

"I know that you Americans like your eggs in the morning."

"You know, I'm not really that American, but I do like my eggs."

"Yes, you're a citizen of the world! Therefore, you need your protein and greens!"

I've never seen him so goofy. It's probably because we're not keeping secrets from each other anymore. I devour the meal and finish with a sigh.

"Do you want any more food? Can I get you anything else?"

I stretch my arms upward. "No, thanks. Maybe we can go out for a walk?"

The sun is blazing through the window and making all the room bright. I squint. As he reaches for his Ray-Bans and hands them to me, I see my reflection in the lenses. My dreadlocks! Will I ever get used to them? Will they ever go away as my hair grows? And yet, I kind of like them. . .

He puts the glasses on me. "I guess we need to go find you something more girlish, or at least smaller. These are huge on you." He strokes my cheek and come really close to my face, taking off the glasses again. Now I'm not so comfortable anymore.

"You still seem hungry. What about something sweet, like a dessert?"

"What do you have?"

"This."

He leans toward my lips and starts kissing me. I give in. His lips are warm and moist and taste like the fresh peppermint he has just chewed. I let go and allow him to hold my arms, and the kiss gets stronger and faster. Suddenly, I taste heirloom tomatoes, and the taste quickly changes to blood, but it isn't blood from the raw carpaccio beef; it tastes very rich in iron like fresh human blood as if I'm biting his lips and drawing it out, only I'm not. And now the saliva tastes like tears, salty and light. I manage to pull free from that kiss and look at him. I see Josh in his face for a fraction of a second.

"What happened?" he asks.

"Nothing."

"But why did you stop? It was so nice!"

"You didn't taste it?"

"Taste what?"

"Nothing."

"What's going on, Cami?"

"I have someone—a boyfriend. I can't do this."

"Oh, really? And where is he now?" He sounds sarcastic, almost angry. Little blue sparkles flicker from his eyes.

"I don't know. Somewhere in South America, apparently."

"Oh, I see. Looks like you and he need to talk."

"Yep."

"What's his name? Is it that guy, Josh?"

"How do you know his name?"

"You screamed it during the whole night."

A moment of awkward silence ensues. I pick up my phone, as I always do when I find an empty minute that I need to fill with information, entertainment, or, as in this case, an excuse. I try to check my e-mail. No Wi-Fi. Why am I not surprised?

"Is there an Internet café in this town?"

"Why?"

"We need to write to Ken, Rori's boyfriend, and give him the good news."

"My dear, several European secret police agencies were involved in this case. By now, her whole family, and probably Ken as well, already knows, and maybe they're even flying here to see her."

"Okay, but I just feel I need to send Ken a personal message."

"Go ahead. It's a pretty long walk. Do you need company?"

"No, I'm fine. Thank you so much for your hospitality. You're very welcoming."

He smiles a sad smile as I stuff my few belongings back into my pockets, but then scratches his throat and puts on his now-familiar poker face.

"If you can't find the place, just give me a call. But it's really hard to miss."

I thank him again and leave wearing his flip-flops and a borrowed pair of jeans.

The road is rather empty this time of the morning, and the walk is beautiful. The two different blues—sea and sky, peppered here and there with green leaves and pink, purple, and yellow bougainvillea flowers—fill up most of the view. The tiny town center, a maze of up-and-down staircases, is jumping with tourists. I feel a lonely tightness in my chest as I reach the Internet café and walk inside. The café serves homemade gelato, and I have to order something to sit down at a computer and get online. I don't mind, but these pants do: I already need to leave the button open to fit my waist inside his jeans.

I order the gelato, sit down at a computer, and sign in eagerly. I haven't opened my e-mail for ages. I scroll down past all the junk mail and see a message, its subject line screaming in capital letters: "CAMI, MY CARAMEL, WHERE ARE YOU? I LOVE YOU, MISS YOU, WANT TO HEAR FROM YOU."

It's from Josh.

The message itself is a little calmer: "How are you, pumpkin? Sorry I didn't get in touch much. The Andes trip took a couple of unexpected turns. To make a long story short, after running away from a sect of ayahuasca drinkers that kept me captive for weeks, I got lost in the Amazon rainforest and now I'm finally in Manaus, Brazil, from where I'm going to fly back to San Fran tomorrow. I've been worried sick about you. I hope you're doing fine. I had horrifying dreams and only got calmer after a bunch of Brazilian native shamans led a drumming circle to send you protection and blessings. Did you hear the beat? Hope to see you soon at home, J."

There was an e-mail message from Ken as well. He was pleased to inform me that he and Rori's father were jumping on a flight and coming as soon as possible to bring their little girl home, and he was most thankful for my efforts.

I'm crying and laughing at the same time. The server looks at me from behind the gelato counter and waves in a just-checking-on-you gesture. I wave back and smile broadly. He smiles back and leaves.

I look for mirrors around me; I must be looking quite pathetic. I don't see one, so I take a picture of myself with my phone. My eyes are red from crying, my dreadlocks are sticking out from my head as if I've stuck my finger in a light socket, my shoulders are broad, and my muscles are bulging. I decide to send it by e-mail to Josh to prepare him for the freakish new me, but just when I'm about to hit

Send, the phone's Wi-Fi connection drops. I take it as an omen and give up warning him. "He'll just have to deal with the surprise," I mumble.

Lots of people are running inside the café now, all of them soaking wet, and I can't stand the crowd, so I leave under the newcomers' astonished eyes. Rain is pouring down, and everyone is seeking shelter. I'm the only one walking out. The strong drops of water soak me from head to toe, and the rain that drips from my dreadlocks is deep purple. I can feel my hair slowly softening and my muscles shrinking. My core isn't as strong and tight as it's been since my night in Subterranean Heights. When I'm almost back to Marco's cabin, the rain is over and a rainbow is dipping into the sea.

He greets me from his window. "Welcome back! I see you're my sweet Carmela again!"

I take off his Ray-Bans. I don't need them anymore; the sun isn't hurting my eyes now. I wave to him.

"Keep them as a souvenir from me!"

***

After treating me to lunch at Ristorante Bruno overlooking the sea, he drives me to Napoli Centrale station where I buy my tickets. Luckily, my credit card was unharmed by my sea bath. I take the fast train to Rome and the local train to the airport. The Benevento police was so kind to pick up and bring my luggage that Ila and Rick prepared for me.

Sitting on the plane waiting for it to take off, I go through the pictures I took on the amazing journey I've just finished. I stop at the last one, the muscular, dreadlocked woman I was for a couple of days. I look at the palm of my left hand. The purple, croissant shaped stain is still there, and no matter how often or how hard I scrub it, it doesn't fade away. What will I say if people ask me about it? I'll find an excuse. Maybe a tattoo, decided upon in a drunken moment? Not that it matters. They won't believe me, anyway.

As I'm about to turn off my phone, a message pops on the screen:

"*Ciao, bella.* I hope to see you again sometime soon. I think we worked well together. Maybe it's some kind of . . . magic? ;)"

What a player.

ABOUT THE AUTHOR

Judith Sakhri lives in California. Catching Red Herring is her first novel.

Made in the USA
Lexington, KY
22 October 2018